Disaster

Drill

Daniel B. Silver

For my friend
Millard E. Starling, Jr.
The Medic's Medic

1.

There's a simple drill taught to children to deal with the apparently significant danger of being physically on fire. It is three words to imply three different lifesaving actions: *stop, drop* and *roll.* If you can memorize the recipe for a peanut butter and jelly sandwich, you can save your own life, kids.

Clearly, this is a necessary drill as you almost never know when you are going to be on fire. Only self-immolating monks protesting horrific human rights violations and entrenched WWII German soldiers hearing the unmistakable snap-hiss of the flamethrower as it prepares to roast their meaty bodies in a concrete bunker are granted that gift of knowledge.

In the drill, the child is supposedly engulfed in a raging inferno, like one of those aforementioned monks in Tibet but probably acting way less Zen about the whole ordeal. Why the child is on fire, how it started… these things don't really matter. The time to act is now.

But, for argument's sake, maybe the emergency starts out as a youthful, curiosity-driven experiment with gasoline-soaked outerwear and one of those long matches that probably are in your junk drawer right now, like the kind your grandfather used to light those Duraflame logs on cold winter nights. Maybe the child is in chemistry class and fails to abide by the teacher's warnings about combining pure sodium and water. Perhaps the poor, youthful victim's friend somehow gets his hands on a giant can of Aqua Net and a butane torch, and with this combination of items is able to make a propelled jet of destruction that leads to predictable results.

Like I said, it doesn't matter how this calamity comes about. The kid is on fucking fire. The events, accidents and/or mistakes that lead up to that point don't really factor into the drill.

This is why we have drills: to simplify intrinsically complicated situations. This is why we, in first world nations at least, have one, easily memorable number to call in the event of any range of emergencies.

What you don't want to do, so it's taught, is to run around thrashing your arms in the air, crashing through the plate glass windows of commercial storefronts or fall into the roadway to be struck by passing cars while frantically looking for a body of water to immerse your burning body in. You definitely don't want to attempt to hastily assemble a bucket brigade. There's simply no time to solicit such a complicated act of spontaneous, altruistic volunteerism. And where does one even get a bucket at that point? Those aren't just *around*. People don't pay attention to the clearly lit exit signs, let alone the presence of buckets. You never want to rely on anything that involves logistical challenges to save your ass.

We don't bother explaining to the children the difference between partial and full-thickness burns, the varying degrees of catastrophic tissue damage. All burns are bad, we tell the children. All burns can disfigure and kill, we tell them if they are old enough to grasp the concepts.

We don't usually get into the specifics of the matter, about how full-thickness burns destroy the nerves contained in the roasted layers of skin. We don't speak of these blackened messes of charred, destroyed, never-coming-back epidermis, dermis and hypodermis. We don't speak of the ensuing infections that have a good chance of sending the kid horribly into the great beyond, even if he or she initially survived being on fire.

We don't talk about the inhalation of super-heated

gasses into the lungs, how they cause the body's natural inflammatory response, which causes the airway to constrict with swelling to the point where the victim can no longer pass air into the lungs. We don't speak of the mortal terror of those last few moments trying to gasp for air but being completely unable to do so, hiding under the bed with a stuffed animal, unable to see through the thickness of the smoke, trying to scream so that someone, anyone, will come to the rescue.

In the drill there are no backdrafts or flashovers for the firefighters to contend with. There are no roof collapses, highly combustible solar panels or exploding propane tanks. No sociopathic maniac with a downloaded copy of the *Anarchist Cookbook* has been stalking the halls of the elementary school with homemade Molotov cocktails bent on correcting some sort of perceived, collective social wronging by the popular kids. The responding firemen don't themselves get trapped in a room without multiple points of egress and become slightly better equipped victims in need of rescue as well.

We don't talk about the borderline barbaric methods used by burn nurses, people of indescribable willpower, to deal with such suffering, to slough off the dead skin with vigorous scrubbing to lessen potentially fatal and disfiguring side effects, to ignore the whimpers and cries of agony, to do what is terrible because it is right and must be done, damn the short term cruelty.

We don't tell the children about the antibiotics, the skin grafts that may or may not be rejected by the body, and the slew of powerful pain medications that create physical and mental addictions and ensuing withdrawals. We never mention the scarring that will never fail to turn heads, the ongoing surgeries simply to make the victim look vaguely human again, the lasting ridicule from ignorant and insensitive classmates and passers-by, the therapy, the looks of horror and shame, and the depression and self-loathing.

Just stop, drop and roll, kiddo. That's the best we got.

We teach our children all sorts of ways to deal with calamity that they don't fully comprehend. Then those children grow up, and they take those lessons with them through their lives, those simple answers to highly complicated problems. We have it all reverted to its most basic form.

In the event of an earthquake, the child is instructed to take shelter under desk or table until the shaking ceases. Then exit building as soon as possible in an organized fashion before aftershocks kick in or fires break out. Proceed to the assembly area and await further instructions. Remind your parents to maintain a stocked disaster survival kit at home. This kit could include, but is not limited to:

- One gallon of water per person, per day, minimum of a three-day supply.
- Easy to prepare, high energy foods that do not increase thirst.
- Food preparation/cooking supplies.
- Eating utensils.
- Flashlights and/or lanterns.
- Fire starting materials.
- Fire extinguishing materials.
- Batteries.
- A well-stocked first aid kit.
- A stash of necessary prescription medications.
- A variety of commonly used tools and household items such as aluminum foil, a multi-tool and duct tape.
- Toilet paper and a trowel or small shovel.
- Personal sanitation supplies.
- Household sanitation supplies.
- Shelter and bedding.
- Important, useful and irreplaceable documents.
- Insurance policy information and claim hotline phone numbers.

- Climate specific, functional clothing including increment weather gear.
- Portable transistor radio.
- Utility knife.
- Firearm with ammunition so no assholes take any of the above.

In the event of a house fire, moisten a cloth and hold it over the nose and mouth. Repeatedly call out, "Fire!" Check doorknobs for heat before opening. Do not attempt to save belongings or pets that are not readily accessible. If Ms. Purrfect is hiding, she will have to fend for herself, I'm afraid. Exit the residence as soon as possible. Close interior doors behind you on the way out to try to contain the fire. Call 911.

In the event of a chemical attack, stay indoors. Close all the windows. Turn off any external ventilation sources. Seal all doors and windows with plastic sheeting and duct tape. Turn on the TV and wait for that distinct sound that used to interrupt your Saturday morning cartoons to announce the activation of the much-revered Emergency Broadcast System.

Call 911.

The first responders will be there shortly. There's no need to panic. They're professionals. They are trained for this.

2.
October 2009

The dispatcher tells us, "Oakland 527, copy code-three," and Ben groans. We're already held over an hour past our twelve-hour shift. We work four in the afternoon until four in the morning, Wednesday through Saturday. It's Friday night turned Saturday morning. It's 0500 hours. The sun threatens to creep in and ruin our chances of tricking our bodies into thinking it's still a normal time to sleep, if we ever get to go home.

I'm in the driver's seat of the ambulance backing out of our parking space at Highland Hospital, the Alameda County trauma center and big city emergency room always on the brink of absolute pandemonium.

Ben isn't supposed to be in the passenger seat when I'm backing up the rig. He's supposed to be out on foot behind me, guiding me with hand signals so I don't take accidental advantage of the many blind spots that the ambulance holds and crash into a car, another rig, or a person smoking in the parking lot in a backless hospital gown while pushing around an IV pole and exposing his or her infirmed, unwashed ass to all passers-by. Maybe that person has on a nasal oxygen delivery system, which is hopefully turned off to prevent the need for stopping, dropping or rolling. But you never know. People don't always listen to instructions. If they did, they wouldn't be smoking a cigarette with some sort of debilitating lung disease. Then again, if people always listened to important instructions about safety, we likely wouldn't have jobs.

American Emergency Response – AER – is our employer, a giant, corporate healthcare enterprise providing pre-hospital emergency care and special needs medical transportation. AER is a business with the awesome power of abundant capital and years of experience providing 911 emergency ambulances to major municipalities that do not wish to bother with the pain of establishing a publicly run emergency ambulance department, or "third service" as it's known in the trade. Many cities and counties don't have a third service, just the PD and FD. Some did and realized it was logistically easier to have the fire department run the ambulance service, like San Francisco did with its Department of Public Health paramedics, who as of the last decade are all SFFD employees. Some places had contracted other private ambulance providers that were then underbid by the Costco-like buying power of AER, or "The Borg" as Ben and I like to call it.

AER policy dictates that at all times, under threat of suspension and/or termination – as most draconian rules at AER threaten – that at no time shall an ambulance be placed in reverse without a member of the ambulance crew standing behind the rig to ensure a collision does not occur. This rule, along with many others, is loosely obeyed as fatigue sets in and day becomes night, especially on nights like tonight when seemingly every possible sick, injured, annoying and/or emotionally needy person in Oakland, California has felt compelled to call 911 during our twelve hour, and counting, shift.

Nevertheless, company policy be damned, Ben is exhausted, like me, and he picks up the ambulance's onboard radio microphone from the comfort of his verboten passenger seat to say, "Go ahead," to the dispatcher.

The dispatcher sends us in lights and siren mode to a priority one emergency, a call of a motor vehicle accident on Highway 13 a few miles away from our current location. Being that it is after 0200 hours on a Sunday morning, the drunks have hit the roadways, and from the sound of it at least one of them has hit something stationary and solid. The rapid cessation of forward movement has caused a 911 call. The Oakland Fire Department is sending an engine and a truck company with extrication gear.

It's now hour thirteen-plus. We are entering hour number two of overtime. We have ten calls behind us. Nine of them were transports, meaning we took someone to the hospital, meaning we had to do longer paperwork and then clean the ambulance between calls as fast as we could. We flip-flop who drives and who "techs," or handles the primary patient care and ensuing paperwork, on every transport. So far, we've flip-flopped quite a bit. Yes, ten times now if you are counting.

Our blue jumpsuits smell like sweat. My breath smells like coffee, chewing tobacco and Mexican food from a taco truck on East 14th Street. Ben's breath is the same, minus the coffee. He's a tea, soda or – *shudder* – energy drink guy.

We are both out of gum. I chew Kodiak wintergreen tobacco and spit into an empty, opaque coffee cup. Ben has a giant hunk of Red Man chaw in his mouth like a squirrel storing acorns for later. He spits into an empty, clear plastic, twelve-ounce water bottle. A brown, viscous liquid sloshes around inside. It's not pretty, and we know it, but we will not cultivate any new sexual partners at this point in the shift. Why put on airs?

We both need showers, toothbrushes, a variety of specialized hair care products, exfoliating rub downs, nail brushes, dental floss, pedicures, manicures, mud masks, saunas, hot tubs, massages, hand-jobs, vodka cocktails and eggs benedict – hollandaise on the side, please… wheat toast and fruit instead of potatoes, maybe. Gotta keep the waistline trim.

We need sleep more than anything but it's not gonna happen yet. Thank Christ for chewing tobacco and shitty 7-11 coffee.

Ben spits into the bottle he's holding with his free hand and I tell him, "Hey, you got blood on your forearm."

He looks at it and seems ambivalent, stating, "Probably ain't mine."

One of the saving graces at this point is the night differential, extra pay that kicks in after 2100, so on nights like tonight that bolsters the overtime rate even more. Long hours mean good money, though we usually spend it as soon as we make it.

We tend to go out after work. We buy beer, toys and gasoline for our motorcycles. We go through sixty-goddamn-dollar Xbox 360 games like they are tissue paper. We take girls out on dates and pay for everything out of stubborn pride. We are, frankly, terrible with money. We are young-ish men living each day like it is our last, like *they* always say to in the self-help books and on bumper stickers but is probably a stupid idea in practice.

The accepted dollar-store wisdom says that it's not where you are going; it's *the journey*. They say that not all who wander are lost. Shit happens. Visualize whirled peas. Keep honking, I'm reloading. Don't blame me, I voted for Whoever.

Delirium is definitely settling in.

I switch on the red emergency lights as we pull out of Highland's driveway. The lights flicker off the facades of nearby houses. A block from the hospital, at the first intersection, I make the siren wail.

After acknowledging our response to the call, Ben yells, "Fuuuck!" and slaps the radio microphone back down into its retention bracket. "Mother-fucking-fuck!" he growls as a follow up. Ben was hoping all day to slide out of work just after midnight and catch last call at some bar where girls are impressed by stories of his heroism.

To date, we have yet to find this place, but it has not stopped us from regularly looking.

Ben looks to his right as we pull up to the intersection. I look to the left. No headlights. "Clear right," he tells me with a tone of resignation. I trust him.

The ambulance's turbo kicks in as I press the accelerator pedal sharply down towards the floor with my boot. The boot is leather and has a few obvious droplets of dried blood on it from an IV line that got away from me for a second because of a rough patch of road that Ben drove over. That was nine hours ago now. I keep meaning to clean it and getting interrupted.

Regardless of visual biohazard, I usually clean my boots with disinfectant wipes at the end of the shift. Most paramedics who have been in the field for a while pay the extra money for footwear that has some sort of biological barrier so that nastiness doesn't soak into the leather. Not all do though. Some prefer to spend as little money as possible and just throw their shoes away when the muse moves them. There are two schools of thought here. Both are valid. I opt for the former.

It's late, and I don't really need to keep the siren on, but I do. Ben and I jam up the hill towards Highway 13 in the Oakland hills. We have this standing policy, the two of us: if we have to be awake, all those other fuckers – you people at home in your beds or having crazy sex after the club or the bar – do too. Because, seriously, fuck you. Why should we be the only ones awake while we save your asses?

Halfway there, on the center console, my cell phone lights up with a text message. It's from a girl. I shouldn't, because I'm driving an ambulance code-three to an emergency, but of course I pick it up to see what it says, briefly. There's not a car in sight on this stretch of road. It's not the part of Oakland that's still alive with activity. The message reads: *What R U up 2??? Want to come over?*

I toss the phone to Ben. "Read this. It's from the one that I made out with at the Ruby Room last week. Remember her?"

"Yeah, I remember. She was cute but had those crazy eyes where you can see the whole iris. Geez, I wonder what she wants at this hour?" Ben asks, sarcastically.

"Well, it's after the bars are all closed on a Saturday night," I say, because it never feels like Sunday until you go to sleep and wake up, then have that mimosa or similar beverage even though it's like two in the afternoon already. "She probably wants to play Scrabble."

"Chess."

"Chess with my boner."

"Chess with your boner and your tongue at the same time."

This reminds me of a related thought. "You know, sixty-nine is never as fun as it sounds," I opine. "I mean, it's not like a bad time or anything, but I always get kind of distracted. I need something else going on there. So, how about chess with my boner and my tongue and a knight or rook in the ol' dirt-button?" I then blast the air-horn at nothing to make as many household dogs bark as possible.

"Nah, that chick is clearly bisexual. All girls are these days. She wants chess with the boner and your tongue and the *queen* in her ass."

"Wow. You win. That's totally it," I concede. "We going east or west on the highway?"

"East. You should call her after this run. She sounds nice... and interesting. And sixty-nine is for Christian teens who have made promises of abstinence to their creepy pastors."

"I'm pretty sure that the 'Christian side hug' generally evolves to be the man-on-child hug... from behind. Not that I'd know or anything."

"What is the Christian side hug?"

"Something I saw on the internet. Like, a way for teens to hug so they don't get awkward erections, I guess."

We hit the next intersection. Headlights are closing in from the left. I blast the air horn. Ben watches them slow their approach.

"Not clear. Not clear. Not clear... okay, clear. Go."

The dispatcher's voice interrupts our typical, juvenile banter as we jam up the hill towards the accident scene. "Oakland 527, the fire department is on scene and beginning extrication."

Ben picks up the radio mic and says, "Yeah, roger that." He puts the mic down, turns to me, and says, "This dude is gonna be *fuuucked* up, watch."

"Yeah, I'll take those odds."

3.

Who drives a Pontiac Fierro these days? I mean, really? They haven't made the goddamn ugly shit-heap since 1988. It's old enough to drink legally. And who drives one drunk as all hell and then, seemingly without any attempt to apply the brakes or slow down one bit from what I would guess to be about fifty-five miles per hour, just rams into the only tree capable of bringing such a vehicle traveling at such a velocity to a dead stop? Because there's only one tree on this whole stretch of road big enough to stop a speeding piece of American crap that no doubt contributed to the company tanking and having to be spared by the US taxpayer a year ago.

That's what I'm thinking about while crouched in the tiny nubs of broken glass and airbag dust that cover the remains of the passenger seat. In the driver's seat, there's this guy who looks about twenty-three but it's really hard to tell because his face is covered in blood from his smashed nose, mouth and teeth. He isn't talking. He's breathing in a deep, slow, agonal way – the kind of breathing not made by the intelligent and evolved part of the cerebrum. It's the kind of breathing made by the lizard brain, the place just at the top of the spinal cord before the gray matter, the part that makes a human respire steadily in defiance of the increased oxygen demand made by what I assume is significant internal bleeding.

The firemen are busy cutting the Fierro's driver's side door open with the hydraulic spreader, the "Jaws of Life" as they are known by news reporters. Ben is in an odd, contorted position with one foot in what used to be the small rear seat area and another up by his left ear on the driver's side rear passenger armrest. He's holding the patient's head up, stabilizing his spine and keeping his airway from collapsing on itself. Ben uses a bag-valve-mask/BVM to force more air into the patient's lungs. It's not a perfect situation: holding the spine in place and also doing rescue breathing, but you do what you can with the two arms God gave you in such cramped quarters.

We have both, during the thirty-odd seconds we have been with our patient, reached the same valid medical diagnosis: our patient is a twenty-something-year-old male weighing approximately sixty kilograms who is, without a doubt, all-fucked-up due to massive blunt force trauma secondary to a high-speed auto vs. tree collision.

Ben says, "I can smell the booze coming off him."

"Yeah, me too. I'm jealous."

The portable suction machine I will use to remove broken teeth, clots, blood and other nastiness from the patient's mouth makes a deep farting noise when I turn it on. Ben pulls the BVM away and I shove the plastic tip of the suction stick into the patient's mouth and watch the clear plastic tubing turn red as it fills the reservoir bucket with the biological material already mentioned. I feel his pulse on his wrist as I use the suction and it's fast and weak.

When I'm satisfied his airway is clear, I grab for the heavy-duty shears on my belt. I don't feel them. Ben continues ventilating once more.

"Motherfucker!" I yell out, causing even the firemen using the incredibly loud heavy equipment in front of me to momentarily look up at me quizzically.

Ben glances over at me and says, "You lost your scissors again, didn't you?" Before I can even answer him, he says, "On my belt, man."

I reach over the blood-soaked cloth seat and retrieve Ben's shears from his belt, stating, "Think there's some asshole out there with like a hundred pairs of my shears in his garage?

There fucking has to be, I swear." Then I set to work cutting off the victim's clothes so we can assess his injuries. This, in emergency medicine, is known colloquially as the *strip and flip*. The flip part happens when we put the victim on a hard, plastic backboard to minimize spinal movement and briefly roll him to the side to check his back for injuries.

I cut off the patient's shirt, fake gold necklace, watch and belt. It'll all stay in the car. I don't have time to collect that stuff and it's all soaked in blood anyhow. Hopefully, the CHP collects it before the tow truck dude steals the patient's wallet.

Ramming my head into the bent steering column in the process, I manage to flay open both pant legs to the thigh. I'll finish the job when he's in the ambulance. I do a quick head-to-toe physical exam:

- Head – significantly banged up. Fluid draining from right ear. This is very bad.
- Face – significantly banged up. Obviously broken nose and teeth. Generally nasty maxillofacial trauma. Also, very bad.
- Neck – trachea deviated to the left. Super bad. Cervical spine in line without obvious deformity. Finally, something in the good column.
- Upper trunk – left, anterior flail chest segment, which is a series of three or more broken rips moving independently of the other due to the movement of air during respiration. Breath sounds are positive on that side. Breath sounds are absent on the right side. Right chest wall is intact. Imprint of steering wheel present across upper chest. No seatbelt burns to left shoulder, because of course he wasn't wearing one or it failed at a crucial time. Very, very bad.
- Abdomen – somewhat rigid upper right and left quadrants. Non-distended all quadrants. Soft lower quadrants. Probably filling up with blood/badness up top.
- Hips – stable. No deformity. Good.
- Right thigh – no external trauma. However, massive internal instability. Obvious closed femur fracture. Very bad, but on the current bell curve, could be worse.

- Right lower leg – no deformity but trauma present. Right ankle likely broken. Bad-ish.
- Left thigh – obvious external trauma. Massive instability. Obvious femur fracture considered an "open" fracture due to the presence of an open wound. The bone could have popped out that hole and gone back in. All bad.
- Left lower leg – banged up but seems solid. I'll take it as a win.

"Ready for the rundown, my man?" I ask Ben.

"Hit me with it," he answers.

"Dude is all *fuuucked* up, as predicted. Probable brain bleed. Flail segment on left side. Pneumothorax on right. Bilateral femur fractures. Probably also has a grenade shoved up his ass for good measure."

"I expect him fully healed by the time we leave this car," he mocks.

"Yeah, thanks," I say. "But it's your tech, remember?

"Ah, fuck, you're right."

I laugh in his face.

In ten-ish minutes, we get the guy out of the car, onto the backboard, into the ambulance, and are about to be underway. Just before the back doors of the ambulance close, one of the newer firemen from the engine company asks Ben if he needs a hand in the back of the rig. Though probably a good idea, Ben is always passive or overtly aggressive to firemen, so he answers with, "Depends. Are you single?" The fireman shrugs and steps in the rig, closing the doors behind him. Romance clearly in the air or he just is used to the harassment from us.

"Naughty boy. I guess you'll do in a pinch," Ben tells him. "Go ahead and take over bagging him."

The fireman moves to the jump seat, the seat behind the patient's head. As he scoots his butt by Ben's face, Ben goes, "Damn, do you work out?" The fireman continues to ignore it.

I pull the rig back into traffic, lights and sirens still on, and I can hear Ben in the back talking to the unconscious victim now. He mostly does this for my benefit, but I also know it helps him stay focused.

"Don't worry, sir. I've already bandaged the part of your chest that came undone when your drunk-ass hit the steering wheel, and now I'm just going to stick this huge needle through the tissue between your ribs on the right side so we can relieve the pressure and make you breathe again. I'm sure it won't hurt a bit!" I momentarily hear the suction turn on again. Then Ben goes, "You know, I'm pretty sure the chess player chick can suck way harder than this stupid machine. You should take this home tonight and test that."

Rumor is that the last thing to go when you are truly, massively, catastrophically screwed and circling the proverbial drain of death is your hearing. Listening to Ben, I hope very much that this is not the case.

I drive in as smooth a manner as I can, trying to avoid potholes and roadway detritus because Ben is about to do a very delicate and invasive surgical procedure. While doing so, I request via the Alameda County Mednet radio to be connected with Highland Hospital so I can inform them who we are bringing them, what treatments were are doing, and when we will be there, the basic ambulance report diatribe. A few moments after Ben tells me to have Chess Girl suck me like a portable vacuum, the trauma team nurse staffing the radio says, "This is Highland. Go."

"Highland," I say into the radio, "this is Oakland 527 en route to your facility code-three with a critical trauma activation. Our patient is a twenty-five-ish year old male who was the solo driver of a small convertible that head-on'd a tree on Highway 13. The car was pretty much demolished. Starred windshield. Bent steering column. Significant passenger space intrusion from the engine compartment. Significant head and face trauma. We are suctioning his airway. Trachea deviated to left. Flail segment on the left. Pneumothorax on the right..."

Ben chimes up in the background, "Hemo-pneumo,

17

man. It's ugly. Blood City back here."

I hear the fireman utter, "Gah, Jesus."

I continue, "Okay, hemo-pneumo on the right side described as 'ugly' by my partner. Bilateral femur fractures, one open and one closed. Pulse weak at 140. He still has a radial pulse, though I think its days are numbered. Respirations agonal at 8 per min. We are bagging him and treating all of the above. See you in less than five."

"Copy 527, we'll be waiting. Highland out."

Ben doesn't miss a beat. In the rear view, I can see him taping down a giant IV to the patient's left arm. "How about this: we both go over there to that nice lady's house. I bring the suction. You bring the chess set. You use the chess pieces as previously stated. While you do that I get busy with the suction. Then we double-team and when we both finish we give each other high fives and from the side it'll look like the Eiffel Tower."

I hear the fireman announce, exasperated, "A little unprofessional, man."

"Ben, can we stay on task here?" I request as we motor down the mountain. In the rear-view mirror, I can see Ben winking at the fireman, who apparently has no further comment regarding our planned fantasy sexual escapades. The patient's legs are bandaged and in splints and I have no idea when Ben found time to do that. The dude is a perverted, inappropriate healing machine, a superhero of pre-hospital medicine and dick jokes. I laugh, and I say over my shoulder because I cannot even abide by my own request, "At some point can we trade positions? Might as well, right?"

"We can hammer out the details later. But what if I really start to like this girl? Won't it be weird that I won't be able to keep anything about her sexual prowess in reserve, just for me to know about? Don't you worry that such a thing could turn into animosity between us and drive a wedge in our partnership?" Ben punctuates that statement by reaching through the bulkhead and giving me a wet willy in my right ear and I swerve just a little before realizing he's done this a thousand times before.

The fireman sighs loudly, clearly regretting his decision to ride along.

"If that's blood on your finger I will fucking kill you."

Ben replies, "Well... let's just say it isn't... blood."

"Dude!"

I hear another sigh from the fireman.

Moments later, we pull into the ambulance bay at Highland. Two nurses in paper gowns and masks stand at the entrance. I wave at them, pick up the PA microphone and say out loud, "We're *baaa-aaack*."

As Ben opens the back door up to unload our cargo, he yells, "Did I tell you I have a date tomorrow? Seriously. Figured I might as well because you are working overtime with Tay-boobs, you poor, poor sap."

The fireman, who has had enough, says, "That is some kind of miracle for either of you to get a date."

Ben answers, "Jealous?"

I meet Ben at the rear of the rig and he looks like a goddamn movie slasher. His blue jumpsuit's knees and stomach areas are covered in blood. His overgrown, black Mohawk is stuffed under a ravaged baseball cap that reads, *OAKLAND PARAMEDIC* and it is now canted way back, no doubt from Ben wiping his brow with his forearm.

Ben's right arm has a full sleeve tattoo based on the movie Alien. Ripley, the Nostromo and the iconic monster all are streaked with the patient's blood, adding to his previous collection. His heavy boots are unzipped to the ankle, as usual. He's smiling like an idiot. I would be too.

That was a ripping-hot call. It's not every day that you get to shove a needle into somebody's ribs and smile as the trapped, lung-crushing air an

4.

We call Paramedic William Tabor "Tay-boobs" – not so much to his face, mind you – because he's fat and has man boobs. It's not that his physical appearance is entirely unique in the profession, that paramedics aren't fat in the same percentage as any other branch of healthcare or public service, but Tay-boobs is kind of a whiney bitch who complains every time he gets a call for service like he's being specifically targeted by AER dispatch. Fact is, he is clumsy. He's a boob. He's fat. It's a double entendre, a twofer.

When you work with Tay-boobs, you just gotta resign yourself to the fact that you are going to:

1. Stop at 7-11 at least four times in ten hours so Tay-boobs can refill his Big Gulp.
2. Not have any say, whatsoever, in an eating location. He makes the call. You deal. Furthermore, he is a cheap bastard and will never pay one cent over the cost of his meal, which means that you will have to handle the tip if you don't want to look like an asshole in the eyes of the waitress who is probably cute and now hates you because she's had to deal with your dickish partner.
3. Have to listen to him complain about god-knows-what for the entire ten hours of the shift, unless he falls asleep, which actually happens pretty often despite the many gallons of Pepsi he consumes in a day.
4. Put up with the worst radio taste on earth. Pop country and conservative talk radio only. White dudes singing either a twangy ballad about inane bullshit or white

dudes complaining that a black guy got elected to president last year but hiding it in some other thinly veiled gripe like the status of his citizenship.

5. Want to kill yourself before the day is over – preferably a murder/suicide scenario.

When stuck with Tay-boobs for a twelve-hour shift, I just keep in mind that I am on overtime, which is good, and bring plenty to read and plenty to chew. Granted, I could buy tobacco during the many 7-11 trips, but I relish too greatly his absence, even if it's just the time it takes him to fill up his soda and try to communicate with the disinterested dude behind the counter for a minute or two.

In short, I do not like working with Tay-boobs, but I do it sometimes because private ambulance companies don't pay all that well, and even though Ben and I share an apartment and that helps keep the rent down, I do on occasion like to do fun things. Fun things cost money. Supply and demand. I'm sure you get it.

Overtime acquirement works like this: I have this giant pager like it still is ten years ago. So does Ben. All the field employees, paramedics, critical care transport nurses and poor – literally, they get paid less-than-dick – basic EMTs do. Ours is the only business in the western world that still uses pagers for anything. The scheduling department pages out the open shifts several times a day. The first one to the phone to answer the page is the winner, like a radio show but the prize is to work more.

Openings on ambulances happen for several different reasons: vacation, family emergency, sick calls, etc. However, some ambulances always have openings on them, because the person who usually works that shift doesn't have a regular partner. There are many possible reasons for this. Perhaps the partner got pregnant and went on maternity leave? Perhaps the partner is healing an injury for a few months? Perhaps the partner is on a vision quest in the Sahara Desert? Or, in the case of Oakland 526, it could be because the person who normally works the shift is insufferable and hasn't found a tolerant and/or desperate enough person to overlook this fact and tie the partnership knot.

I left the house for my shift when Ben was still asleep. He planned to get an early "dinner" with this person that he identified as "Blondie" at 1700. I was to start at noon, which was a somewhat brutal turn-around considering the laborious nature of the previous night. I couldn't even fall asleep until just before 0800. Part of that was my fault, and not just because I was amped up from the shift. Ben and I like to play cooperative video games on the Xbox 360. We both have our rooms set up with consoles and TVs, so it's easy to know when there's at least one person who can join me online because he's right there in the next room.

So, when we finally made it home, we gamed. Even though we were both fighting the same alien horde, Ben and I still dealt one another some serious trash talk. He insisted that he was carrying my weight whenever his tally of dead enemies was greater than mine. When my kill-count surpassed his, I just told him that his date, Blondie, could never fuck a man who can't even triumph in the digital arena. And down from there it continued to go. Anyhow, I slept for less than four hours.

The shift with Tay-boobs started out pretty status-quo:

Stop 1 – 7-11 in San Leandro near the AER deployment center.

Stop 2 – Responded to a call near the same 7-11 in San Leandro as we were the closest unit. The call was for an old man who fell and probably broke his hip. We took him to Kaiser Hospital in Oakland.

Stop 3 – Tay-boobs wanted to go look at the new BMW M Series at the dealership on Broadway, near Kaiser. He talked to a half-interested salesperson acting like there was any way in hell that this potential customer could afford such a car, until we got another call.

Stop 4 – Old lady with mild trouble breathing in the Acorn housing projects, in deep west Oakland. Chronic emphysema patient. Not an acute condition. Family just didn't want to drive her to the ER themselves. We took her to Summit. The triage nurse knew her by name.

Stop 5 – 7-11 on Grand Avenue. Tay-boobs thumbed through a Playboy while I sat in the car, read the latest issue of Game Informer and sent Ben a text message instructing him to wake up and get ready for his big date.

Stop 6 – Oakland Police put a psychiatric hold on a guy. We strapped him to the gurney and took him to the emergency psych services center, back down in San Leandro.

Stop 7 – Swung back by the deployment center because Tay-boobs can't bring himself poop in any bathroom but the ones he is familiar with. By now you probably have deduced this process took about half an hour. I napped.

Stop 8 – Got sent to a post at the Eastmont Mall in East Oakland. We sat for thirty minutes. Tried to nap but Tay-boobs turned on talk radio and listened to Michael Savage, agreeing with everything he said. I tried to tune this out because I think Michael Savage is a braying penis. Finally, I had enough and stood outside the ambulance chewing Kodiak and pacing. Ben sent me a text message saying that he *"looked so good"* he was *"going to bring some saran wrap for Blondie's seat at the resto."* Gross, but painted an interesting mental image.

This brings us to the present tense.

"Oakland 526, copy code-three?" The dispatcher says at 1631 hours, forty minutes of conservative and angry radio banality later. Still outside the ambulance, I pick up the portable radio out of my pocket, key it, and say, "Thank God. Go ahead."

"Oakland 526, this is code-three for the shooting at 82nd and MacArthur. OPD is on scene and advising the scene is safe."

"Acknowledged. Responding," I reply.

I open the driver's side door and hop into the driver's seat. Michael Savage is talking about the scourge of illegal immigration. Tay-boobs is passed out and snoring. I jab him in the flabby arm.

"Wake up, dude. We got a call."

He opens up one thyroid-troubled, bugged-out eye and says, "Mmmff."

I turn the big, rumbly diesel engine over and give it a few revs with the pedal for good measure. Before we even start moving, I flip on the lights and blast the yelp, scaring the crap out of people walking into the nearby McDonalds, the security guard going by on his ragged golf cart, and the fat paramedic sitting next to me.

In his nasal tone, Tay-boobs blurts out, "Goddamn, Harlan. Will you stop doing that please?! I told you to wake me up first."

I glance at him and make a sound similar to, "Shhnaaa." He looks at me quizzically. I don't bother explaining what that meant, because I don't know either.

"What call are we going to, now, for Christ sakes?" Tay-boobs whines.

"Shooting at 82nd and MacArthur."

"Well, slow down there, kamikaze. That could be dangerous. We have to let the police get there first. And you are only half a good driver by genetics, and all."

Oh, great. Here come the Asian driver jokes. Brilliant.

"The cops are there already. Dispatch said so," I inform him, which he would know if he could stay awake long enough to hear the radio. The thing is, I love shooting calls, no matter if the police are there or not so I would have lied to him anyways. I add, "And regarding the obviously racist comment you just made, you should know that I disconnected your airbag before we started the shift, dipshit."

24

A bit about Harlan Takumi Finnegan, Mobile Intensive Care Paramedic, state license number P15912:

- My father is an American mutt with genetic ancestry from most of the major northern Atlantic Drinking Islands.
- My mother is Japanese American and has been in the US since she was 20.
- I am as of the fifth day of this month twenty-eight years old. I am 5'10. I am a lean 160lbs. I am still blessed with a young man's metabolism.
- My hair is dark brown and goes down to just below my shoulder. I usually wear it pulled back in a ponytail when working and loose when not.
- I have lots of tattoos. I technically have more than Ben and like to shame him for this. Ben is probably going to catch up eventually, but not for many years because he is extremely picky and indecisive about such things.
- My hobbies include listening to punk rock and heavy metal, playing first-person shooter video games, riding my new Ducati Streetfighter, drinking beer and whiskey, watching baseball, and often kissing a variety of pretty girls now that I am single again. More on the last part later.
- I grew up in Berkeley and I was a rebellious youth with ripped jeans, a denim vest with local punk band patches sewn on it and spikey hair.
- I live in Oakland now.
- I've worked at AER since 2004.
- I harbor simmering hatred towards firefighters as I am a proud and increasingly bitter paramedic who will not leave the ambulance to be a, well-compensated, "hero" or whatever. More on that later, as well.

Tay-boobs picks up the radio, and while glancing at me incredulously asks, "Um, Oakland 526 are we the closest unit to this run and are the police saying the scene is safe. I don't feel like getting shot today."

You're a big fucking target, but safe unless the bad guy has an elephant gun, I think to myself.

The dispatcher answers, "Yes, you are the closet unit, 526. I know that because we have GPS on all the ambulances, 526 – as we've been over before. The police are on-scene advising that it is safe," the dispatcher spits out. This is so embarrassing, being branded with the 526 stigma by the dispatcher, who clearly thinks Tay-boobs is as big a tool as I do.

I blow five red lights in a row at a pretty good clip, and we pull up less than a minute after getting the call. Tay-boobs white-knuckles the handle above the door in response to my driving. He looks at me with venom in his eyes and says, "Oh, thank you, dispatch; I guess we're on scene then." He glares at me a second and states, "Glad we made it in one piece."

I somehow resist the urge to tell him to shove it up his ass and scream, *"The only person here who wants to murder you is me!"*

The shooting scene is pretty standard. You got your yellow police tape. Shell casings being marked by little cones. It's in a rough neighborhood. There's about forty people milling around, none of whom seem willing to talk to the police. The firefighters are in the center of it all allegedly attending to the victim but mostly just looking confused as to what to do with the obviously dead guy. A gaggle of what I assume to be family members and friends holds back a crying, screaming and hysterical woman who I assume is closely related to the shooting patient. I assume this from seeing this same drama play out countless times. Several times at this same location even.

Tay-boobs and I hop out of the rig and grab the gurney out of the rear doors of the ambulance. Even though the dude is dead, we can tell that OPD is going to want us to transport him to the ER. It's a tried and true fact that if you take the body away from the crime scene, the crowd tends to dissipate. Family will show at the hospital, but most of the random neighborhood uproar dies down. The cops like this because it makes the scene easier investigate, to take photos, collect evidence and such. Maybe a witness will be more inclined to come forward if not being closely scrutinized by those sympathetic to the shooter.

We leave the heavy plastic box full of our medications behind. It's a trauma call and we likely won't need any of them. Our jump-kit is already on the gurney with everything we are going to need for the time being.

We get to the patient. His T-shirt bearing the photograph of a young black man with the word *RIP* above the photo is specked with some blood, but not too much because his head is facing downhill. Looking from his feet up to his head, I glean the following: he's quite dead.

I make this immediate assessment because, though about 95 percent of his body is in pretty good shape, all things considered, there does seem to be a scarlet river running down the declining pavement, with his head as the origin point. Another thing stands out, rather impressively: I can see what appears to be a bullet trapped just under the skin of his forehead. It's a big bullet. It looks like a grape implanted under his skin. I've never seen this and think that it is pretty interesting, but that's a thought that I don't vocalize because people in my profession have skewed ideas as to what constitutes *interesting*.

I crouch down by the patient's head. Tay-boobs busts his shears out and starts cutting off the victim's clothes. The firefighters should already have done this, but they were probably still too frazzled from having to leave their recliners and/or workouts to run this call properly.

Despite the death thing I mentioned, the patient is breathing deep, gurgling, snoring breaths, much like the car crash victim the night before – probably about six to eight times per minute and slowing. I push his forehead back and tilt up his chin to open airflow, then put a plastic airway in his mouth to keep his tongue from occluding his breathing passage. I look at a nearby fireman and say, blankly, "He isn't really breathing. Get a bag please."

Then I see that some brain matter is coming out from a large hole behind the patient's left ear, the same hole providing all the blood flowing downhill. I wipe the brains and clotted blood away with my gloved hand to look at the hole. I suppose don't need to do this, but I'm curious about the wound and it can't make anything worse. It's a big entry wound. I see powder burns around it, indicative of a close-range shot.

Someone got the drop on this dude. He's medically deceased but the part of his brain at the top of his spinal cord doesn't know this yet because his body is so young. So, it continues to tell him to breathe and make his heart beat for now.

With my clean hand, I grab a stack of 4x4 inch gauze pads and cover the hole in his skull with them. I mean, hell, might as well go through the motions for the family, right? Then I use some ugly applications of tape to hold everything in place. The fireman crouches down next to me and asks, "Want me to start bagging him?"

I barely resist the urge to say, *No, genius, I just had you get it to hold and look busy and all heroic and stuff.* What I really say is a deadpanned, "Yeah."

Tay-boobs has gotten the guy completely naked in the street, searching for more bullet holes. I can hear the strained screams of a woman, hoarse from yelling over and over again, "Good Lord Jesus! Good Lord Jesus! Oh, my baby! My baby been shot! Good Lord Jesus, help him!" Vocalizations like this are traumatic the first times you hear them. They make you want to hide under the blankets of a warm bed. Via enough exposure, it becomes background noise. This is probably not good for the soul.

The air smells like neighborhood barbeques and lighter

fluid. It's about eighty degrees. Half the bystanders are holding cans of beer in brown paper bags, the usual rabble outside of the liquor store. About a block away I can hear the repeated *boom-boom* of a thunderous subwoofer and the rattle it causes the aging car containing it. Then I hear tires squeal. Thankfully no more gunshots. The cops don't take off running to the new shooting scene.

Another summer evening in East Oakland.

It feels like a modern-day version of the Old West. It's still not over redlining, crack wars and the newly dubbed Great Recession. Parts of this joint are well and truly fucked up.

I love this town.

Oakland is a great place to be a paramedic, provided you want to *work* for a living. But the benefits pretty much blow in comparison to the public sector. Half the time we wonder why we even have a union due to their absenteeism.

"You gonna C-spine him?" one of the firemen asks, wanting to know if we plan on putting a plastic cervical immobilization collar on the guy and strapping him to a backboard. The collar is basically pointless in this case. Yeah, okay, *maybe* the guy somehow managed to break his neck falling from standing when the bullet entered his cranium, but I think we have bigger fish to fry at this point.

"Um, no. Don't need to," I say. I look up at Tay-boobs and ask, quickly, "Ready to load and go, Fatty?"

He darts an angry look in my direction, "What did you say?"

Did I mention Tay-boobs says he's part Irish too?

"Ready to load and go, Paddy?"

"Um, yeah. Sure. Flip him on your count."

I totally got away with that one. I say, "One-two-three," we roll the patient over and check his back for additional injuries. Seeing none, we roll him down onto the board and then I call, "On the gurney on my three; one-two-three." We lift the patient off the ground, blood dripping from

29

his head, and plop him down on the gurney.

Tay-boobs and I jog the gurney back to the rig to maintain appearances. One of the firemen opens the door for us. A kinda cute female OPD officer asks me as we load the victim in, "Going to Highland?"

"I can think of nowhere better," I say and flash her my creepy smile. I get an about-face-march in return. All business.

I close Tay-boobs in the back with the patient and the OFD probie who is working the BVM. I jump in the driver's seat. A cop helps me back out of the crowd without hitting any grieving family members. AER policy probably doesn't allow this either, but it's successful regardless. A three-point turn later, we are on the way to Highland with the lights and siren on. I pick up the Mednet radio and talk to Highland.

"Highland base, go ahead," a male nurse responds.

"Highland, howdy. It's Oakland 526. We are coming to your facility code-three with a trauma team activation. We have a teenage male weighing about 65 kilograms with a single gunshot wound to the head. He's breathing agonally at twelve times per minute. Blood pressure is..."

Tay-boobs chimes in, "Eighty palpated. Pulse at 100."

I continue, "... eighty palpated with a pulse of 100 and I imagine slowing. Doing what we can. See you in five."

"Highland base copies, 526. Out."

"Any change back there?" I call out to Tay-boobs.

"Nope, he's still shot in the head, Harlan. Can't imagine any change will be for the better."

"Okay." What a fun-vortex this man is. Ben would have thought of something witty to say at least.

My phone rings. The caller ID photo shows Ben in his underpants in a very sexy pose holding a beer and eating a huge turkey leg. I took that picture one night when he was drunk. It makes me laugh. I like to have him call me when we are talking to girls in bars. About forty percent of them think it's funny too. The other sixty percent look totally disgusted by both of us. Thank god the forty percent doesn't hear the stuff we say in the ambulance.

I pick up the phone. The siren wails in the background. Ben speaks first.

"Oh, so you've clearly got time to talk."

"Meh, I'm a good one-handed driver."

Tay-boobs yells from the background. "Great, just great. He's on the phone now while driving code-three. Do you know how illegal that is?"

Ben obviously hears this, "Tell that fat turd to stick the suction up his ass and lose some weight."

I whisper, "I'm totally going to fart on his Big Gulp later. Swear to god, dude. This is torture, like a hate crime torture. Anyways, how can I help you? Cold feet about the date?"

"No. Just a question. Can you get beer on your way home?"

"Yes. Wait, what the hell? I just bought beer. You have been at home all day. *You* go get beer."

"I drank it all. You helped a little; don't get your panties all in a bunch. I recognize your contribution and commend you for it."

"You have a *first date* tonight," I say as I drive in the opposite lane of traffic around a line of stopped cars to get onto the westbound 580 freeway. "How many beers did you feel compelled to have before this?"

"Only four."

"Dude."

"Look, don't judge. I was playing *Modern Warfare 2* and I cannot fucking stand those little pimpled, suburban, racist runts shit-talking me so I had some beers."

"I don't have any problem with that, but this girl you are taking out is not some tramp you met in a bar, right? So far, you've told me that she is a nurse. She has a job. She has a car. She is in her thirties. Like, she has her shit together and she probably doesn't like drunk assholes... or at least not anymore since the divorce or whatever."

31

He puts on a pathetic baby voice and says, "Like your ex-girlfriend didn't like me, you mean?"

"Yes. Exactly that."

"By the way, you really did a nice job on that one there, Romeo, so fuck you. I'm fine. Your advice is invalid."

Tay-boobs yells out, "Are you going to hang up and drive at some point, Harlan?"

I turn to Tay-boobs and give him a hissed, "No," and then say to Ben. "You are not fine. Nor have you ever been. Drink a Red Bull and get your head in the game. And, for the record, my ex-girlfriend didn't dislike you. She just didn't like it when you acted like an asshole, which is always."

"I'm comfortable with that label," Ben says. "But it could just be that she was stuck up?"

"I'm not talking about this with you right now. Wait – is that the only reason you called, so I'd get beer?"

"No. I also wanted to tell you I borrowed a hundred dollars from your money stash in your top drawer."

"No, dude! How did you even...? I am savin-"

He interrupts me and goes, "Buy beer, cock-monster." Then he hangs up.

5.

Things you should know about Ben:

- Ben is thirty years of age, two years my senior.
- He is 5'09 and about 200lbs, an inch shorter but a good amount heavier. Most of the weight is muscle. Some is beer.
- Ben and I have lived together in the same apartment in Oakland for five years.
- Ben also has been at AER since 2004.
- Ben has identified as a punk rocker for many years. Now he is an aging punk rocker. An aging, bitter, money-stealing, beer-embezzling punk rocker.
- Considering his stories of his youthful indiscretions, it is by no small miracle that Ben is not an outlaw biker, in jail or both.
- Ben loves video games too.
- Ben loves riding his motorcycle, a Buell 1200 that he has done some cool aftermarket mods to. I would never tell him that I think his bike is cool, because I am a motorcycle snob and don't generally like American bikes.
- Ben and I met at work, and soon realized we had some mutual friends. We partnered up at work and got along famously, which led to getting beers and such after our shifts. We became roommates shortly after his last girlfriend kicked him out and I finally took the financial plunge and moved out of my Mom's in Berkeley. I was in a serious relationship with a girl at the time, who

was not really all that pleased that I didn't move in with her instead. In my defense, I found this out after the move was already complete. Though, she swore she told me before. This was a bone of serious contention.

- Ben can drink me under the table.
- Ben complains about his body fat while drinking his fourth beer… of the morning (days off only).
- Ben hates firefighters as well.
- Ben grew up in semi-rural Virginia, so he's genetically a redneck.
- Ben moved to San Francisco when he was eighteen years old and worked as a doorman at bars and nightclubs primarily before becoming an EMT and then a paramedic.
- Ben says he hates Berkeley even though he did not grow up there.
- Ben met the girl, the nurse he's going on a date with, at work. Her name is Kaylee. She is white. She is twenty-seven. She is cute. She is short. She has a nice body. She has blonde dreadlocks and a tattoo of a yin-yang on the back of her neck. She works at the Alta Bates ER in, ironically, Berkeley. Ben has never seen Kaylee out of her scrubs. Ben seems to be either unaware of or ignoring the fact that Kaylee is most definitely a hippie.
- Ben hates hippies.

Anyhow, I'm really looking forward to hearing how this date goes.

Ben picks Kaylee up on his motorcycle. She lives in a cute little cottage in West Berkeley by University Avenue. The exterior of Kaylee's house is that dark wooden shingle stuff that looks really earthy, like it would be well suited for The Shire. There's a vegetable garden out front. There's a Toyota pickup truck in the driveway. Ben does not see the sticker in the rear window of the pickup that is of the terrible jam band

Phish. Ben also doesn't see the "BRC" sticker on the rear bumper that identifies the owner of the pickup as being a fan of the dirty dance festival known as Burning Man.

Kaylee hears Ben's bike pull up and bounces out of her front door a few moments later. Ben is dressed in a black flight jacket, a Ramones T-shirt, black work pants and black boots. Kaylee has her dreads pulled back in a ponytail. She's wearing an olive drab tank top, a long skirt that goes well past her knees, and flip-flops.

Ben starts the date off with a hum-dinger of a line, "Is that what you are wearing? You do know that asphalt is bad for your skin, right?"

Kaylee takes it in stride, "Oh, should I change? I didn't even think of that. I've never really been on a motorcycle before." In Ben's mind, one point has already been taken off the board for Kaylee with this statement.

Ben kind of shakes his head and rolls his eyes. Kaylee apparently ignores this non-verbal sign of annoyance or doesn't see it. That or she's very, very sweet and/or naïve.

Ben says, "Pants. Shoes. Boots are best. Heavy jacket if you got one – denim or something."

Kaylee smiles, bounces back towards the house totally undeterred by Ben's flat delivery and says, "Okay, sugar. I'll be right back out."

About five minutes later, Kaylee reemerges. She's now wearing a blue denim jacket with a giant Grateful Dead patch on the back, the same olive drab tank top under, some jeans with holes in the knees and pink Doc Martens that are not really laced up.

"Better, I hope?" Kaylee asks rhetorically. She turns to lock the door exposing her Grateful Dead patch to full view. "I haven't worn this jacket for like eight years! I'm glad I can still fit into my college clothes. This will be a walk down memory lane."

"Um… Yeah," Ben deadpans, resisting the urge to immediately peel away.

Kaylee has to take her dreads down to fit the motorcycle helmet on her head, but after a few moments of wrestling manages to get it on. Ben remains pretty much silent during this time, making the situation even more awkward for a time. That is until Kaylee fumbles with the chin strap and Ben sighs and helps her with it, resigning himself to the fact he's really going through with the date. His fingers brush her neck gently as he fixes the strap. Ben notices how soft her skin is. He's close enough to get a whiff of the vanilla scented perfume she's wearing. Ben expected Patchouli. He is pleasantly surprised. A smile creeps across his face despite his efforts to remain aloof.

Kaylee straddles the bike behind him. She asks, "What do I do?"

"Just hold onto me. Lean where I lean. Ready?"

"Sure," she bubbles. "This is fun! Where are we eating?"

"It's a surprise. Hold on," Ben says, and guns the throttle sending the bike roaring away while triggering every car alarm on the block on their way to San Francisco via the Bay Bridge.

Ben isn't a moron. But he is set in his ways. So that's how and why Ben decided to take the vegetarian, hippie girl to the mid-range steakhouse. In his defense, he wasn't aware until they sat down in the leather booth of the place that she didn't eat meat. And then when she said that she'd just have a side of asparagus and some bread, the ensuing line of questioning caused him to feel somewhat bad. Ben, in a rare display of chivalry, had his meal packaged up and they went from Ruth's Chris on Van Ness to *her* favorite restaurant on Valencia Street in SF's Mission District. And this is how Ben wound up calling me from the bathroom of an all-vegan Mexican café, while eating a bone-in rib eye with one hand.

I'm in the back of the ambulance using a million paper towels and this weird foaming disinfectant spray to soak up the shooting patient's blood. It's everywhere. It's all over the gurney, the floor, the tailgate, the cabinets, the seat at the head of the gurney; it's a mess. I blame Tay-boobs. Luckily, there aren't a million calls hanging so I have time to clean up as well as I should.

Ben is excitedly whispering on the other end of the phone.

"Why didn't you fucking tell me she was a hippie?!" he goes. I can hear him chewing. It's louder than the whisper he's speaking in.

"And risk not hearing the story of this train wreck? I've been waiting for this call for like an hour. It's the highlight of my day."

"Prick! A prick is what you are, I say!"

"You try working a full shift with Tay-boobs and not do something cruel. By the way, how on earth didn't you put that together yourself that she was a hippie?"

"I don't know. I was thinking of her ass too much. It looks really good in scrubs, and I wanted to bite it. I don't know if I can see it now. I bet she's got more hair on her than an Armenian porn-star in the Seventies."

"I don't think they made porn there back then. I bet she has more hair on her beaver than Robin Williams' armpits."

I hear Ben's giggles echo in the bathroom of the restaurant, which he told me is called, *The Earth's Vulva* but I think he made that up. I picture Ben eating his steak while seated on the toilet. I like to think it's one of those tomahawk cuts and he's holding it by the protruding bone. I later find out that I was correct about all of this.

He counters, "I bet she has more hair on her beaver than the floor of Supercuts in Newark, New Jersey on a Saturday afternoon before Easter – like around 1500 hours."

That one gets me – so layered, so nuanced. I die laughing in the back of the ambulance with a wad of paper towels in my hand containing a portion of a Jello-like mega-clot of cranial blood. A sheriff's deputy walking by who works at the hospital looks towards the source of the laughter. No sooner does he look than half of the giant clot slips out of the paper towel and falls back on the ambulance floor with a splat. The deputy makes a face of disgust while I try to hold onto the rest of the clot. He shakes his head and keeps walking. I spray more foamy stuff on the floor.

"That was funny. Oh, also, we just had this shooting call. I had to wipe the dude's brains off his head to see the hole the bullet made. There was like a creek of blood going down the hill behind him. I always underestimate how much blood is in heads and now I'm trying to pick up a coagulated pool from underneath the gurney in the back of the bus. It's fucking gross. Hope you enjoy your steak."

"Like you've never seen a head all engorged with blood," he goes. I set myself up for that one. "What was the scene like? Did Tay-boobs help at all?"

"Meh. Kinda. He bitched a lot per his norm. Anyhow, dude, go back to your date. I gotta clean up and this is a two-hander. If you wanted to be here, you shouldn't have stuck me with fatty and we could have taken a shift on 532 or something."

"You know I don't do morning shifts. And I don't want to go back out there. There's nothing here to eat that won't make me shit my pants, man. It's all lentils and tofu and gluten. People say you aren't supposed to eat gluten now."

"You know there's gluten in beer, right?"

"I'm going to pretend you never said that."

"It's for the best. Anyhow, finish your steak. Take your time. Also, please tell me you aren't talking to me with your pants down right now."

Ben laughs and goes, "Maybe I am. Maybe I'm not." I hear a toilet flush in the background.

"Dude! Not cool. Just get out there and drink until it's fun. I know you can do that. Booze is vegan."

"Yeah, I guess. Are we gaming later?"

"No, *I* am gaming later. You are going to be at that

woman's house working your seductive magic. No Xbox for you. Go make it happen, Casanova. Bushwhack your way to home plate."

He sighs and concedes, "Fine. But I'm coughing up the hairball on your pillow later."

"Gross."

6.

I come home with a twelve pack of Bud in my messenger bag, and it's heavy as hell. Carrying that and my helmet, I kind of bang through the front door and make a bit a racket. The lights in the living room are off, and Ben's door is closed. He's home, I think, because his helmet and his spare are on the kitchen counter. I glance at the couch. There's a blue denim jacket there with a Grateful Dead patch.

Son of a bitch, I think. *He did it! He humped the hippie. Good for him!*

Smiling, as I know how much new material I'll have to torture him due to this development, I put the beer in the fridge, tear open the cardboard container and grab two cans out. Then I walk to my room, strip, throw my jumpsuit in the hamper, leave my boots by the door, and take my ritual after work, anti-cootie shower. The hot water carries away the microscopic spots of blood, brains and left-over stink of Tay-boobs' mildew body odor.

I pound the first beer in the shower, get out, grab the other, and walk into my bedroom where I turn on my big TV that's perched atop a wire shelf unit purchased from Bed, Bath and Beyond for too much money. I fire up the Xbox 360 for what I intend to be a two-hour session. It's about 0100 hours. I won't be sleepy until 0300 at the earliest. I don't hear any sex noises coming from Ben's room. I figure he and the hippie must be passed out. That or she's passed out and he's trying to have diarrhea quietly, which is an impossible endeavor.

I sign into my Xbox Live account. I know two people currently online. One of them is my most recent ex-girlfriend's nephew, Nathan, A.K.A. *BiggsDaddyGanjaXXX*, his obnoxious Xbox Live profile name. I haven't spoken to him or played online with him since I split with said girlfriend. He's sixteen. We don't really have anything in common. I'm not entirely sure what to do about this situation. I feel like I should delete him as a friend on my account, but that seems passive aggressive and unnecessary. The complication is that I still think about her but he *is* also kind of a moron, as should be obvious by his online handle and his age. Any gaming handle that has an unsubtle reference to marijuana generally means that the person who controls the account is a douche. It's a plain and simple truth, infallible even. Anyhow, I'm conflicted.

I decide, as I have for many months, to ignore the fact that he is playing online and deal with the situation later. No doubt, he's doing the same because when I signed in online it automatically sent an alert to him of that fact that I was on the Xbox Live server and he didn't exactly rush to greet me. I imagine that somewhere he's talking over his headset with his dumbass friends playing *Halo 3* and saying, *"Oh, my aunt's dipshit ex-boyfriend is online. If he joins our game, frag him and call him a fag."*

The other person online is our friend, Dougie. Ben and I met Dougie randomly while on the same team in a capture the flag match of Halo. Dougie works as a cop in SF, and just made the rank of detective a few months back. He works on some sort of late shift major case squad, so on his days off he's usually up for a game. We don't see him much in person. Dougie lives in The City. We live in Oakland. We tend to stay on our side, and he on his, except for special occasions like taking a vegetarian to a steakhouse. It's just kind of the way things work in the Bay Area. Sometimes he makes it out here to see a show or meet us at Le Cheval for the much feared "Snake Juice" cocktail. He's always by himself and always takes BART if he's going to be drinking. He's far more responsible than one would think after seeing the dude for the first time.

I invite Dougie to a private chat group. It takes him less than fifteen seconds to respond.

"Yo, dude. How goes?" Dougie chimes in. I can hear the familiar sound of explosions and gunfire in the background.

"Just got off work. What are you playing right now?" I could easily just see what he is playing with the push of a button, but I'm lazy.

"Left 4 Dead. Want to join? Every character is available but the hot girl. I'm playing her."

"Cool, I'll be the biker dude then."

"How's that maniac roommate of yours?"

"Good… I think. He just went on a date and I think he is either having very quiet sex or they are both all humped out and sleeping."

"Oh, good for him! What's the lucky fella's name?"

"Nice. I have no idea. Let's just call him Bruce to keep it easy."

"Ooh, Bruce. That's a strong name. Maybe he's Australian. I like that sexy accent."

"That makes one of us," I say. "Ever since that Australian chick was on *Lost,* I just can't help hearing nails on a chalkboard when I hear that accent. God, she was annoying. I couldn't stand the way she said Charley's name like, 'Chaaahleee'."

"I get that," he says. "Is it weird that I kind of wanted to see her naked in the first season when she was pregnant?"

"Yeah, kinda. Pregnant women are strange. I'm not into it. I always want to look away when I see them. It's like we are all supposed to ignore the fact that they in the very recent past had unprotected sex, like there's this social contract. Someone came in you and we all know it. It's not right. It needs to be addressed by Congress."

I pop in the game disk and cue up the game with Dougie. Shortly thereafter, we are running around shooting

42

hordes of zombies with various weapons. I decide to choose the black businessman over the white-trash biker. Soon, we are in the middle of a city street, and a mob of zombies is sprinting towards us. Dougie blasts controlled bursts from an M-16. I run around in circles with two pistols pumping round after round into the undead. The two pistols are good because you have unlimited ammo in this game. I have no idea why, but I'll take the cheat.

"Good lord, it's hot to watch you slay the undead in that snazzy outfit."

"If we survive this and you play your cards right, I'm going to take you to bed and show you that the rumors are true."

"Keep dreaming. I'm saving myself for my beloved, Shaun of *Shaun of the Dead* fame."

"Ooh, very good choice. I can't even be jealous. He's both charming and efficient at zombie murder."

We get past the first level in about thirty minutes. We are evenly matched for kills. Suddenly I hear rapid footsteps, and my bedroom door flies open. It's Ben. He's wearing boxer briefs and that's it. He's holding a beer, one of *my* beers, and a piece of cold pizza.

I report on the development: "Dougie, Ben has entered my room. And, surprise, he's almost naked... and drinking *my* beer."

"Say hello for me," Dougie instructs. "Then slap him on the ass like he scored a touchdown."

I turn to Ben as he plops down on my little loveseat couch next to me. "Dougie says hello."

"Say hi back to that pig," Ben says.

"Ben sends his greetings, Dougie. And he called you a demeaning word for a policeman."

"Ask him how the date went," Dougie ignores.

"How did the date go?"

Ben gives me a look. Then he says, "Well, we banged, and it was pretty good. She wasn't as hairy as we thought, by the way. Then she split."

"Did you notice that she left her jacket here?" I ask.

"Oh, yeah. That."

"So, what's the deal with *that*?" I ask.

"She kind of left in a huff," he says.

"Um, dare I ask why?"

"Ask why," Dougie adds in. He can hear all of this over the microphone attached to the headset I am wearing.

"We humped once and I told her that I'd never banged a hippie before and I was stoked to see that her downstairs wasn't as hairy as I thought it would be, like I just told you now. I don't think she was pleased about that. She was rolling her eyes and saying, 'I gotta go now. I got to be at work in the morning.' Then she left."

I am suddenly overtaken by a swarm of flesh eaters. The screen goes red as they demolish me on the ground. Dougie can't save me, despite the loud report of his M-16 indicating that he's trying pretty hard.

"Remember my sacrifice!" I rasp.

"I shall and tell Ben he remains an asshole," Dougie says. "The world needs all kinds. Those with bush and those without deserve equal space and respect, much like the Jews and Palestinians, if you will."

"Dougie says good job and he hopes you are well," I relay to Ben.

"That is not what I said!" Dougie exclaims.

"Thanks." Ben then adds like it's minorly important information, "We humped in your bed. That's what you get for that little stunt you pulled last week when you drew the butthole on my chin when I was passed out."

My eyes dart to my bed, now recognizably disheveled. I hate my friend, but fair is fair. I expected retaliation eventually. I underestimated his cunning.

On the headset, I hear Dougie laughing.

Jesus, if cops don't grow up, what hope do we have?

7.

Ben and I are both off work and sitting in my room watching *Dirty Rotten Scoundrels*. We love this movie. We have seen it approximately ten thousand times. It's towards the beginning of the movie, and Steve Martin is laying a con on a girl in the dining car of a train so she will buy him lunch.

Ben is drinking a beer, *my* beer, again. He is also eating slice upon slice of cold pizza. I don't have any clue where he keeps getting this pizza. There is none in the fridge. He doesn't have a fridge in his room. Why is it cold? This is just one of the many mysteries of being a dude who platonically lives with another dude: a lot gets left to the imagination. Generally, this is a good thing.

Ben sticks his belly out and burps loudly. It's noonish. We both just woke up.

"I gotta get to the gym today, man. I am a fat fuck," he says and pats his belly with the bread side of the slice he's holding.

"Well, smart guy, maybe you shouldn't be drinking beer and eating pizza then? Maybe you should have yourself a little protein shake and motivate?"

"I'm gonna do that later, after the movie is over. And then I want to play video games for a bit. Maybe have something to eat."

"You are eating now."

"I mean something healthy."

"Where are you getting all this pizza? Actually, forget it. I don't want to know."

"Good, because I wouldn't tell you anyhow."

"Have you thought about calling Kaylee back and apologizing to her for saying that you were surprised she wasn't as hirsute as you thought she'd be?"

"I don't even know what that means."

"Yeah, you do. To be hirsute means the lady's southern face has quite the beard."

"I figured. I just wanted to hear you describe it. Hirsute also could mean that the curtains and the drapes have similar length."

"Correct. It could also mean that the kitty-cat loves her some Eighties rock bands."

"You kinda lost me with that one."

"I mean her vagina likes Poison or Twisted Sister. It's all teased up and such."

"Eh, not bad," Ben goes, "but not your best material. How about, *hirsute* means that she's always got nice a soft place to sit?"

"Gah." I laugh and admit, "Funny."

We talk more for a while about Kaylee's muff situation and then Ben tells me that he has decided to wait for her to call him first. I am not at all surprised by this. Before I can chime in, he changes the subject.

"So… you have a date tonight, right?"

"Yeah. Supposedly."

"Is it the girl who wants to hump the chess pieces, the one we decided is bisexual?"

"Yes, indeed." I am lying about this fact.

"I imagine the conversation will be riveting."

"We can always talk about chess."

"True," Ben concedes. "If you need another unit when you are banging, shoot me a text and I'll come running."

"I'll keep that generous offer in mind."

We watch the rest of the movie. At the end, Janet "The Jackal" (artfully portrayed by the vastly underrated Glenna Headly) puts her arms around Michael Caine and Steve Martin. She delivers the all-time classic line, "Are you ready?

46

Then let's go get 'em." The characters walk away from the camera into what we are to assume is a life of comedy, leisure, friendship, opulence and happiness – shallow and manipulative people who find redemption by being the exact same assholes that they were in the beginning. Frank Oz made that movie. He also voiced Yoda. There's no small coincidence there, surely.

The paramedic's first day off is always filled with generally mundane and mildly laborious tasks-turned-torture. Few people work a twelve-hour shift and then decide that they really, really want to clean the bathroom or do a load of laundry. After the end of the flick, Ben and I part ways. He, surprisingly, heads to the gym. He was off yesterday so he took care of all his necessaries.

I reluctantly Skype my mom at her home in Las Vegas – where she moved after I moved to Oakland – and tell her, in answer to her interrogation, which is pointless because she already knows that I'm still single, that *no*, I'm still not getting married, nor do I have a grandchild on the way for her. I can hear and see her live-in boyfriend milling around in the background, adding his thoughts on the matter. He's got a heavy Japanese accent. He usually chooses not to speak English, which means I don't understand most of what he says. But between his demeanor and the words I do understand, I think he doesn't like me because I'm not his child. Mom refers to him as "Mr. Man" and doesn't blink when she says it. His last name might be *Man*, even though I'm pretty sure that's an unusual name.

Mom grills me about my recent ex. Mom says I should win her back by proposing. She says I won't do any better for a wife. She says my ex has a great job, one much better than mine because it pays more. She says that my ex has a good family. It seems to me that my mother is in total denial that we are broken up. I highly suspect that my mom and my ex's family are still in contact and she is no doubt horrified by stories of my behavior.

After that call is finally, thankfully over, I phone my dad on his cell and we talk about our offseason predictions for the A's while he takes a break from restoring the old boat he bought a few months back. We talk about Barry Zito struggling with the Giants all year. We both feel badly for the guy even though he's rich enough to not need sympathy from two plebes such as ourselves. We talk about the 49ers sucking. We don't bother talking about the Warriors continuing to suck, because that's nothing new. We both could give a shit about the Raiders. Then we talk about the Sharks. Dad is more into hockey than I am, but I'm glad at least one Bay Area team isn't shitting the bed for once.

Dad met mom when bellbottoms were in style. Dad was recently out of the Army where he served in Vietnam as an engineer, a line of work that is apparently rougher in reality than it sounds on paper. Dad lives in San Rafael and has since he and mom split when I was twelve. He asks if my mom is still busting my balls about getting married and having kids. Dad tells me not to get married, despite what my mother thinks, because I'm not mature/ready enough for it and he wasn't at my age either. Thing is, he was about my age when I was conceived so I'm not sure how this makes me feel.

Dad tells me not to worry about not being a father yet. He says that being a parent is really hard and it costs a lot of money. Then he says, "But, really, fucking have one eventually. I know *you* aren't gonna take care of my ass when I'm old and crapping my pants because your retirement sucks and my V.A. benefits are total bullshit. And then get married, for Christ-sakes." He laughs. I think he's been drinking beers all day. I don't blame him. He and Ben have similar personalities.

I wash my uniforms. I eat a light lunch consisting of cottage cheese, salsa and corn chips at the kitchen counter while standing up. I vacuum. I go for a run around Lake Merritt. It smells of stagnant brackish water and goose poop, per usual. I shower. I trim my nails. I man-scape. I do my best to clean up all the little hairs from the bathtub, so I don't have to hear my roommate go on about me grooming my nether parts.

Ben gets back from the gym. He goes into the bathroom. He closes the door behind him.

"Ooh, you must like this girl. You shaved your balls again, didn't you? I can tell by the short-and-curlies around the soap scum ring."

Damnit. I'd make a poor janitor, it seems.

"Yes, but I shaved them for you, big boy."

"You shouldn't have." I hear the shower start. Ben raises his voice and calls out to me, "I hope you don't mind if I use your razor to smooth out my butt crack!"

"Nah, it's cool. I used yours on my nuts. Hey, you know how I know you're gay...?"

My phone lights up with a text message. It reads: *Six at my place?* ☺

I type back: *Absolutely. Look forward to it :)*

Ben responds, "How? You are the one who just shaved his balls. Remember that. That isn't a stereotypically 'straight dude' thing to do, dude."

I ignore him and say, "Because you looked at shorn man-pubes and knew exactly what they were."

A brief side note: Ben and I do the *"You know how I know you're gay?"* thing all the time. People always assume we are quoting the brilliant film, *Forty-Year-Old Virgin*. However, this is not the case. If we stopped to think about this, we would probably realize that it isn't socially acceptable. Yet, political correctness aside, Judd Apatow simply was able to introduce the rest of the world to the uncouth antics of our immature demographic.

Ben and I also frequently riff on the following topics, among many others:

- The woman you marry is gonna... (Be really into her prized show dogs, have a haircut like a show dog, actually be a show dog – etc.)
- If you had sex with an animal, it would totally be... (A unicorn, because there's just no pleasing you is there? – etc.)
- The first time you got drunk you... (Made out with a circus clown because he tied you a cool balloon shaped like a sword; or, were in your mother's womb because she's a raging alcoholic – etc.)

"You are one to talk," Ben yells out from the shower. It's muted by the closed door and white noise of the water spraying, but I can still hear him. "You are so gay that your first car was a Mazda Miata convertible, pink with a Playboy bunny airbrushed on the hood and cinnamon smelling air freshener."

He must have been thinking about that one at the gym. The level of detail is far too precise for him to have come up with it on the fly.

"It was like four-grand below the *Blue Book*!" I yell to him. "Tell me you wouldn't have bought that?!"

Ben gets out of the shower a few minutes later and wanders into our shared living room space where I am seated on the couch's end table. We could totally put the televisions in here and have a cool Mission Control vibe going, but we are lazy, and then we would have nowhere to fly remote controlled helicopters or shoot one another with Airsoft rifles without breaking expensive things. These are things that often happen in here. We refer to this room as *The Rumpus Room*.

"What're you up to tonight?" I ask.

"Dunno. I was thinking about watching internet porn for a while and then going out drinking."

"Where are you going to go drink after you jerk off to tentacle rape anime?" I ask him, which on its face seems innocent enough to the untrained ear. But I have an ulterior motive. I don't want to run into him on my date, especially if he's been drinking. Ben doesn't know this, but the girl I am going out with tonight is not Chess Girl the bisexual. Chess Girl was a one-night stand that drunk texts me now and then. My date tonight is The Ex, my ex-girlfriend who I was in a serious relationship with when I moved in with Ben – and then was summarily dumped by when she found out that I screwed around on her a few times. It's the same woman Mom wouldn't shut up about when we were skyping, earlier.

I talked about this girl for months with anybody who would listen after she kicked me to the curb. Unfortunately, that person was usually Ben. I was a depressed mess who rarely left the house to do anything but work. Ben was at his wit's end, but true to his best friend form, never blamed me. Instead, he took out his frustration with my general state of misery on her, even though it was my fault from the get-go.

The Ex didn't speak to me for months… then one night on her birthday I drunk-texted her, randomly. I passed out right after. I woke up to a message from her, cringing inside at what it might say. Surprisingly, she didn't respond in anger – quite the opposite. She seemed like she was a little happy to hear from me.

It's been two months since her birthday. Two months that we've been talking about our failed relationship. First it was just text message exchanges. Then it was a phone call turned plural. We went out for coffee a few times. We went to lunch two weeks ago. We made out during a walk in the park with her new dog last week while Ben was still asleep. I snuck out of the house early so I wouldn't get caught and returned in my running clothes. It was perfectly executed.

We talked about my maturity and commitment problems. I accepted that it was all my fault: the infidelity being but a symptom of my immaturity and irrational fear of serious relationships. I admitted my shortcomings and told her that I was ready to be a different man. I was ready to commit to the idea of *us*. I told her I was tired of not being complete in the eyes of my mother, like I knew Becky – that's her name, Becky – was as well.

We wept together and held hands on that walk. I pledged never to lie to her again. She asked me if I was willing to move in with her, sooner than later, should we ever give another go at dating. She told me that she didn't expect me to cease being friends with Ben and that she would never ask me to abandon a friend... but added, "If you do reduce the influence of Ben in your life, I think that we can more effectively work on your problems and bolster the strength of our relationship. I feel like we were so much stronger when you were still living at your mom's place. I know that's weird."

I told her she was probably right, and then said something kind of stupid – a lie but one I meant to retroactively make true at the time. I have that problem. I say things without thinking them through because at the time I think it's what I should do... another maturity issue that needs to be resolved.

I told her, "I don't really even hang out with Ben anymore. We just live together but we barely see one another, honestly."

I shouldn't have said this, but I knew it was what she wanted to hear, and her smile made me beam. When I saw that smile, I had every intention of growing up and moving out of my bachelor life with Ben. I wanted to be with her, and I wanted to be the man that she thought I could be.

It made sense: I had been unfaithful and dishonest. It was the same story for my entire dating life – the one constant in my failed relationships was me and my behavior.

I needed to grow up.

After that last night, we started sexting. It was hot. We exchanged sexy photos and written fantasies. We began reminiscing about prior erotic experiences. She sent me graphic pictures of her body with subject lines like: *Wish you were here with that big cock.* All of it drove me crazy with desire, even though she did very much exaggerate the size of my quite normal penis. Maybe it's above average? I hope it is.

I'm off track, sorry.

It's just that our sex was so good when we were together. Why did I ever stray? What was wrong with me? She let me pretty much do anything I wanted to, as sex was concerned, and I still wanted to be with other girls. Dr. Phil would tell me I was a total scumbag. He would probably be right. I acted like a scumbag, a slave to my genetic programming, testosterone and youth.

So, tonight is the night that I'm going to re-close the deal, I think. I won't lie and say that I haven't had sex with any other girls since we broke up, but I haven't loved any others since her.

Her full name is Becky Ribakoff, and she's beautiful, and smart. She's sweet and kind. She thinks I'm funny. She comes from a big, supportive family. They are all nice people. Mom and I agree on that point.

Becky is a Senior Deputy Sheriff with the Alameda County Sheriff's office and works at the North County jail. She'll be a sergeant soon, aced the test. She's fluent in Spanish. My mother loves her, *loves*. My mother still has not forgiven me for losing her even though I didn't even tell her the whole story about how I screwed up leading up to me getting dumped.

I am equally as pissed at me as my mother is.

My mind wanders: *Senior Deputy Ribakoff, permission to handcuff you to the bed and rock that body till you can't take it anymore?* I defy you to tell me that concept isn't sexy. You can't. I know.

Despite the perfection that this woman embodies, I do not want Ben to see me hanging out with Becky. Becky thinks Ben is a bad influence on me because of our shenanigans when we are together: the drinking, the immaturity, the occasional brawl, the wheelies at three A.M. - all typical jackass stuff that only a minority of women think is funny and then only when their boyfriends, husbands and/or sons have nothing to do with it, and then only when it's on a TV screen... or you live in the American South. Plus, you know, she's a cop and has professional standards she expects to be upheld. The problem is, Ben knows of her disapproval.

In turn, Ben thinks Becky is stuck-up and a killer of fun. His nickname for her is, "Fun Police."

Ben generally thinks every woman I talk to for more than five minutes is a buzzkill. He never approves. He finds fault in everyone I date on anything more than a casual level. I think it's all because he hates anyone who threatens the time that we get to spend together.

So, they can't meet. I have to keep them separated like fighting dogs, Hatfields and McCoys. The mere thought of coordinating this charade stresses me out a bit but I repeat the mantra: *I am getting laid tonight, god willing. Ben shall not fuck this up for me.*

"I dunno," Ben answers. "I was thinking about going to the Ruby Room."

Crap. Crap. Crap. That's where we were going to go. I chose it because it's easy to make out in the back. You basically need a flashlight in that place to find the can. It's so dark that if you had a medical emergency you would just have to make your peace with death because ain't nobody finding you.

No matter. We will go to the Radio Bar. It's a few blocks away, but far enough. It's not as dark as the Ruby Room, but it'll do. When drinking alone, Ben only ever goes to one spot, maybe two, anyhow. He knows every bartender in town and always wants to hang with them all night because it's cheaper and he can be the coolest guy in the bar, in his own mind. He says there are too many hipsters that go to Radio, so I'm safe. He hates hipsters. He only ever goes there with me.

"Cool. I'm just going to play it by ear... see where she wants to go."

"Okay," he goes. "Good luck with your chess game!"

I chuckle in response. Hopefully, I am convincing.

Before I leave, dressed to impress but not *too* eagerly, I tell Ben, "You know how I know you're gay? Because you liked the movie *300*."

"What's gay about that?"

I stare at him for like five seconds and then deadpan, "Really?" I walk out the door and think to myself without any awareness of how far ahead of myself I am: *How am I going to juggle these two when I'm married?*

8.

Basic Tsunami Safety:

- If in a coastal area, please stay alert for broadcasts and emergency sirens warning of any approaching giant, killer death-waves.
- Always have an escape route in mind that leads to higher ground. Keep in mind that others will likely be using the same route. Plan alternative transportation options, such as off-road vehicles, to reach sufficient elevation. For those of you in more remote stretches of coastline, have you considered purchasing a 4x4 side-by-side – like the Navy SEAL version of a golf cart – to have as backup transportation?
- Pay attention to offshore seismic activity. Earthquakes cause tsunamis. The reports are available online.
- Be cognizant of the tide. A suddenly retreating sea likely means a tsunami is inbound and about to crush your puny existence with ferocity of the Old Testament God's terrible wrath.
- A tsunami is a series of waves, not just one. Do not go back to the shore until the proper authorities give the all clear sign.
- For the love of all that is holy, do not go down to the beach with your video camera. Don't be that moron. Nobody has good things to say about the person who goes to the coast to see a tidal wave and summarily, predictably dies.

Becky and I get Vietnamese food at Le Cheval in downtown Oakland. I have the cubed filet of beef with green beans. It comes with a salty, lemon and garlic dipping sauce. I try not to eat too much of this to keep my breath in the realm of kissable. She has cashew chicken. We share a steaming, silver pot of jasmine rice. She has a glass of white wine. I have ice water and a glass of the snake juice. The snake juice is a concoction consisting of grain alcohol in a big jar with herbs and dead snakes in it. Yes, it has actual dead snakes in it. It looks like death in liquid form, like if Satan invented cough syrup and nobody dared tell him to use an opaque bottle so as not to inspire terror.

The jug sits in the corner of the bar daring people to drink it. The bartender will not touch the stuff to his lips or with his bare skin. Nobody orders it, really. It's supposed to help with virility, as the legend goes, like everything that's both horribly gross and meant to be consumed by humans who have a healthy strain of courage.

I can't help myself. I have to prove my virility to this girl, again. Why? I don't know. Regardless, I do, and it tastes like cherries and mystery. Becky laughs at my face while I drink it, but I finish the glass eventually. Then we have Vietnamese coffee, which is delicious. Now we both have coffee breath. This is a plus.

We talk about old times. We talk about vacations we took. We catch on another up on how life is. We talk about our mothers and how much shit they give us for not having kids yet. We talk about how we must be disappointments for only being a deputy and a paramedic as opposed to a lawyer and a doctor. We are that unique brand of successful that any parent in their right mind would be happy to report to his or her coworkers and friends. However, we do not come from families with realistic parental expectations.

The server comes to the table with the check and two additional shots of snake juice. He says, "You two have fun tonight! This will give you *energy* for later." He winks and walks away. Becky laughs nervously and winks at me back. We down our shots, shuddering as we slam our glasses down.

After dinner, we walk from the restaurant to our next drinking establishment, the Radio Bar, holding hands and talking. Becky is a little light on her feet. She's smiling and enjoying her buzz.

It's a lovely night. The sky is clear. There's a soft breeze making the leaves rustle. It's relatively warm and smells like the bay. Traffic is light with intermittent cars and bicycles. There are a few people out walking dogs, a few dudes loitering suspiciously in shadows and a number of couples doing what we are doing.

When we arrive at our destination and I see two seats open at the bar. Mike, the bartender, is pouring drinks tonight. He greets, "Harlan, how goes?" when we walk in. He looks at Becky and adds, "And there's a face I haven't seen for a while! Welcome back. Giving this asshole another shot, eh?"

Becky smiles and says, "Well, we will see about that." She laughs. He laughs. I laugh, only a tad uncomfortably.

I like this bar more than Ben. Mike is a good bartender. He always says the right thing to a female companion. He makes people feel welcome. It's a weeknight, so there's no bouncer at the door and a far thinner concentration of faux-sullen youths who ride fixed-gear bicycles smoking hand-rolled cigarettes, or skunky joints, out front.

Becky and I continue to hold hands. Our date is going perfectly. We get our drinks and raise them in a toast. She gets a vodka and cranberry juice. I have a whiskey and soda. "To a lovely night so far," she says with that sweet voice of hers, clinking my glass. "I hope you know how much I missed you, Harlan."

"I missed you too, baby." I lean in closer to her. We kiss, passionately. Robert Smith of The Cure belts out the words, *"I will always love you,"* over the jukebox in the background. Perfect timing. We put our drinks down on the bar without taking a sip and continue to kiss. The feeling of her lips against mine, the smell of her hair and shape of her body in my arms makes my chest warm and anxious. I want her. I want her now.

Tonight, is the night. It's the night that I put things back in order. Tonight, is the beginning of the rest of my life – I can feel it. My mind races with sexual fantasy as our tongues dance and our hands begin to search around.

We *could* live together. I *could* cut the cord with Ben and grow up. Screw that guy anyhow. I *should* marry this girl. I could give the enterprise another shot. I could take the vows and mean it. We could have a house with our dual income. Our moms could dote over our children. I'll have a minivan. I'll sell the motorcycle. I'll do work on our house. Dad could teach me to remodel the bathroom. Maybe we could have a hot tub. I could play video games with my kids, non-violent ones, but the ones about happy little critters doing happy things on farms or whatnot. I could introduce the kids to baseball and basketball when they are old enough. This could work. I could be one of those people: domestic, content, normal – happy even.

I want her so bad. I want my parents to think I'm not a fuckup. It's highly confusing to have these two thoughts running through my brain but I go with it. Tomorrow, I'm telling Ben that I'm going to move out. Maybe the next day. Definitely this week.

Then I hear a sound like a net pulling my thrashing fish-body out of the water onto the cold deck of a boat where I flop around for a few moments before being unceremoniously clubbed over the head until I am forever still. It's something so horrible and unwelcome that I want to wake up from my nightmare immediately and take that first gasping breath that means it was all just a bad dream and I'm not really watching the world crumble from the end of a pier with my high school math teacher and Luke Skywalker.

But it's real… very, awfully real.

"What the fuck is going on here?! She's Chess Girl?!"

Ben yells as he meanders into the bar clearly on the express train to Drunk City.

Becky pushes me away with both hands, suddenly. "God-damnit, why is *he* here, Harlan?!"

And Ben slurs, "Get bent, you cow. I can be where I want to be. And don't talk to my friend like that! He's too good to be spoken to like a damn child. Harlan, gather your things. *We* are going home!"

"Dude," I plead, "fuck off! Please not now!"

Becky gets up and grabs her purse, moving to the door. I put my hand on her arm and say, "Baby, don't leave! It's all good; I got this."

In no way do I got this.

"You told me you were done with him, Harlan Finnegan! Don't you *baby* me. You lied. Again! You're fucking compulsive! What the fuck is wrong with you? Can you say *anything* that's true? And what the fuck is wrong with *me* for thinking that you had suddenly changed?! You probably have another date with some other floozy tomorrow you conniving, lying... slut!" She's in full Rage Mode now. The gloves are off. All the vitriol and bitterness harbored for months boils over in front of me.

I am speechless, standing mouth agape trying to conjure up words but nothing comes out except a lame, "Baby, no! Baby I'm sorry! It's not like that!"

It's totally like that.

"I am out of here. We are done," she says coldly and storms towards the door.

"Baby... come on, don't..." I beg, but it's no use. She shrugs my hand off her shoulder at the door and orders, "Do. Not. Ever. Touch. Me. Again."

She marches outside. In the corner of my eye, I see Ben shrug, pick up her drink and take a sip. The front door slams. She clops away down the sidewalk in her heels, her gorgeous self now disappearing from my life again.

Everyone in the bar is quiet and looking at me. Mike

looks horrified. I look at Ben through slit eyes. My reptile brain takes over. The veins in my neck are showing.

"I don't actually care that you lied to me, man," Ben says, nonchalantly. "Just glad I nipped that in the bud. I knew there was a reason I wanted to go here instead of the Ruby Room. Well, after Ruby Room, I mean."

Slowly, I turned.

"Look, Becky is *no good* for you, man," he says. "She never loved you for who you are. That's just one more relationship failure waiting to happen that you are going to blame yourself for and get all upset and 'woe is me' and shit. I'm not gonna sit around and watch you mope for another six months or try to drink yourself to death when that ship crashes and burns, which it definitely would," lightly slurring all the while.

Step by step.

He stares at the bottles behind the bar now as he continues. "You are fine the way you are. You don't need to go changing for some chick. They are a dime a dozen. You are young still. There's no hurry to settle down or settle for someone who doesn't want the real you. Drink your drink. You'll feel better," he tells me and pats the seat of the barstool next to him.

And then I start to strangle him with both hands.

9.

I don't really know what the over-under is on Bad Brains' "Pay to Cum" being the next song on the jukebox, but it does not matter. However unlikely the odds, its frantic staccato roars pretty much as soon as I decide to murder Ben. And if you are going to be in a bar brawl, I highly recommend it as the soundtrack. The lyrics aren't really fitting, but boy is the hardcore thrash vibe A-plus perfecto for the overall ambiance. It's fast. It's angry. It's chaotic. Pretty much the sonic mirror of what comes next.

With a hard shove, Ben sends me flying over a bar table onto my back. I hear him coughing. I jump up and come at him with a chair like a battering ram, like the lion tamer in the circus finally snapping at the uncooperative lion and shoving two of the legs into his stomach.

Ben turns to the side, averts the legs and covers his balls with both hands so I wind up ramming him against the bar with the bottom of the chair. "Ooof! Watch it, Harlan! Those were almost my nuts you hit!" he exclaims as he wrestles the chair from my hands after a brief tug-of-war. He has an unfair numb, drunk-guy advantage... drunker than me, at least. He doesn't seem to be too concerned with pain.

I throw a right cross at Ben, but the force of him ripping the chair from my other hand sends him backwards into the bar again, and I spin sideways, over-committing to the missed punch. Ben kicks me in the right thigh with a roundhouse kick causing me to yell out, "Motherfucker!" and hop around on my left leg for a brief spell. Ben slaps me on the back of the head with his open left hand, right in the base of the skull. For a brief second, I see stars.

I turn to face him as Mike yells for us to break it up. But I ignore the bartender's orders. Rage courses through my alcohol-loosened veins. I want blood, Ben's blood.

High on snake juice, I charge forward, and connect with a lunging left jab into Ben's nose. I follow it up with an overhand right to the left cheek and then limp a few steps to my left, sticking and moving the best I can with a dead leg.

Ben advances and counters with a jab of his own that glances off my forehead. I try to trap the jab like Bruce Lee, miss completely, and then Ben's big right fist slams into the right side of my face. The world goes dark for a moment. I still hear sounds around me. A multitude of voices yell for us to stop. I drop to my knees. I hear an effeminate voice call out, "They are gonna kill each other!" and Mike saying, "I'm calling the cops!" and some clearly educated asshole saying, "Fight with greater proficiency, you raging, plodding, uncompromising dipshits."

Yes, the hearing is the last thing to go. It's official. But I'm not dying; it's only a flash knockout. I wake back up, try to stand, and fall all the way down.

"Dude, stay down," Ben says, looking down at me. Then I hear glass break. Ben falls to the ground next to me holding his head. He groans, "What the fuck was that?"

Mike stands on the other side of the bar holding the neck of a broken beer bottle. He spits, "You two get outta my god-damn bar! You are both eighty-fucking-sixed!"

"Okay. Give us a goddamn minute," Ben answers from the fetal position. Laying there on the floor, we make eye contact. Ben goes, "Hey, you okay?"

"I think so, maybe... you raging, plodding, uncompromising dipshit."

Ben chuckles like a psycho and notes, "I think he hit me with a bottle. That's kinda cool."

10.
September 11th, 2001

I am twenty years old and I'm asleep in the in-law apartment I've converted into my little cave of perceived independence, even though I still don't pay rent or utilities as I live with my mother. I dream contently. My worldview is the luxurious, carefree sort that only a twenty-year-old who lives in a college town, works a stupid job and has no clear direction in life can fail to properly appreciate.

All of the past twenty of my years on this earth have been free of the fear of foreign-owned bombs falling from the sky, free from the fear of conscription for revenge upon the droppers of said bombs, free from the fear of my life being ended prematurely by the horror of war and the pestilence it totes in its aftermath. I know that this fear has existed in the minds of other citizens of other countries in my lifetime, yet having been born as a citizen of the United States in the era that I was, I have never had to worry much about it.

I am asleep when it all starts.

In 1981, the year of my birth, the Vietnam War was already over. And as I came into consciousness and learned what nations and governments were, the fatherly and charismatic Ronald Reagan went on TV and told the bald, Russian man with the birth mark on his head to tear down The Wall his people had built in Germany, back when the world was captured in black and white.

The Wall was built at the end of an era in which my grandfathers on opposing sides of the family fought a war that consumed nearly every region of the globe. My mother's father never came back from it, but prior to his untimely demise on some little gore-soaked atoll of tactical importance but little else, he fathered two children. He was nineteen. I've seen one more birthday than he ever did, and I have the audacity to complain that my mother stomps around on the hardwood floors too early in the morning or afternoon.

My American grandfather did come back from WWII, having fought in Western Europe, another gore-soaked theater of war made up of otherwise idyllic fields, rivers, towns and forests, all of which are still there and mostly bare little trace of the cataclysms that took place in the 20th Century, minus the occasional discovery of an unexploded bomb by a farmer. Upon his return to the ticker-tape parades and presumably consensual make-out sessions with women in heels and red lipstick, he fathered many children, my dad being the second of five.

After Reagan commanded his Russian counterpart to destroy The Wall, the news programs that my parents watched showed people in high-waist jeans ripping down a graffiti covered, concrete monument to misguided nationalistic pride, much to the seeming elation of everyone involved. But the elation and triumph I witnessed was impossibly far away from anywhere I had known, just a different colored section on my spinning, desktop globe, one not simply across the vastness of the Atlantic Ocean, but also all the way across my own country, which I had never before crossed.

I knew of war because of TV, movies, school and from the tales of my American grandfather. I knew of war because of my mother's explanations about my father's refusal to talk about his times in the Vietnam jungle. My father, depicted in a photograph that I had in a frame on my bookshelf showing his younger self in a green helmet with an M-16 rifle, shirtless, sinewy and tan with a smile on his face and a cigarette dangling from his lips, in defiance of his circumstance, a warrior captured in his raw form.

When I was nine, I saw my first images on television of a brand new war, images that were nearly overshadowed by the coverage of protests going on in my home town and across the San Francisco Bay, and then on the Bay Bridge itself. I saw young people yelling while holding signs and helmeted policemen yelling back while holding long sticks. Anger all around.

My parents watched news programs showing our young men in a desert I had never been to, our battleships and carriers in a sea I didn't know the name of, our tanks, our jet fighters and our attack helicopters framed by sun-drenched sand. From GI Joe toys, I knew the names of the M1 Abrams tank, and the A10 Warthog and I wanted to know what the rest of the destructive machines were called. In secrecy, where the parents of my friends would not see them and accuse my *Baby Killer!* of a father, and mother raised after the fiery setting of the Empire of the Sun, of child abuse, I played with my war toys that the other kids weren't supposed to know about. I pretended my plastic soldiers were going to go get the bad man named Saddam. I pretended I piloted the same helicopters that I saw blowing up vehicles on that long, desert highway of horror and mayhem.

Mom said that I wasn't supposed to watch the violent, late night news broadcasts, but my dad's commentary about such footage was contagious and I would sneak into the room and catch glimpses of depleted uranium rounds decimating ramshackle buildings and vintage artillery instillations. I remember a hodgepodge of scenes of more protests, more violent GI Joe battles, coffins draped in American flags, GI Joe funerals, and charred bodies in smoldering vehicles on the Highway of Death. I remember clearly the late nights of seeing my dad, who did not talk about his own war, riveted while watching a war that he said wasn't like the one he knew. Then as quickly as it started, it was over.

A few years later, Mom and dad split. I never really

understood why, but I knew my dad was the one who left.

Now let's cue the early Nineties in all its grungy prosperity and distortion-pedal driven rock n' roll glory.

In my last year of middle school, I walked into second period's Spanish class with a flannel shirt tied around my waist and unwashed, greasy hair long enough to touch my chin. I found that the teacher had rolled one of those mobile television stands with the VCR on the shelf beneath it into the class. But when I sat down, I realized we weren't going to watch a movie. Instead the TV displayed images of a building in Oklahoma that looked like it had been ripped in half by Godzilla. It turned out to be the work of a different kind of monster, one born, bred and injected with hatred right here in the U-S-of-A. There was horror and death. There were dramatic rescues and shining displays of heroism. People were pulled, alive or dead, from impossible piles of rubble by professional rescuers and volunteers alike.

Not long thereafter, an angry white man was arrested for the bombing, a man who had played GI Joe in real life the Gulf War, a soldier like my father had been. This arrested man's expression of his hatred and radicalization helped radicalize me against the system that could make such people in the first place. I found my hatred of the "establishment." I found my hatred of warmongering. I found my hatred of the institution of racism and the patriarchy. I wanted to fight those things with fists and guitars. I was angry at my father for leaving us and I knew my new ethos could bite him back. I cursed him as a war pig, a *Baby Killer!* and all that shit.

Cue the protest songs and insolent hair. Cue puberty and teenage angst. Cue me flipping off cop cars while skateboarding in traffic. I pogo danced at every show at Gilman Street and my ears didn't stop ringing for years. I lifted cans of malt liquor and Strawberry Hill wine from the corner store and dodged apprehension by Cal's campus cops.

Over time, my steadfast dedication to the punk subculture waned, no doubt tempered by exhaustion with having to be angry at something all the time, go to protests, read the right publications and zines, argue with my father about American foreign policy, consider democrats to be far too conservative… et cetera, et cetera.

Then some assholes drove a skiff into the side of an American warship and blew a giant hole in its side. I didn't really give it much thought. It happened in the Middle East, and for as long as I had been alive that place had been a mess. Plus, I was busy bumming around Berkeley Community College taking not-really-useful courses like *Introduction to Film* and *Native American Studies 101* with no clear plan to do anything other than keep on working at Rasputin Records and attempt to seduce UC Berkeley girls who thought I was cool because I got to grow up going to Operation Ivy shows.

There's the knock at my bedroom door and I yell, "Jesus, Mom, it's fucking dark out still!" She stops knocking and says, "Turn your TV on." I'm completely confused. Due to years of me complaining, she normally waits until at least daylight to wake me up, on purpose or otherwise. She says it again, "Harlan, turn your TV on… and call your father." She sounds genuinely disturbed. So, I grab the remote off the bedside table and comply as ordered.

My groggy mind can't quite comprehend what's going on. I see two World Trade Center towers billowing smoke like impossibly large candles. A giant hole in the side of the Pentagon makes about as much sense as a bite taken out of an angular donut. The shit takes a while to register as a real thing that is indeed happening.

In New York, there are people jumping to their deaths rather than burn alive. Their bodies fall at terminal velocity to the ground below where rescuers try to save what lives they can.

Sirens.

Screaming.

The red lights of every imaginable type of emergency

vehicle.

FDNY dudes, cops and medics run into the buildings. Victims walk out way too slowly looking shell shocked and staggering. Cops and bystanders hold them up and pull them away from the flaming buildings and falling bodies. So many firefighters file in.

I lose track of time as I watch. Reporters struggle to come up with things to say. Nobody cuts to commercial.

On live TV, a skyscraping tower implodes. Then another. Faces full of horror and panic run from the billowing clouds. Pandemonium. I hear my mother's voice upstairs scream twice. Maybe I do the same. I don't know.

I hear my mother weeping and don't know if I should go to her. I call my father. We don't say much. He asks, "You watching this?"

"Yes."

Calmly, he says, "Son, listen to me, okay? The world is going to change. More people are going to die. It would be hypocritical of me to ask you to not fight. I just want you to know that I love you and I'm sorry that my generation couldn't keep this shit from landing in your generation's lap. Just remember that there's more than one way to serve your country. You don't have to go kill anyone. You don't have to die in some pile of sand, and you don't have to lose your soul. Take that from someone who wishes he had been told that long ago."

"I love you, Dad. Let's go to an A's game soon, okay?"

"Absolutely. Son, I love you too. We will go to the first home game we can. Who knows, they might even make it to October."

"Okay, Dad."

"Go hug your mother for me."

"I will."

I hang up. I walk upstairs and find my mother on the couch staring at the TV with the puffy, red eyes of someone who has managed to gain a margin of control over her tears. I sit down next to her and embrace her. I tell her, "I love you, Mom."

The news reports another plane down in a field in Pennsylvania, far from any landmark. Nobody knows what to make of it.

More screaming.

Replays of the second plane impacting.

Replays of the towers falling.

Images of humans plunging to their deaths.

I'm angry. I want to revenge. I want to kill the people who did this to my homeland, to wave our flag in their evil faces. Blood for blood.

I have never felt this way before.

Mom grabs my face with both hands. She looks me dead in the eyes. She holds my cheeks and says like a telepath, "Don't you go die, like all your father's friends."

11.

None but terse dialogue has pockmarked the opening two hours of our shift. Perfunctory conversation about where to park, where to get coffee, some other banality, but that's about it. Ben and I have spoken of nothing of substance, and certainly nothing about the previous night. Granted, everyone else has asked what, in the name of all that is holy, happened to us. We both have black eyes. Ben has a lump on his head that looks like one from an old cartoon. We are obviously beat up and broken. Coworkers ask me what happened, and I just say, "Ask that guy," and point to Ben who says, "I don't want to talk about it." And vice versa.

We stubbornly refuse to address the elephant in the room. I am still upset. Ben probably thinks I am being unreasonable. None the less, we aren't budging. The uncomfortable atmosphere is made worse by the fact that today, of all days, is uncharacteristically slow going. It's been two hours and we haven't even had one call. We are the crew of a ship waiting on still water for the wind to pick up. Rebellion brews in the meantime.

Ben makes the loudest possible noise he can spitting tobacco juice into his empty plastic soda bottle. I try my best to fart as much as possible, but silently like a gaseous, ninja assassin. It's a psychological war. We rattle our sabers like rival superpowers. Somewhere, our coworkers are playing Frisbee or driving around looking at girls. They are relaxing and reading the paper or visiting with hospital staff. Two crews might be shooting hoops at a public park. Some EMT or medic is texting a prospective sex partner. They are no doubt loving the relaxation, catching up on a good book or browsing in some bespoke shops on Grand Avenue. But we just sit there, trying to push one another's buttons. We are North and South Korea. The space between our two seats is the DMZ.

"Oakland 527?" the dispatcher calls over the radio.

I glance at Ben. He glances at me. Neither of us move. We are sitting in the rig in a parking lot at the Eastmont Mall. The mall is a failed economic venture. Only a few stores are left. Most of it has been converted into houses of basic services, a police substation, a health clinic, the cable place… and, of course, the obligatory McDonalds.

Shootings happen in the parking lot a few times a year, which is basically the parking lot of a police station and everyone knows it, but this only seems to be mild deterrent to violent crime. Good thing there's a fire station just across Bancroft and usually an ambulance in the area. Nobody prefers posting out here. It feels like being banished away from the relative splendor of downtown.

"Oakland 527?" the dispatcher calls again, a bit louder.

Neither of us move.

"Oak-land-five-two-se-ven!"

I pull my chew out of my pocket, pack the can with my finger and put a dip in my mouth.

The Dispatcher says, "Negative response from Oakland 527. 527 is out of service. Can I get a supervisor to copy?"

The Supervisor's voice sounds, "Oakland S1, I copy. Any idea what's going on with 527?"

"They aren't coming up on the air. I show them stationary at 73rd and Bancroft on the GPS."

I lose the standoff and pick up the radio. "527. We are here," Then I lie, "We were on portable and had the volume too low. Go ahead with your traffic."

Ben lets out a satisfied and victorious sound, "Hmmmf."

"Okay, 527, please post at 10th and Clay."

This is normally good news. Downtown: the land of

food, coffee, newsstands, bookstores, women in business attire, and things to look at and do away from the drab landscape of the east. We would normally be stoked. Instead, I just say, "Copy that," because I refuse to show positive emotion in Ben's presence.

I turn the engine over and drive up the hill to the 580 freeway in silence. Halfway to our post downtown, just before the exit for Highland Hospital, dispatch calls us again.

"Oakland 527 copy code-three?!" the dispatcher blurts, obvious panic in his voice, which is troubling.

Ben looks at me with a raised eyebrow as if to ask, *"Wonder what got his panties in a twist?"* Ben picks up the radio this time, curiosity getting the better of him.

"527, go ahead."

"527 this is code-three for the infant not breathing. 2210 east 19th Street at 22nd Avenue. Fire and PD responding, copy?"

"527 responding," Ben says. He adds, "Fuck."

"Yeah… fuck," I agree.

I hit the lights and siren and go diving across three lanes of traffic to make the off-ramp. I take a left onto Beaumont headed down to the near-east section of Oakland, home to the infamous *Murda Dubbs* area. It houses a maze of streets that are blocked off by concrete barriers to deter drive-through drug traffic and calm the speed of police chases and drive-by shootings.

One minute into our response, we get an update from the dispatcher, "Oakland 527, OPD is on scene reporting CPR in progress."

I hit the gas and blow through stop signs but take no such chances at red lights. We are no good to anybody if we don't get there in once piece. Ben sits up in his seat and puts his gloves on. We are five blocks away.

"527, OPD is requesting an ETA?"

Four blocks.

"We are almost there," Ben says into the radio. "They

should hear our siren."

Three blocks.

Two.

Ben relays, "Oakland 527 is on the scene."

I kill the siren in front of a yellow apartment building. The unit on the ground floor is open. There are four police cars out front. An OPD sergeant waves both hands frantically at us. The fire department still isn't on scene, but I can hear their engine's air horn in the near distance. It's that hour of dusk that movie makers call the *Magic Hour*, the same lighting as when Luke saw the two orange suns over Tatooine and all the teen girls in 1977 swooned at his boyish good looks. I spit my dip out on the ground as I exit the ambulance.

"Get the shit," Ben says and confidently marches towards the front door. The cop clearly wants him to run, but Ben knows how to keep his heart rate down. He's done this enough to take precautions, so his hands don't shake uncontrollably. Cops run; we don't. Cops don't have to start intravenous infusions in tiny veins. Gotta keep control over fine motor skills. Gotta mitigate the adrenaline dump to be an effective rescuer. There's no time to explain this right now, though.

I move to the side doors and pull the gear out. I whip the doors closed and I can hear the fire engine getting closer. From inside the house, I hear voices. A woman screams, "My baby! My baby! Help my baby!" There are loud bangs and crashes. The police sergeant disappears inside. I race-walk towards the open door with our equipment.

Almost in slow-motion, Ben strides out the front door with a small baby draped across his left forearm. The baby's dark brown skin is far too pale. Ben covers the infant's nose and mouth with his lips, giving no-mask CPR, caution for communicable diseases abandoned. He uses the pointer and middle fingers of his right hand to give chest compressions to the infant. Ben nods at the ambulance between breaths and marches towards it.

I turn around and hustle to the back doors, dropping the bags at the tailgate. I climb inside. Ben meets me at the back of the rig and hands me the kid.

"Your go," he says and offers me the child with both hands. I take the baby from him, a male. He's nude and only lukewarm. His eyes are slits of white with brown centers. There's nobody home behind them. Vacant.

I continue CPR as Ben loads the gear onto the gurney. He says, "Four months old. Mom took a nap with the kid down an hour or so ago. Woke up and he was like this next to her. No obvious trauma. No medical history. Vaginal delivery without complications."

The fire engine arrives.

I can hear the police trying to calm the mother and other family members. I hear more female voices. They sound angry and young. Mom wants to come in the rig with us and bring a bunch of baby stuff in tow. She's not any older than twenty. I hear Ben tell the cops no, we can't. We are leaving right now. More screams follow.

Two firefighters get in the back with me and close the doors behind them. I look up for a second. Wide eyes on both, understandably. "Take over CPR, please, and I'll start ALS."

I'm so polite.

One firefighter climbs past me to the head of the gurney and slides open a cabinet, retrieving the smallest size BVM that we have. Ben hops into the driver's seat after closing the side doors. A cop bangs on the rear window telling us to go. I still hear a commotion outside. I glance up to see him holding family members back from the rear doors of the ambulance.

I place the kid down onto the gurney and the firefighters take over CPR. Ben puts the rig in drive and starts to head to Highland, the closest ER. He immediately picks up the Mednet radio. I put the EKG leads on the child's chest. The monitor shows a flat line, no electrical activity.

"Dude, the kid is asystolic. Gonna intubate and get an

I.O. going, copy?" I call out.

"Roger that," Ben responds.

First, I drop down to the floor of the rig at the head of the gurney. I affix the smallest blade to the laryngoscope and ready a tiny airway tube, matching it up with the thickness of one of the kid's fingers. After a round of CPR, I put the dull metal blade into the kid's mouth and lift up slightly, opening his epiglottis so I can see his tiny vocal cords. I pass the tube between them. It's probably the only invasive procedure that's easier on a baby than on an adult. The fireman tapes the tube down and starts bagging the kid through it. I confirm the tube placement with my stethoscope.

"Easy, easy, easy; nice and gentle," I instruct the firefighter. Don't want to blow the kid's lungs up. "Tube is in," I update Ben.

After that, I take out a needle designed to be inserted into the bone of an infant to secure a route of access for fluids and meds. Babies are usually too fatty for a field IV; it's impossible to feel their veins. I've done this before, but it's no less brutal with every attempt. After cleaning the kid's thigh, I push the large metal needle down into the flesh until I feel it scrape against the bone.

"Stick!" I call out to Ben, who takes his foot off the gas and lets the ambulance coast gently. Then, using a slight twisting motion, I gently push until I feel the little crunch indicating the needle has passed through the bone's surface into the marrow, and hopefully not all the way through the other side, as is extremely easy to do by accident. The fireman hands me the end of the IV tubing, and I attach it to the needle, now sticking out of the kid's leg like an impaled object. I tape everything down quickly and turn on the flow of fluid. The quick drip-drip means it is working. Good placement. I grab the cardiac meds.

"I-O in place, man."

"Nice… three blocks away."

I ready a dose of epinephrine and inject it into the IV

tubing. There's no change on the monitor. CPR continues.

We arrive. A gaggle of medical personnel meets us at the back door of our ambulance. Everybody wants to help the kids when they come in. My coworkers swarm too. Ben puts the rig in park, gets out and opens the back door for us. I hold up the IV bag. The firemen keep CPR going.

The firefighter doing compressions, an Italian bodybuilder looking guy with traditional nautical flash tattoos (anchors and such) on his thick arms that push the limits of his tight T-shirt asks, "You think he's gonna make it?"

I think about lying for a second and then admit, "No, man. Dead babies in asystole like that stay dead."

He winces. A nurse takes over CPR.

"Sorry."

He frowns and a moment later asks, "What happened to your face?"

Accepted preventative measures for Sudden Infant Death Syndrome (SIDS):

- Always put a baby to sleep on its back.
- Babies should sleep in the same room as parents, but not the same bed.
- Put babies to bed in cribs, by themselves, with no other children or adults.
- Make sure the temperature in the room is not too hot. Babies should be the same temperature to the touch as you or I.
- Babies should sleep on a firm mattress covered by a sheet. No quilts, pillows or overly soft bedding.
- Note that home breathing monitors have been shown to have little to no effect in the prevention of SIDS.
- Keep the child in a smoke-free environment starting at conception.
- Breastfeed.
- Offer the baby a pacifier.

- Never give honey to a child under one year of age.

Keep in mind that nobody knows the actual cause of SIDS. Absolute prevention is not yet possible. There are no symptoms. There are only contributing risk factors. These risk factors can include:

- Being around cigarette smoke while either in the womb or after being born.
- Being in an economically depressed environment.
- Having limited or no prenatal care.
- Sleeping on the stomach.
- Soft bedding.
- Sleeping as the same bed as the parent.
- Babies born in twins, or greater number, multiple births.
- A short time between pregnancies.
- Teen mothers.
- Use of illegal drugs by the mother.
- Babies born prematurely.
- Having a sibling who also died of SIDS.

12.

It's twilight, and the sun has already set. We try to clean the ambulance quickly. Don't say it out loud, but we are both thinking the same thing: *Let's get out of here before the parents find out their child is dead. I don't want to watch someone fall to pieces right now. I don't want to think of this as anything more than just another call. We aren't done today, and the next call could be the same thing.*

For about five quick minutes I reassemble the monitor and reposition the bags and IV supplies while Ben wipes down the gurney and changes the paper sheet on it. That finished, I start to hammer out the patient care report, my report of the incident and the treatment given. Using the times we arrived on the scene, left in the ambulance for the hospital and arrived at the hospital, I do my best to estimate the times I gave meds, started the IO, intubated the kid, hooked him up to the monitor, etc. Each major treatment modality gets its own time stamp, along with an ensuing description of what, if any, change there was. In this PCR, the descriptions are brief. I use medical shorthand, a bizarre collection of symbols made up by some unknown, bloodletting doctor long before my time.

We finish readying the ambulance for the next run. We still haven't spoken. I walk the hospital's copy of the PCR in through the ER doors to drop it off at the nurse's station. Ben follows behind me, presumably to take a leak. I'm not sure why else he'd come in as well. He's right behind me as we pass the door of the family waiting area, where worried relatives are sequestered awaiting the destructive news of the fate of their cherished little bundle of innocence, pride and hope.

Three steps past the family room and the most god-awful, blood curdling scream I can imagine, a wail like a banshee awash in the torrent of grief comes blasting from behind the closed door and reverberates down the halls. The scream stops dead in their tracks all who hear it: orderlies, nurses, physicians and patients alike. I imagine that somewhere in the hospital that an obtunded old man in a coma can hear the horror of the sound and it traps him in a nightmare.

The scream goes on for what seems like an hour. Then it's followed by more. The mother of the dead baby trying with all her tenacity to scare away the news of her child's passing. Hairs on the back of my neck stand up. I slap the PCR down on the counter of the nurse's station and hurry out of the ER where I hide from the noise behind our ambulance, seated on the tailgate with my bruised face buried in my hands.

Seconds later a familiar hand touches my shoulder.

"Harlan," Ben says.

I jump up and fail to choke back tears. It's too much drama to take in the span of a day.

Ben puts his arm around me and embraces my sullen form. And uncharacteristically softly, he tells me, "You are okay, man. You always do your best. *We* do our best. Everything is fine. This isn't our tragedy."

I nod and he lets me go. With both hands on my shoulders he looks me in bloodshot, bruised eyes with welled up tears and says, "Also that was my tech and you totally didn't even say anything, again… dumbass."

I sigh and wipe the moisture from my eyes with my forearm. I say with a reluctant grin, "You are such a raging, plodding, uncompromising dipshit ."

13.

A little over an hour goes by since the dead baby call. OPD calls us for a medical evaluation of a custody. When we get there, we learn that the patient punched a cop and was summarily treated roughly. The punched cop, an athletic looking Asian dude with a flat top who has a bit of a fat lip but is otherwise in good spirits, waives off any concern for his injuries and tells us, "Just let us know if we have to take this custody to Highland for medical clearance." Then he tells us that said custody did a purse-snatching of some hipster girl who thought that it was totally a good idea to walk around the side streets of downtown at night, by herself and with her iPod on full blast. I see said hipster gesticulating wildly while talking to another cop who is holding a clipboard and writing down her version of events.

The patient is a young and African American. He wears an oversized, weed-reeking hoodie that clearly hasn't been washed in a good while. As I examine his superficial injuries he says in a rather perfunctory manner, "The police whooped my ass for no reason."

I ask him if he was just minding his own business and he makes an affirmative noise. After taking his vitals, doing a quick head-to-toe in which I discover a number of bullet scars and determining that the primary injury is to his ego, I tell the cop, "He is cleared." I make the cross of a catholic priests blessing in the air as I say this.

In response, the patient tells me unpleasant things about my mother, which causes Ben to audibly cast doubts as to our patient's heterosexuality. The cop sighs.

We take our "lunch" break at the Temescal District Walgreens. Neither of us are hungry per se, so we buy six-dollar cigars, giant bottled waters and a Twix bar to split. The clerk cards me despite my uniform and barking radio sending calls to units around the city, which means it's busy and our lunch break might be short lived. Ben thinks this is hysterical and says to the clerk, "He's only sixteen. Don't believe his fake ID. He's the Doogie Howser of Oakland paramedics."

I tell the clerk, an older gentleman who doesn't speak a whole lot of English, and who I am sure doesn't know NPH from NPR, "Ignore him, please." I present my work ID that doesn't even have my birthday on it, but I don't think the clerk notices when he nods, satisfied.

We head outside. It's a pretty warm night. There's a light breeze coming off the bay that smells like kelp and sand, and I deduce that means the tide is out… or in. The blustery winds of the Bay Area's unique sunset have subsided considerably. The moon is bright but not quite full. We light up our cigars and lean against the front of the rig, which is parked pretty much by itself in the nearly empty lot. Walgreens is the only open business. It is nights like these wherein I wish Genova Deli was open late.

Sometimes on our lunch breaks Ben and I play Frisbee and listen to *Loveline*, lamenting the absence of Adam Corolla who relished in mocking callers whose smoke detectors were chirping in the background. Sometimes we rock out to college radio if the DJ isn't too annoying or acting like he or she is the first person since the Woodstock generation to discover Jimi Hendrix. We tell stories about high school memories triggered by the occasional occurrence of the correct song, Pavlov taking control of the moment, if you will.

Today, though, we smoke shitty cigars in relative silence because I am lost in my head. I think about the dead baby. I think about the mother's life, maybe growing up in public housing projects, indentured to welfare. I think about how crack helped destroy a generation and regressed its successor, further turning the ancestral victims of slavery into victims of mass poverty and all the shit it carries in tow.

I think about the jerk of a patient that I just evaluated and the circumstances that brought him there. I think about the nonstop meat grinder of gang revenge. I think about the disappointed looks of grandparents whose houses bought after the war, with so much hope for better circumstance, wound up in decrepit states of disrepair, adding to the blight that accompanies the plague of violence.

I close my eyes and see dead faces: old men killed by heart attacks or strokes or awful diets, crackheads in their final seizures from cocaine-induced delirium, gangsters and random bystanders from gunshots, drunks and random commuters in mashed cars, babies from SIDS or neglect – ghosts all around me, a gamut of despair. The one common theme is that I couldn't save any of them.

I feel guilty about my fortunate upbringing, and lucky that I wasn't born a couple generations earlier in an internment camp.

I look over at Ben and am halfway convinced that he's thinking about the same things as me. He quietly blows smoke rings into the sky, staring at the moon, and then takes a bite of his half of the Twix. Tonight, we went from dealing with a dead baby to a person living on borrowed time, who is aware of this fact and behaving accordingly. Now we smoke cigars, eat candy and are both very much alive. Situation normal: all fucked up.

Ben breaks the silence by asking, "How old is the oldest woman you would bang?"

Clearly, I was incorrect as to my assumptions regarding Ben's thoughts. He is not meditating on social issues. No matter. It's a fine distraction. I answer, "Is there any duress or coercion involved? Am I receiving payment or being held at gunpoint? Or is this like a genuine attraction thing?"

"No, it's not a *fuck to save your life* thing. Just think of the oldest woman you would have sex with and please provide an example."

"Alright. Creative, I must admit."

"Thank you."

"I can't believe we've never had this conversation before." I tap my foot for a bit and search my brain, switching it back over to my normal, idiotic, man-brain. I take a drag from the cheap cigar. A face pops into my head and I answer, "That blonde lady from the last *Ocean's Eleven* movie that wanted to hump Matt Damon when he had the fake nose on. I totally would have sex with that actress, but I don't know how old she is. I'm guessing fifty-something... and her boobs are probably half that age."

"Ellen Barkin? Good call," he says. "And the movie is called *Ocean's Thirteen*, goofball."

"Whatever. What about you? Got anyone in mind?"

"Kim Cattrall. Hands down. I know for a fact that she's in her fifties, but I would ride her like I stole her. Whatever dust is on that saddle would be knocked right off."

"Kim Cattrall, eh? Well there's no dust on that saddle. You are delusional if you think so. Her boyfriend is probably younger than I am and with better abs."

"Well, just saying..."

"You a big *Sex in the City* fan? Cuz, if so, I hear there's another one of those movies in production soon, or so the internet tells me."

"No, dildo. If you recall, she was in *Big Trouble in Little China*, one of the greatest movies of all time. She was sexy and awesome and had green eyes and she courageously defied the villainous Lo Pan. Perhaps you've heard of this film?"

"Don't start with me on John Carpenter flicks. You know I am a veritable encyclopedia of Carpenter knowledge."

"Then you should know that she has a respect boner, for life, from me."

"I totally concur. I must say that this is a solid choice you have made, and I support it."

"I still feel like I could bang Carrie Fisher out of reverence for her impact on my sexual development. I mean, I have mentally made sweet, sweet love to Slave Leia about seven thousand times, if not more."

"She's really not very sexy now though, dude. I mean, seriously. She's got that old smokers voice and, and just... no. I don't think I could do it. Not that I don't think Leia was attractive. Leia is also a respect boner recipient for life no matter what. Carrie is just not Leia anymore in my mind. And she's never coming back, I'm afraid. No amount of Jazzercise or whatever can fix that."

"That proves you aren't as big a man as I am."

"Well," I say, "so be it, Jabba. Keep pulling them chains."

"Call me Han."

"No way."

The conversation peters out and we take the last drags off our cigars in silence for a while, listening to the sounds of the freeway in the North Oakland night. You can hear the freeway from everywhere in Oakland, its persistent white noise refracting off the giant bay windows of the expensive houses in the hills down to the valley below. In the distance, I can hear the farting noise of giant car stereos rattling the bolts and plastics of auction-purchased jalopies. Some tires squeal. Maybe a female voice screams in either drunken joy or mortal terror. Maybe that was a backfire in the distance and not another shooting, or so we hope.

I look up into the night sky again and see clouds lazily drifting past the moon. I see Orion and the Big Dipper. I make up some other constellations in my head: Jabba's Frog Bowl, Lo Pan's Hat, Dead Baby.

I picture other people looking up at the same moon and stars, but they aren't in Oakland. Maybe some couple is walking along the beach in Maui with cocktails in their hands that are sweet like fruit punch. They have their shoes off. He's wearing a Tommy Bahama shirt. She's wearing a light dress over a bikini top. They are talking about going skinny dipping away from the soft glow of tiki torches. The ocean is calm and makes a soothing bit of white noise to mask the giggles and splashes. They'll make love on a beach chair in defiance of common decency, in the spirit of love and mischief, even though nobody really minds.

I've never been to Hawaii, but I imagine this is how it is.

I break the silence this time, "I really want to go to Hawaii."

"Okay. Random. When?"

"Well, we got to save some money first, I think," I tell him. I have no idea how much a trip to Hawaii costs. I think probably like four thousand dollars. I don't know why I have this number in my head.

"Cool. Let's do that," he agrees without protest, to my surprise. "When do you want to go?"

"I don't know. The end of summer after school starts, again? Prices probably drop then, I would think."

"Cool," Ben says. "Use your fancy phone to see how much tickets are."

"Cool," I agree. "Wait, you use *your* fancy phone to see how much tickets are. I thought of the idea. You work on planning." I know this is a lost cause; he will not plan a damn thing. He will endlessly surf the net and bring up a funny video of someone falling or a picture of a man being penetrated by something not biological in nature or otherwise *not* designed to do the task as a simple dildo would, like a souvenir statue of the Chrysler Building or an old Ninja Turtle toy. Ben is not mature enough for the internet.

The radio tells us to stop planning our tropical vacation for a moment, "Oakland 527, copy a code-two med-eval for OPD."

"Again?" Ben whines.

"I'm finishing my cigar first. I'm sure this can wait."

14.

An airline's pre-flight briefing is more or less standard across the board. No matter where you are flying to, your final destination, you are given instructions of what to do in the unlikely event of a water landing.

Say, for instance, you are on a commercial flight leaving out of JFK. Then, and this is just hypothetical, both turbines are immediately clogged with the shredded carcasses of a flock of waterfowl. The pilot makes a split-second decision to belly land the plane in the Hudson River. The plane jostles and skips across the surface of the water to an eventual stop, where it slowly begins to sink. You had better:

1. Recall that your seat cushion is *not* a flotation device.
2. Reach under your seat and remove the life vest from its pouch.
3. Place it over your head and pull on the red tabs or blow on the red tube to inflate.
4. Secure your own vest before helping others, such as the elderly, disabled or children.
5. In an orderly manner, proceed to the nearest emergency exit.
6. Hope a crew member will activate the yellow rubber exit slides that also serve as rafts.
7. Proceed onto the rafts, or onto the wing and then into a raft.
8. Leave all personal belongings behind.
9. Await rescue. Do NOT swim for it.

This is a perfectly valid strategy when down in the Hudson River, wherein a number of people enjoying a jog along the shoreline witnessed your near death and called it in. In the middle of the Atlantic, Pacific, or Indian oceans, it's probably less of a high percentage drill. But, then again, what the hell else are you supposed to do? Your plane just crashed into the ocean. Do you really remember where your life vest is? How great is your cell phone service? Can you resist trying to sneak your laptop off the plane with you? Is there a nearby vessel with capacity for two hundred-plus passengers within rescue range? How hungry are the sharks and orcas and shit?

I wonder if submarines have an emergency plan for crashing onto dry land. Are there emergency flip-flops and sunblock located under the bunks of the crewmen? Beach towels? Cold beers? Picnic food? Frisbees?

Nobody ever bothers to mention the elephant in the room when flying over water: if that plane goes down, you are friggin' screwed. And if the plane goes down anywhere else, you are probably just as screwed. This is the price we pay for our modern convenience of being able to traverse the country in five and a half hours: the very real possibility of screaming for several minutes while the oxygen masks drop and inflight magazines fly around the cabin before instant, fiery oblivion. And as you plummet, you'll wonder why you couldn't get more than two micro-bottles of Jack Daniels or why only the rich people in first class had blankets provided to them without having to beg like vagrants back in the cheap seats.

We all fly the friendly skies while rolling the dice of fate. At least the first-class fuckers die first. In that, take solace, my fellow proletariat coachmen.

15.
Late November 2009

1700 hours and Ben and I are eating bagels with cream cheese. I'm drinking coffee. It's our morning, so we act like it, sliding into the local bagel shop in San Leandro on the way to the westbound 580 freeway that will soon take us to Oakland. We always arrive in the last hour before the place closes with the rest of the ambulance crews, cab drivers, tow truck drivers, meter maids, cops, hospital staff and the other folks that work nights.

We like this place because they always give us giant slabs of cream cheese with pretty much whatever topping we want in an effort to make their closing process easier. We won't know until years later after visiting Montreal that this bagel place is comparably crap, but that's a story for another time.

Ben reads a paper next to me while he devours a plain bagel with garlic and chive schmear. Right as we ordered, dispatch posted us in San Leandro to provide coverage in the northernmost city in the South County area.

The San Leandro/Oakland border delineates the two zones of Alameda County AER coverage into North County and South County, and the two radio dispatch channels we use correspond thereto. We are tuned into the South County channel, *South* as it is known, and listening to familiar dispatchers broadcast unfamiliar street names in Fremont, Hayward, Union City, Livermore, Dublin, Pleasanton, Livermore, Castro Valley and the rest of the small municipalities scattered about the East Bay. It's a huge area of coverage for one dispatch channel, but it works. However,

Oakland is busy enough to warrant its own.

The bagel shop is near the location that we are posted at, so it works out okay for us to be lingering there, but we both despise working calls in South County. We hate it here because there are overly eager paramedics on the fire engines. Many were trained by their departments with a pay increase being the motivator to undergo such training and they don't have much ambulance experience. Many of them, frankly, suck in our non-humble opinions, which are self-righteous, unreasonable and tainted, but there you go. We much prefer the utter disinterest of Oakland fire crews in the medical aspect of the job. It gets in our way less and – also in our opinion – too few cooks in the kitchen is much better than too many, especially when it comes to jabbing humans with needles or shocking them alive with electricity.

Earlier this morning, I woke up to the sound of Ben leaving the house at 0830. Seeing as he went to bed at nearly five in the morning, this was obviously meritorious. I conduct a brief inquiry now that we have a free moment.

"Where did you go this morning?" I ask. "You only slept for like three hours."

"Nowhere special. I had a Bloody Mary at Geo Kaye's with the hippie girl after she got off a night shift."

"How many did you have? You better not be asleep all day between calls. You know how much I hate that," I warn.

"Just like two and then half of her second one. I took a nap after. Don't worry."

"Then what'd you do between the bar and the nap? You two bone again?"

"Nothing. I came home and went to bed. Now I'm here. Is the fucking interrogation over yet?"

In my head the time frame doesn't really work out for him to be gone so long, but I don't actually care what he was doing, so I don't press him. I'm more interested in another question, one that just popped into my head, so I ask him, "Why do you think that people drink tomato juice on airplanes and *only* on airplanes? Isn't that weird?" I have no idea why I am thinking of this; might be my mental Hawaii vacation planning.

"I don't know if I've really flown enough to weigh in on this issue. People don't drink tomato juice normally?"

"Nope. Not that I've seen."

"If they don't then why can you buy it at the supermarket? It's not like you cook with the stuff, right?"

"No, you do not cook with it, which is weird that you would have any idea about that because you have never cooked anything for the duration of our friendship. And, no, not unless it's in a Bloody Mary or on a plane do people drink it. I'm serious about this."

"No, I get that."

"Maybe there's some sort of like intrinsic thing in humans to consume vitamin C and sodium when traveling? Like maybe it's stuck in us from when people got the scurvy."

"Uh, I guess. Mexicans drink tomato juice though, with beer. I forget what they call that, but it's delicious. You can buy cans of it at the liquor stores on International Boulevard. Some of them have clam juice in there."

"Clamato, yeah, I know. I mean *plain* tomato juice, not with booze. Nobody drinks it plain."

"Unless they are on a plane?"

"Yes, that's what I'm saying." I nod. Then I take another bite of my bagel. I have managed to come up with an entirely original thought, or so I am convinced, and I smile smugly. There's a moment of dead air.

"Or there's booze in it?" he clarifies.

"Now we are going in circles. Who's on first, asshole?"

"I don't know," Ben answers, playing into the bit perfectly.

We look at one another and then simultaneously belt out through full mouths, "Third base!" This is not the first time we have said this in concert.

And right on cue, the radio announces, "San Leandro

527, copy code-three?"

I sour at hearing our call sign slandered so. Sometimes I wonder if the dispatchers can hear us in their little room located somewhere unknown in what I imagine to be a drab corporate plaza.

Five minutes later Ben and I meet the Alameda County Fire Department on the outskirts of a parking lot for a strip mall at 151st and International. There's a San Leandro police car there too. All the various public safety professionals are standing around the body of what appears to be a white guy in his mid-fifties, but it's hard to tell his exact age because he's three quarters of the way to face down on the ground. The presence of the cop means that he was probably called first, someone reporting a drunk down on the ground or the like. The cop then recognized the situation was medical in nature and here we are.

I stop the rig. We don our gloves and hop out to see what's up.

A fireman in full turnout gear emblazoned with *PARAMEDIC* across his shoulders and his last name of *FOREMAN* across the bottom part of the jacket stands up from a kneeling position by the patient's torso. He turns to us and says, "Guy reeks of booze. He's not really responding to voice or pain."

"He a regular down here?" Ben asks because we don't know the frequent fliers in this neck of the woods. Sometimes they jump the border, as it's known, but generally stick to familiar territory.

"No, I've never seen him. Nobody else here has. We got called by the PD."

"Sooooo..." I butt in, "anybody at all know how our boy here wound up on the ground?"

Foreman says, "No, we aren't sure about that. The officer asked some bystanders and they said there wasn't an assault or anything out of the ordinary and nobody knows the guy. I just did a D-stick on him and his sugar is normal, so he's not in a diabetic thing or any, uh, situation like that."

Medical jargon is clearly not his strong suit.

"How about that whole *airway-breathing-circulation* thing?" I ask. "Are we confident that he is alive?"

"Yeah, he's got a fine carotid pulse."

"Physical exam...?" Ben leads, fishing for more info.

"Uh, haven't got that far yet," Foreman answers.

"Okay, so you had time to do a D-stick, an ALS procedure, but did not do any of the BLS stuff. You know the B stands for *basic* and that comes before A, which stands for *advanced*, right?" Ben can be an asshole, but he's right.

As Foreman starts to get all defensive and ramp up his verbal retort to my partner, I kneel to work on the patient. I get my face way down to his level and see that he has a bit of dried blood in the corner of his mouth that looks kinda old. I call out to the guy and pinch the skin on the interior of his bicep, but he doesn't stir. He does reek of booze; that much is correct so far.

The patient breathes regularly but not very deeply at twelve times per minute. I feel his pulse, and it's regular at about eighty BPM at the radial artery, which means his systolic blood pressure is at least 90. I cut the back of the patient's shirt with the new shears I've not yet lost and look at his back. Seems to be normal. In an abundance of caution, I direct a fireman to stabilize the patient's head and he and his cohorts help me roll the patient over to his back. I begin a physical exam of the guy looking for any further evidence of head trauma or spinal injury. When I touch the vertebrae in the middle of his neck, the guy groans. This sets the hairs on the back of my neck on an outward ascent. It sucks to get pinched on the interior bicep. It *really* sucks to get tattooed there. It usually doesn't hurt to get touched on the back of the neck.

Ben is now arguing with the lieutenant on the fire engine about their medical exam and the cop seems to be backing away slowly, obviously uncomfortable at the awkward exchange. I don't blame the guy. I'm kinda cringing inside but try not to show it.

I call out, "Hey, Ben, collar, backboard and high-flow oxygen right away would be great, if you finish arguing soon."

Ben immediately shuts up, turns and walks to the ambulance to get the gear.

Foreman asks nervously, "What's got his panties in a bunch?"

"Probably that you skipped some obvious shit, but that's not important now. Just help me strip and flip this dude. I'm gonna bring him in as a trauma activation to Haven." I call out to the cop, "Officer, can you see if there's video of this guy falling?"

The cop goes, "Sure thing," and heads towards the closest store.

Foreman asks with a hint of embarrassment in his voice, "What did you find that makes you think he's a trauma activation?"

As Ben tosses down the C-spine gear and opens the oxygen bag next to me I deadpan, "Well, this seems like a bad place for a face-down nap. But, truthfully, I just have a hunch and I'm bored and want to jack up this guy's bill as high as possible. He interrupted my riveting conversation about tomato juice."

Ben adds, "Hope you got insurance, sir!"

I hear a couple of firemen harrumph in disgust at our lack of professionalism. They are easy marks. There's no use trying to explain to them now why I think the patient is in trouble. The feeling's genesis is the hairs on the back of my neck going up. We can talk about it later if he's really interested, but you either got it or you don't.

Ben crouches down next to me and puts a high-flow oxygen mask on the patient's face. Then, Ben sizes and affixes a cervical collar around the neck. Foreman cuts the man's clothes off as I tell Ben what I've found so far, particularly the apparent tenderness at about C4, the fourth vertebrae in the neck southward of the skull.

After my report, Ben says, "Copy," and he continues the physical exam. The patient still doesn't respond to any other stimuli below the neck. Ben tries to tickle the bottoms of his feet with a pen. Ben pinches the guy's inner arm skin. Nada. Foreman and his peers seem to be clueing in.

We take positions to roll the patient onto the backboard and the firefighter holding C-spine gives a quick, "Okay, roll to the right side on three... one-two-three roll." Ben re-examines the patient's back while I work the backboard in place behind him. The task is completed without a hitch. Another, "One-two-three roll," and we have him in a supine position on the board.

The same firefighter gives the directions to center the patient on the board. "We are gonna slide him up on three... one-two-three slide," and we move the patient into position so I can tape his head down.

We buckle him into the board with the attached seatbelt-like straps. Ben brings the gurney over and a three count later he's packaged for delivery to the trauma team at Haven Medical Center. All he's missing is the bow.

Ben and I wheel the patient to the back of the rig and roll the gurney inside. Ben jumps in.

"You want a rider to help you out?" I ask him.

"No," he answers decisively.

"Don't blame you. Plus, I doubt anyone here wants to be stuck in an ambulance with you after that charming display of goodwill."

I trot to the driver's seat and call out, "Please have the officer bring the video to Haven if he finds anything."

Foreman looks kinda stunned and nods. The other firemen just look like they don't ever want to see us again, like we are yahoos making mountains out of a drunk molehill with a sore neck... and no intelligent nerve response in his extremities.

We pull away from the scene with lights and sirens ablaze to Haven Medical Center in Castro Valley, just off the 580 freeway at the base of the hill that shades Dublin, Pleasanton and Livermore from all fun and/or redeeming aspects of living in the Bay Area. Haven is the South County trauma center and though not as busy as Highland is still not by any means slow. Hayward and San Leandro have plenty of violence and major freeways scar the whole of metropolitan California, so they get plenty of carnage to deal with.

Ben calls out vitals as I hear him working behind me: "Pulse at 110 now. BP 100/50 and I think it's fishy. Respirations at twelve. This guy is too old for a pressure that low, right?"

"That or it could be a combination of his superior physical conditioning and frequent imbibing of Budweiser's Clamato beer."

"This guy hasn't seen a gym since... ever," Ben answers. "And he smells like whiskey so there goes your theory. Now I'm poking needles into his feet and he hasn't moved at all."

"Ouch, seriously?" Did he really poke a needle in the dude's foot? Yes, yes he did, I find out later. "I think that combined with neck pain is a bad sign, isn't it?"

"Unless you are a huge fan of controlling motorized chairs with your tongue, then yes. I'm going to put a line in his arm."

"Need me to slow down?"

"Never have and never will."

"Braggart."

I pick up the Mednet radio and ask for a channel to Haven Medical Center. As the dispatcher dials up Haven, I call back to Ben, "You doing anything else cruel and unusual that you want me to tell them?"

"Yes, tell them that every time you hit a bump he groans but has zero movement associated with guarding. He's like a limp noodle. Also, I got the IV line now and his blood sugar is, so I was told by that fireman, normal."

"Ah, mustn't forget that, yes."

The nurse at Haven answers, "Haven, go ahead."

I give my report, "Haven, howdy, it's *Oakland* 527 coming with you from sunny San Leandro with an approximately 55-year-old male found down by the PD. Fire did a D-stick on him and it was normal. We arrived, did an exam and now believe that what we have here is an un-witnessed fall possibly secondary to alcohol. Our patient is unresponsive except for some apparent point-tenderness in the mid cervical spine area at about C4 and he has zero movement of his extremities. His vitals might be crashing; got a BP of 100/50, heart rate of 110 and respirations at twelve. We have him in spinal precautions, on high flow oxygen and are establishing IV access as I speak. We think he broke his neck, to put it bluntly. See you in five. Oakland 527 clear."

"Haven copies the trauma activation, possible spinal injury. Haven out."

I lay on the air horn to clear and intersection and try not to hit any bumps while Ben sits and wishes there was more he could do for the guy on the gurney. I know this because he says, "I wish there was more we could do for this guy." But Ben knows that medical science is only so advanced and enlightened. Ben further knows that this guy will probably never walk again, if he even lives. Ben further, further knows that *shit happens* to the human body, and stem cells research is our only current brand of hope for this particular kind of shit.

We drop the guy off with the trauma team and stick around to watch for a while, long enough for the X-ray films to come back. Both of us are curious if the guy indeed has a spinal injury. If he does not, we will feel like epic dildos and hope we never see that fire crew again. That said, this could have been one of those situations that all paramedics dread: finding some drunk down, under-treating it, and having that now sober quadriplegic man come back with a big, face melting, ass-biting lawsuit and then wheel into the courtroom in a chair pushed by his youngest daughter in her Sunday best with a single tear dripping down her cheek. Luckily, we did our best. We didn't let jaded attitudes prevail, as is always a danger.

The X-ray tech walks in with the films after about fifteen minutes and the attending physician, radiologist and trauma surgeon view them on the light box on the wall of the trauma room. A flurry of activity goes on behind them as the staff tries to minimize the horrible impact of such a devastating injury. It doesn't take the docs long to find obvious fractures with cord damage at C4. I was on the money. Not that it matters for the guy; the dude will never move or feel a body part below his neck again unless a major scientific breakthrough happens.

I feel a twinge of genuine sorrow for our patient. This was a freak accident. Maybe we can get the dude to some AA meetings, grow the guy back some spinal nerve tissue like on *Star Trek* and he probably won't fall down and break his neck a second time? Eh.

That or he kicks the bucket, goes to hell, get repeatedly poked by the Devil (not in the feet) with a pitchfork and is roasted for eternity in the same dungeon as Hitler. At least we meant well, St. Peter, you cold bastard.

I take the last bite of my, now cold, bagel.

16.

Throughout recorded human history man has been trying to meet woman (and vice-versa) to mate with, have a relationship with or otherwise get all cozy with so they can stop trying to look hot all the time and just wear pajamas, all the while farting with impunity and reproducing so that one can be taken care of by family rather than an underpaid and possibly handsy orderly at a hospice facility. Also, man has been trying to meet man and woman has been trying to meet woman-and-man-on-man-on-woman and so on and so forth… basically all the stuff you see on the Casual Encounters section of Craigslist, not that I use it, by the way. But what I'm getting at, is that the business/science/junk-science of matchmaking is as old as the process itself and it is made even more so specific in the Internet Age.

Once upon a time, two cavepersons probably huddled together for warmth and one thing led to another. Bam, nine months later, a little cave-baby arrived. Things were simple then. Nowadays, you have your four-hundred-and-seven question "love profile" to fill out on HappilyEverAfter.com and the like.

You get a couple years past college age, and a couple failed relationships under your belt, like pretty much everybody does as thirty approaches, or at least everyone who did not marry their high school sweetheart, then welcome to Baggage City USA! It's home of the biological clock that is no longer the slow moving one that adorned the wall of your fourth period math class, the class wherein you probably did *not* sit across the row from your future spouse who you were to grow old with and cherish, and all that shit that Hollywood loves to ram down our throats. Instead, this clock is now an angry, red, digital display of the sort used to time the launch of ICBMs outfitted with nuclear warheads of parental dissatisfaction with your lifestyle choices, perhaps voiced in a delightful phrase like, *No son of mine is gonna be a homo!* Or maybe it's another, equally horrible thing an asshole, drunk family member says when you finally let them know who you really are during Thanksgiving Dinner because there's no time like the present, right?

It gets worse even. Because if age forty approaches and you are still alone, well there must be something wrong with you, right? Regardless of your level of self-worth, there will be doubts along this line because you *used* to be so cool, the envy of all early-married folks for staying single and free for so long. You took all those cool vacations and had the whole bed to yourself! But soon you have your midlife crisis and shortly thereafter, your hair turns gray and your genitals shrivel up (so I hear). Then nobody wants you except your many cats or your antique baseball figurines and you eventually waste away alone in some government subsidized nursing facility having your few possessions that survived the involuntary estate sale embezzled by the shady orderly who comes in at night to see if you are still breathing and occasionally looks like he's going to diddle you but, best case scenario, does not. So, you have to partner, get hitched and whatnot, right?

The business of matchmaking is booming. People pay monthly memberships to dating services to find the correct person to grow old with. You can't meet your soul mate in a bar, they tell you; that's the express train to rehab and domestic violence. And dating coworkers is a *terrible* idea, they say. How will you lie to them about working late so you can bang your middle manager on the side? So, currently, it's a must for the single man or woman to take their *Matchability* exam for an online dating site or go to one of those speed dating lunch things.

You would have already found your soul mate by now, soon to be thirty or forty-year-old, if you had made this all a priority earlier in life. Now it's crunch time. The peak of the hill is approaching. After that, down you go... hell, sorry honey, you're thirty-five now? Oh dear... you might not even be capable of giving birth anymore unless you shell out enough money to a fertility doc to get a new personal watercraft to store on the aft deck of his yacht.

We in the Western World speak in condescending and negative manners about teen pregnancy, but anthropologists probably would argue that the human body is perfect for breeding at about sixteen. Breeding, yes. Parenting, not so much. It's all about finding that sweet spot, and that sweet spot is probably 25 which you already left in the dirt, didn't you?

What's a bachelor who is approaching thirty, one historically terrible with women but who loves to have sex with them and ride his motorcycle around like an idiot *but* who also has an impatient mother breathing down his neck telling him to start a family and give her grandchildren, to do?

17.

The nametag indicates her name is Dr. Vivian Lopez M.D. and she is insanely hot. She's talking with the trauma surgeon and the ER's attending physician at the bedside of the quadriplegic that Ben and I have so recently delivered. I currently eyeball her like a wolf watching a bunny rabbit that's covered in barbeque sauce. I'm apparently at the horny part of my man-cycle which means that I've gone from the baseline of *rather* horny to *mega* horny.

As I have this internal thought, Dr. Vivian Lopez M.D. looks up at me standing in the doorway of the trauma room and asks, "Can I help you?"

This brief sentence sends me into a slight panic as I truly have no reason to be in the room anymore. Ben is writing the report. I already got another backboard from the stack of extras outside the emergency room's ambulance entrance and, in truth, I saw this hot doctor enter the trauma room from down the hall and was making a fly-by to investigate when I was paralyzed (had to, sorry) by her visage.

"Uh, I, uh was... just about to ask you that same thing." I salvage the ship before it scuttles. "Before we get out of here is there any question I can answer?"

"Yes... actually, you can, come to think of it. Was his D-stick normal at the scene? Want to make sure we aren't dealing with a diabetic baseline. Just need to have all the info before we take him upstairs."

Son of a bitch, I think. "Yeah, the fire department did it right away and said it was fine."

"Thank you. I don't think I have any other questions."

"What, uh, do you do here?" I ask rather clumsily.

"I am a physician and… I try to make people not, like, die," she deadpans while pointing at her nametag which clearly indicates such. She ever-so-slightly rolls her eyes at my obvious flail.

Way to go, Harlan!

"I mean, I saw that on your nametag that you were a doctor. What's your specialty, is what I was asking? I've never seen you before. We normally work in North County." Again, I pull up right before careening off the end of the runway.

The two doctors next to her, both men, roll their eyes not-so-slightly and display expressions that clearly convey, *Give it up. Everyone has tried and everyone has failed, you simpleton dildo.* But I am undeterred, still on an adrenaline high from the last call, and still glad we caught what could have easily been downplayed as a simple drunk dude's drunk behavior or missed entirely by less awesome paramedics.

"I'm an anesthesiologist. I just finished residency and moved here from LA. I like long walks on the beach and drinking chardonnay in my pajamas. Will that be all then?" She raises an eyebrow.

A lump now forms in my throat. *Fuck it, here goes,* "Yeah, okay. Sorry to interrupt. My name is Harlan and I think you are gorgeous. I'm leaving now." The blush response makes my cheeks hot.

The two male docs frown at me, disgusted by my obvious, pitiful attempt to steal away their desired colleague. Dr. Vivian Lopez M.D. cracks an ever-so-slight smile and says, "Nice to meet you, Harlan. Good job on the case. That would be an easy one to miss."

We shake hands. I smile, bow forward in a gentlemanly fashion like I just got done conducting an orchestra, turn around and walk to the nurse's station to scavenge for candy. I don't look back because I just know she's stealing a glance at my perky ass, maybe. Knocked that shit out of the park, pretty sure.

I ask the charge nurse, who is sitting there in the receptionist's chair eating wasabi peas by the handful, for a piece of note paper and she hands me a notepad emblazoned with the AER corporate logo offering superior patient transport services, both BLS and ALS 24/7/365. I take the pen out of the breast pocket of my jumpsuit and write my phone number on it with the message: *Grab a drink sometime? – Harlan.*

I hand the notepad back, grab a handful of Hot Tamales out of a bowl on the counter and walk back over to the trauma room. Dr. Vivian Lopez M.D. walks out into the hall right as I approach the door and we almost collide. Without saying anything I hand her the note, throw the Hot Tamales in my mouth, smile, and walk out towards the ambulance bay, again without looking back… like a boss.

Nothing ventured, nothing gained and I sure as hell don't want to use one of those stupid websites to find a date. I'm not quite thirty, just yet.

Outside I find Ben finishing the patient care report on a metal clipboard balanced on his lap while seated on the tailgate of the rig. He spits tobacco juice onto the ground, looks up at me and says, "You see the body on that doctor in there? How does an ass look that good in hospital scrubs? It was majestic. She must be into yoga."

"I assume you mean my soul mate, Dr. Vivian Lopez M.D., the anesthesiologist who just moved here and now has my phone number?"

"Which, A) I assume you gave to her without her asking for it; and B) she will never call you because she knows you thirst for sweaty man-cock."

"Only ones bigger than your little pecker," I retort and grab my own can of chew out of my pocket. After swallowing the Hot Tamales and packing the tobacco with a quick flick of the wrist, I put a wad just behind my lower lip. The chew and cinnamon combo make it burn. I wipe my fingers off on the thigh of my jumpsuit and ask Ben, "Wait, is their non-man-cock? Why the gender-specific distinction. There's no lady-cock."

"Yeah, totally there is non-man-cock. There's horse-cock, whale-cock, elephant-cock, mouse-cock…"

"Mouse-cock? I've never seen a mouse-cock. I assume they are quite small."

"You've never looked. And don't interrupt… dog-cock, cat-cock, lady in transition to be a dude-cock, lady on too many steroids cock, uhhh… fly-cock… alligator-cock…"

"Flies do not have cocks."

"There's a bunch of kinds of cock, dude."

"I shoulda known you were an authority on all things penis."

"Fuck you for mocking my hobbies. Five bucks says she doesn't call you."

"You're on." I fish around in my pocket, produce a pathetic assortment of crumpled bills of denominations no higher than ten and start counting out singles. "Got the money right here."

"Also," Ben says, "do me a favor and kill me if I ever wind up like that poor dude we just picked up, seriously. That shit sucks."

"Deal. Ditto, man. Pull the plug ASAP in the event of quadriplegia. Or throw me off the Bay Bridge."

"Woodchipper all the way, buddy."

"So sentimental."

We bump fists to seal the bet and the mutual homicide pact in the event of paralysis. A simple instruction in the event of a specific disaster. You can never be too careful.

18.

"Her head hurtin'. What the fuck you think is wrong with her? See how she holdin' it? It fuckin' hurts!" the nineteen-year-old white girl with blonde corn-rolls and a neck tattoo of cursive the name *Andre* in front of me says in reference to her sister, who is probably about fifteen and as pregnant as pregnant can be. The pregnant sister is seated on a ratty couch watching *Spongebob* on a flat screen TV, leaned against the wall on the floor. Funeral pamphlets for deceased young men and plastic rosaries sparsely adorn the walls of the run-down unit we are all currently in. It's in deep East Oakland.

It's a day after I gave Dr. Vivian Lopez M.D., the new love of my life, my phone number and she still hasn't called. I am losing hope but trying not to show it to Ben. This is our first call of today's shift.

"If this is such a problem than why did *you* call 911?" I ask the aggressive sister. "Why didn't *she* call?" I point to the pregnant girl who isn't even looking at us and seems oblivious to our presence. "And why would one call 911 for a headache in the first place? Are you concerned she might be having a stroke in her teenage years?" I ask, trying not to get her too worked up but still convey my annoyance with the situation.

"Cuz, she's busy watching *Spongebob!*" non-pregnant sister says, like this explains everything.

"I am quite aware. Why didn't *she* call for herself? Or why didn't her parents call?"

"I called because I'm her older sister and she pregnant. I look out for her. That okay with you, Mister Pear-ah-medic?"

Oddly, this makes some degree of sense to me, but, "You didn't answer the second part of my question, but I will go ahead and assume that her parents aren't exactly in the picture here."

"They ain't around and ain't *been* around."

"You couldn't have just given her a ride?"

"The police took my car cuz I ain't got a license." She crosses her arms and smirks.

"They don't have taxi's here in Oakland?"

"Taxi's cost money, motherfucker! You think that shit grows on trees? Do we look rich to your ass? Do yo' fuckin' job and take her to the motherfuckin' hospital."

Ben, clearly quite done with the whole interaction, gestures to the younger sister, turns towards the door and says, "Let's go. Come on."

The angry, older sister hollers, "Ain't you gonna put her on your gurney?"

"She can walk just fine and that's a double negative," I retort, accented with a finger point. Our patient, Ben and I walk out of the unit and hear the door slam behind us. The non-pregnant sister carries on in anger behind the closed door, but I manage to tune it all out.

Ben whispers to me, "That was not a double-negative."

God damnit.

It's my turn in the back of the rig. After the pregnant girl climbs in and sits down on the gurney, Ben stands at the back doors and asks, "What hospital do you want to go to, little lady?"

"Highland, I guess," she answers. These are the first words that she has said so far. Ben closes the doors.

I start by asking a few basic questions and deduce the following: she is eight months pregnant with twins. She's had some prenatal care at the free clinics. She's been pregnant before but miscarried. She has no allergies or medical problems. She is taking prenatal vitamins. The twins' father is in adult jail right now, a troubling age difference that I try to not think about further. She has had a headache all day and for some of last night. It's a three or four on the one-to-ten pain scale. It's dull pain. She has had no head trauma.

"How long has it been since you drank anything?" I ask.

"I haven't drank anything since I found out I was pregnant. I don't drink much though. I just smoke weed."

"I don't mean that, not alcohol. How long has it been since you had water?"

"I had two Sprites today."

"Okay, that's problem number one. You gotta start drinking water, lots of it, out of the tap, bottled... whatever. I can tell by looking at your lips that you are dehydrated."

"I ran outta chapstick! Do it look bad?!"

"That's not what I'm getting at. It doesn't matter anyway. You gotta drink water. I guarantee it'll help with the headaches. Soda is full of sugar and makes you less hydrated. It *de*-hydrates you. I know it seems weird because soda and water are both liquids, but that's the way it works. The sugar makes your body move fluid out of the little cells that comprise your body, out of the important parts. That can give you a headache and lead to a load of other problems."

"Oh. I didn't know all that. What about diet soda?"

"Don't drink diet soda either. It might still affect your insulin levels. Insulin is the thing your body makes to keep your blood sugar levels normal."

"My momma had insulin she took in a pill."

"Not to be insulting, but...she pretty big?"

"Yeah, fat as fuck, like one of them big-ass seals that has the teeth in front."

I laugh. She laughs. Up front, I hear Ben laugh.

"I think you mean a narwhal."

"No, not those! They sound like, uh, walnut."

Confused, I silently mouth the word *walnut*.

Ben calls back to us, "Walrus!"

"Yeah, those!" she exclaims with a heavy chuckle.

I've had these talks hundreds of times with patients, about the need to drink water and not eat like crap. I've talked about how horrible fast food is. I've told people to try to eat vegetables and fruit instead of filling up on the ramen that comes in Styrofoam cups.

I've told little girls to wipe from front to back and not the other way around. I've told teenage girls how to use tampons and pads, about toxic shock syndrome, and how to avoid urinary tract or yeast infections.

I've told parents that secondhand smoke is awful for kids with asthma, and that marijuana smoke, yes, is also bad. I've tried to explain the other horrible things smoking does to the body. I've showed the warning labels on the cigarette packets that nobody reads and explained what emphysema means.

I've told boys they need to clean under their foreskins. I've explained how to properly use an albuterol inhaler for asthma or treat a bee sting, twisted ankle or the like and clean a cut or scrape. I've told parents not to wrap babies with fevers in blankets to reduce the risk of febrile seizures.

I've mentioned a few times that bathing regularly has additional benefits besides making one smell better. I've told men with complaints of foot pain to clip their toenails and the situation would be resolved. I've admonished men with fungal infections of their feet to change their socks.

Also, did you know you can get condoms for free at clinics?

Go outside and exercise any way you know how. Just walk if you can't do anything else. Send the kids out to play. Don't let them hide indoors all day. On that note, maybe it isn't appropriate to let your seven-year-old play *Grand Theft Auto*?

I tell people how to live and I'm in my twenties. I tell parents how to parent and I've never been one. I don't get how this makes sense but it's a common occurrence. They didn't teach me this in paramedic school, but it's part of the job regardless.

I have no way of knowing if any of it ever sinks in. I do, however, get occasional complaints delivered via my supervisors from angry parents for telling their sexually active teenage children where to get rubbers. I'll take that hit. The supervisors understand. There are enough neglected children out there already.

There have been countless conversations about basic health and nutrition in my tenure as a paramedic, all topics and skills people should learn in school or from parents or anybody but the person they will only be with for the length of an ambulance ride. Ben says that this is because public school is a factory of standardized testing and institutionalized cheating. There's no more home economics, he tells me. Sex education is constantly met with controversy because of religious zealotry and puritanical handwringing, he says. They will teach you geometry but not how to keep your body from breaking down, he preaches.

Ben and I agree that there are advanced concepts in modern education in place of basic human survival skills, ones that seem more important in the long run. There are efforts to teach existential concepts rather than to avoid the middle aisles of the supermarket. Many of our patients from impoverished neighborhoods will not or did not attend college. So why do we prepare them for a thing that will not happen as opposed to one that will, such as dealing with the reality of having and caring for a human body? Is it because our school systems treat everyone like they have the potential to become astronauts and physicians when that is unrealistic? Not all of us can wind up at the International Space Station. But, guaranteed, most of us will get sick, fornicate, or go to a grocery store.

It seems that many people don't know how to cook. And it's cheaper to eat at McDonalds and die of diabetes and heart disease later down the line anyhow because that is *then* and the *now* is far more pressing. The Number Four, supersized, with a gallon of soda may eventually kill you, but it's delicious and filling. Gunfire will definitely kill you and fuck it, at least you'll be fed when you get to the Pearly Gates or whatever place you think you go to after you die.

So I give my spiel about water and nutrition to the fifteen-year-old soon-to-be mother of two whose babies' young father is in state custody on a robbery charge. I take her vitals and make sure she's not gestationally hypertensive, which she is not and that's the only thing I can think of to be concerned about in her case.

Upon arrival, Ben and I walk her into the triage area at Highland where Tonya, one of my favorite nurses because she has insolent hair, rides a motorcycle, and is attractive, tells the pregnant girl, who is unfortunately named, Obsession, to have a seat in the lobby. Ben and I then chat with Tonya for a minute before getting the busywork out of the way.

I walk by Obsession to do paperwork as she texts furiously on her cell phone. She looks up at me and says, "You think that nurse is cute. You like her. I'm tellin'!" She smiles and laughs.

I tell her, "I might! I admit it," and we high-five. I give her ten bucks so she can get a ride home and she jumps up and hugs me, her pregnant belly bumping me in the crotch, which is extremely awkward.

Then she says while giggling, "I think you're cute too. How old are you? Wanna be my new baby-daddy?"

"Whoa, easy there, young lady. Pump them breaks. You got enough on your plate." I wish her well and make a quick exit because multiple voices in the waiting room start asking for money as well.

It doesn't take long to finish the PCR. Dispatch has us post basically where we are, right near Highland, so we clear the hospital and drive over to Lakeshore Drive by Lake Merritt to get coffee. It's only about a mile away.

Within five minutes, I'm inside Peet's just before closing time adding half and half to my cup of joe when we are sent to a call of an "unknown medical" in the area just east of the lake. I walk out to the ambulance and Ben follows about forty seconds later because he still was waiting for his soy chai *(You know how I know you're gay?)* when we got the call.

The "unknown medical" call is rarely an urgency, but for some reason we get dispatched lights and siren to them anyways, along with the obligatory fire department response. Nearest I can figure, these calls get classified in this manner because they aren't a traumatic event like a car wreck or stabbing being reported. Also, they aren't shortness of breath, chest pains, goddamn headaches, abdominal pain, unresponsive patients, or any other thing that could foreseeably be very serious (or in the event of our last call, not at all serious). It's just that the dispatcher really couldn't figure out what the hell the problem was so, now I'm driving an emergency vehicle while blasting a siren and screwing up the evening commute.

We roll up to the scene and see Darryl the Drunk lying across the sidewalk on his back with a children's bicycle on the adjacent lawn. Darryl's pants are pulled down far enough that I can see part of his cock. He shows no signs of wearing any underwear.

Ben points at Darryl and says, "Darryl-cock."

"Darryl-*dick* works better."

"Yeah, but that doesn't fit with the shtick that I got going."

I put the rig in park next to Darryl's supine form, "Regarding that, Darryl-cock is invalid as it's a subsection of man-cock. It's just drunker."

Ben and I hop out and approach Darryl without any gear. I yell out, "Darryl, wake the fuck up!" and he opens one eye and lazily regards me with it.

Imagine a cross between a drunken homeless guy, a somewhat entertaining redneck and a pirate and you have yourself some idea of Darryl Figgus. Ol' Figgus is one of the most frequent of *frequent fliers* for Oakland Emergency

Medical Services. Darryl really doesn't have anything wrong with him besides the occasional alcohol withdrawal seizure, a penchant to be assaulted by fellow homeless people and a barking, Scooby Doo-like voice further exacerbated by his love for all things intoxicating. For some reason, much like the other regulars of Oakland EMS, he really likes to put himself in positions wherein the services of medical professionals tend to pop up. And this is precisely what I think we have here: a staged situation, a dressed set piece, to convince the casual onlooker to call 911 without having to say anything. Basically, I suspect that Darryl has made himself a nice little bicycle crash scene so that he can get a bed, banana-bag, and a meal on the county's dime.

The engine pulls up and the firefighters don't even bother getting out of the rig. Ben waves them off and they pull away.

"Darryl, I know you didn't crash that bicycle. Get up," I tell him.

Darryl opens both eyes wide. "I did! I did! I fell right down," he barks at me in his raspy voice in reply, sounding rather like Oscar the Grouch today. "I promise I did."

"Prior to starting this argument," Ben chimes in, "can you please put your dick back in your pants."

"Oh, I'm so sorry, Sir. Sorry." Darryl shimmies his pants up while still laying on his back.

"So… what's it gonna be?" I ask. "What are we going to do with you, today?"

"I should go to the hospital," Darryl says, while propping himself up on his elbows and looking up at me with imploring eyes.

"No, no you should not," says Ben. "You should go home on that little bike of yours, stop drinking, take a shower, have a nice meal, get a job, meet a rich lady, and reconnect with your family, becoming an example of success to all those around you."

"I want to go to the hospital," Darryl ignores.

"Okay," I say. "Let's find some middle ground. Darryl, what is the hospital going to do for you today?"

"They are going to make my arm better. I hurt it. I was riding this bicycle and I crashed."

Ben adds, "And somehow during that crash your cock fell out?"

"I don't know about all that. I have been drinking, Sir!"

"Darryl, we know you have been drinking. You never need to tell us that," I inform him. "But, bad news, today is a *no bullshit* day. There isn't anything wrong with you. Get up and ride your happy-ass away on your little clown bike, please."

Darryl looks back and forth at our stoic, stony faces. Both Ben and I shake our heads at him, disapprovingly.

With a huge sigh, Darryl begins an overly arduous and dramatic process of gathering himself up from the ground, making sure to ham-up the vocal expressions of poorly acted pain. What seems like an eternity later, and he's on his feet. Ben picks up the bicycle.

"Here. Ride off," he tells Darryl, and presents the bicycle to him. "Ride off into the sunset and find yourself another bottle of... whatever it is you drink that I hope I do not as well because then I need to have a hard conversation with myself."

I say under my breath, "It's probably not Clamato beer."

Darryl, in what can only be described as the most passive aggressive way I have ever witnessed a person take a child's bike from a grown adult, sighs loudly, throws a leg over the bicycle, and sits down on the tiny seat. He then looks up at me with his puppy eyes and says, "Sorry to be a bother, Sir." He slowly coasts down the gradual incline away from us in the general direction of the lake.

Ben and I nod at one another, happy that we have managed to avoid the judgmental looks of the hospital staff for bringing them Mr. Figgus, who is as known to them as he

114

is to us.

"Good job waving the fireman off," I tell Ben. "The fewer witnesses to us violating federal law by refusing a patient transport the better."

"That's why we are partners: we excel at crime."

We bump fists and turn to walk back to the ambulance.

Then we hear tires screech and whip our heads around just in time watch Darryl Figgus channel his best Johnny Knoxville by riding his little bike off the sidewalk, into the busy intersection and directly into the passenger side door of a now stopped Lincoln Navigator SUV.

Reflexively, I begin to run down to moaning, prone figure of our frequent flier while yelling in defiance of fate, "Fuck you so hard, Darryl!"

"I'm sorry, Sir. I'm sorry!" he groans, laying on the ground, holding his left shoulder and wincing in non-pretend pain.

Of course, now his pants are around his knees and it's a full dick show.

19.

"Highland, it's your favorite crew, Oakland 527. We are code-three to you with a trauma activation. Today, as in many other days, we present to you Darryl Figgus, who you no doubt are familiar with as a forty-two-year-old male with a history of heavy alcohol use. Mere moment's ago, we witnessed him ride a young girl's bicycle into the side of an SUV at approximately fifteen miles per hour. This was totally random that we happened to be in the area, might I add. He was conscious at the scene but is now confused about time and event. Not sure if this is secondary to the ETOH or the collision. He's got some moderate facial and dental trauma. Possible left side clavicular fracture. Heart rate at 110. BP is 140 palpated and respirations at 20. ALS is in progress and we will see you in three. Oakland 527 out." That's how my transmission to Highland sounded before we presented Darryl to the standard eye-rolls and sighs of resignation to the fact that some unlucky hospital staff had to deal with the near-daily occurrence of a visit by Mr. Figgus. We dropped him off telling only a few key people who could be trusted how the whole incident went down, Tonya being one of them. She laughed a deep belly laugh at our/his misfortune and told us to have a good rest of the shift... one far, far away from Highland.

The rest of the night was pretty normal. We had another notable call. This time it was in deep West Oakland. A lady who lived in a grand but haggard Victorian had flu-like symptoms. It would have been an easy run if she didn't weigh 300 lbs. But, as it turned out and as her very biting, ammonia/urine odor indicated, she had a blood sugar level of about 400, which is bad. We took her to Summit and Ben somehow managed to get an IV line started on her to dilute her sugar-blood, no easy task on an obese diabetic.

After that, we had a salesman-type white guy who got whipped with a car antenna by some pimp and it cracked open his scalp, a two vehicle crash with both drivers reporting *severe insurance pain* in their necks accompanied by aspirations of lawsuits, and a one-year-old toddler near the Berkeley border with a runny nose and freaked out, yuppie parents who apparently had never seen a kid with a cold before. All of it was pretty status quo.

We get off on time, just before 0400, so no bars are open. Ben and I ride our motorcycles through the cold, early morning air back to our apartment. There, we knock back a six pack of Eye of the Hawk ale while taking pulls from a bottle of Makers. We are both watching a rerun of *Man Versus Wild.*

"This is the gayest show on TV. I know I have said it before, but I'll say it again: there hasn't ever been a woman on this show and I'm pretty sure there never will be. He always sleeps overnight with other dudes in little snow caves and whatnots. Plus, the dude's name is *Bear.*" Ben says, slightly slurring.

I respond, "Yeah, I'm just always pissed that Mr. Bear kills a snake or a bird and then takes two bites out of it. Like, was that really necessary? You couldn't just demonstrate the fucking technique? You had to kill something with your Swiss Army knife so that your show won't get cancelled? If you aren't actively repressing your desire for penis by doing that nonsense, then you are just a total prick."

"I agree. Everybody knows he's gay but him and it's uncomfortable for us all. I feel like he would be happier if he just came out of the closet, stopped trying to climb every damn tree he can wrap his legs around and started doing dinner theater."

"Totally! He climbed Everest. He was in the Special Air Service. He volunteered to be trained by the French Foreign

117

Legion – not one girl in sight in any of those activities. Just go to some therapy, move to The Castro, realize you are fine the way you are, and go get crazy laid. Leave the goddamn wildlife alone. You'll be much happier, and no wild animals will have to be sacrificed."

"Let's make a PSA," Ben suggests.

"I'm in." A few seconds go by and I ask, "You think that you are at all gay? Like, seriously. Not joking."

"No gayer than you."

"I'm comfortable with that. I *wish* I was gay. That would rule."

"Finally, you admit it! Ha!" Ben yells and smiles psychotically.

"Just think about it from my point of view: dual income, loving relationships that often *include* the fact that you can just go out and fuck other people with impunity, your own neighborhood of town where there's tons of ass to chase, your own special weekends on cruises and in Vegas and stuff, and you can drive little sports cars and scooters and nobody cares. That's awesome. Plus, were I gay, my Mom might actually get off my back about getting married because she would probably never speak to me again: win-win."

"Harsh! Really?"

"Probably."

"You might have to get plowed in the ass, don't forget that."

"So? I like plowing girls in the ass. Who is to say that I wouldn't like it back? Maybe it's the best thing that ever happens to me and totally changes my outlook. There's no way of knowing but to do it."

"Oh, I'm sure you do it already. I suspect you are heavily into pegging and I'd hazard to guess that your colon is like an old, leather boot because of heavy abuse."

"Gnarly. You always take these things too far. Pick a new topic. You are clearly too big a homophobic redneck douche to ever have a serious conversation with."

"A douche who will no longer be sleeping with his door unlocked."

"Harsh! Really?"

"Probably."

We go on to gab about nothing in particular until we are done with the six-pack and then retire to our respective bedrooms. I hear the familiar sound of Internet porn coming from Ben's room before I drift to sleep.

Despite the muted sex noises in the background, I dream not of carnal pleasure but instead that I am a patient who is unconscious but aware of what's going on. Instead, I'm in the back of an ambulance. The siren blares as the crew transports me. Clearly, I'm on the way to the hospital. The overhead lights are bright in my face. At some point, the nameless, faceless paramedic pulls out a needle that's way too big for an IV and starts one in my neck. I feel it in my dream like a painful bee sting that throbs as cold saline solution drips through the IV tubing into my jugular vein. My body becomes awash in what feels like ice water and I begin to violently shiver.

That dream ends when I wake up to the sound of my cell phone ringing, but I just reach over and turn it off. I'm in no mood to answer the phone. Daylight already has begun to peek through my curtains. It is some unknown time in what I am guessing is the morning. I take a drink of water from the glass on my bedside table, roll over and go back to sleep.

The next time I wake is to the sound of Ben clamoring around in the kitchen. I look at the clock and it's 1330 in the afternoon. I should get up and go to the gym, but I am tired and sore from the work week so far. I just want to have a cup of coffee and slowly meet the day before getting ready for work. I pick up my cell phone. There are a few text messages from friends and coworkers, funny dog photographs and the like. There's also a voicemail message from a number that I do not recognize.

I bring up my voicemail and play the message. It's Dr.

119

Vivian Lopez M.D. I immediately smile and pump my fist.

"*Hi, Harlan. This is Vivian. We met the other day and you gave me your number. I was thinking that we could maybe grab brunch on Sunday if you don't already have other plans. Hope that sounds good! Okay, well, you have my number now. Call me back if you are interested.*"

"Fuck yeah!" I yell out. Seconds later, the door to my room flies open and Ben stands there with a digital camera in hand and an excited look on his face.

"Oh, motherfucker! I was hoping I caught you jerking off," he says.

"No, dude. Better: Dr. Hotness from Haven, the one with the epic Pilates or yoga butt, called me back. She wants to go to brunch on Sunday."

He snaps a photo of me in bed and says, "That's pretty cool. Where are we going?"

"*We* are not going anywhere, if you mean you and me *and* her. She and *I* will go someplace nice, where you would not want to go because you are closed minded and a redneck douche as previously mentioned, and they don't allow your type there."

"Suit yourself. I'll take the hippie chick to brunch somewhere even better, like, um, wherever people do that. I've never really been to brunch. Where do I do a thing like that? Have you been to a brunch?"

"Yeah, I have. Women love it, man, *love* it. I think maybe they normally feel bad about drinking in the morning and brunch gives them cover."

"You drink at brunch?"

"Yeah, like bloodies and screwdrivers and champagne and orange juice and stuff."

"Oh, hell yeah. Count me in then. I'm gonna do the shit outta brunch."

"Now I kinda feel bad for telling you about it, for your liver's sake and the sake of the poor brunch-goers around you.

20.

Ben and I are posted at 98th and International, way out in East Oakland. This is one of my least favorite places to post up because of the lack of goods and services I'm interested in. Namely, there's no coffee, at least not the kind served by a disinterested hipster who charges you $4.00 for a medium. The bright side is that if we are posting at this location, which isn't one of the primary posting spots, there are plenty of units available to share the workload.

"People always have brunch, right, but nobody ever has *linner*," Ben tells me seeming proud of the term he just invented.

"You mean like an amalgamation of lunch and dinner?"

"Yes. Exactly. We should look into that. Maybe that's how we make our millions?"

"Okay, sure. But I am also fairly confident that whoever 'invented' brunch doesn't hold a patent on the idea. It's not like William Randolph Hearst or Rockefeller came up with the idea and that's why they all have all that money now."

"I think you are overly negative. I'm totally opening a linner spot. We are going to serve sandwiches as appetizers and dinner entrees as main courses."

"Are you going to have a soup de jour?"

"What's that?" Ben asks with a sly grin, knowing what I'm trying to set up here.

"It's the soup of the day."

Simultaneously, we both say, "Barumbumbum."
And the radio goes, "Oakland 527, copy code-three."
Fuck.

"Aw, Shorty, you shit yourself!" a drunk man in the crowd of fellow drunks who loiter outside the liquor store at 99th and International says regarding his equally drunk, female friend who we have been summoned to deal with for an unknown malady.

And, he is correct about that, Ben and I have gathered, as "Shorty" though previously seated in a wheelchair, had mere moments before miraculously risen under her own steam from the chair revealing a brownish-yellow pile of crap, the volume of which seems to indicate that it had been a while since she had a regular bowel movement.

From what we've learned so far, this seems to be the only reason we were called. Though this call was dispatched as a "possible" unconscious person, Shorty is quite conscious and somewhat alert. But her drawl combined with the copious amounts of liquor she has obviously consumed today make it rather difficult to understand her.

It's Ben's tech, and he's pissed. He's chosen not to wave off the fire crew so that they can share in the horror of this smell. Unfortunately, we have to take this patient to the hospital, as she is far too annihilated to take care of herself and there are way too many witnesses to try to coax her into heading off under her own power.

Code Brown protocol goes as follows:

- Double wrap the gurney in the water-resistant sheets.
- Double wrap the patient in the same.
- Roll all the windows down in the ambulance and put the ventilation system and AC on full blast.
- Drive like a bat-out-of-hell to the nearest emergency room.

- Feel daggers of hate pierce your very soul from said emergency room's staff.
- Make a very quick exit and pray you don't have to come back to this facility in the shift.

We follow the first two parts of the protocol to the letter. I tell her drunken comrade that I trust him impeccably to keep an eye on the soiled wheelchair while she's away. He tells me it won't be any trouble and adds, "She's been hollerin' about her stomach so make that better if you can, my brother."

I answer back, "Can do." He reaches in for a fist bump, which I give him without reluctance as I am wearing gloves.

No sooner is the agreement met than I hear Ben call from the back of the ambulance, "Today, asshole."

I jog to the driver's seat and hop in. Ben calls out, "St. Rose, please, ASAP."

"Your wish is my command." From the front seat I can already hear Shorty snoring.

"If she was you, I'd draw dicks on you," Ben tells me from the back.

"I'd expect no less."

We pull away, headed to the closest hospital just over the border in San Leandro.

I hear Shorty make a noise when I accelerate sharply. Clearly, she is a finicky sleeper. From experience, I know that this annoys Ben, as it would me, because now he has to talk to her and talking to people who are completely smashed, when you aren't, is no fun, especially in the back of an ambulance.

I can't hear much of the conversation between Shorty and Ben from the front seat. Between the diesel engine, exhaust fan, open windows, dispatch radio and FM radio, it's a lost cause trying to discern anything either of them are saying. I drive and hum along with some stupid "alternative" drivel that I hate myself for being familiar with, but what am I going to do? It's not like the ambulances have CD players, and the DJ over at KALX is currently into experimental jazz. AER does not give two shits that two of its picky employees want to jam out to Slayer while they drive code-three to a call. So, it is a continual search for the magic radio station that won't drive us insane in the twelve hours of a shift. To date, we have yet to find such a station. We hate them all more or less equally.

I am able to discern one thing that Ben says during the transport: "You're pregnant?"

To which I say over my right shoulder, "Please tell me you are joking."

To which Ben loudly answers, "No. Apparently not."

To which I sigh and then say, "Okay... noted. Good god, man." Yes, this is not really a nice thing to say about such a downtrodden person, but Jesus, the woman is covered in poop and hangs around in a wheelchair because she's probably often too drunk to stand. The sex drive of the human male, we are continually reminded, is a truly horrific thing and it must be destroyed.

As I try to not think about this any longer, I suddenly hear Ben exclaim, "No! What? No!"

"I don't want to hear any more, dude."

Shorty screams out a wail like she just had her grave walked over and it startles me enough to jerk the wheel a bit.

Ben yells, "Pull the fuck over and get back here!"

21.

An important lesson learned early on in an EMS career: when the medic in the back attending to the patient tells you to do something in a serious voice, you do it. You comply even if you do not want to, even if it is going to be gross, because lives are at stake, seconds count and all that.

When I open the back doors of the ambulance after pulling over in front of San Leandro's Civic Center building where the police station is and such, I realize there is, in fact, gross stuff going on. Shorty is pushed up on both arms like she's on parallel bars. She's trying to climb off the gurney and seems suddenly much more sober than before. Ben is pulling her pants down around her ankles yelling at her to stay still. A gush of fluid hits the gurney, no doubt mixing with the traces of excrement.

As if that isn't enough to process, Shorty grimaces and I see her abdominal and thigh muscles contract. As I climb into the rig, a stillborn baby, looking about half the size that a newborn should be and still wrapped in the amniotic sack, pops out of Shorty's pelvis and into Ben's waiting hand. It takes a mere matter of seconds. I race to put new gloves on as fast as I can. Ben struggles to keep ahold of the slippery, pale kid trapped in its cocoon-like membrane, the cord still disappeared inside its mother.

Gloves now on, I grab an oxygen mask out of one of the overhead cabinets, crank the O2 up and put it over Shorty's head. She's screaming. The ambulance doors are wide open. Thank god there's no crowd, just passing traffic slowing but not totally stopping.

Ben holds the neonate in one hand, and he throws a square of unfolded sheets down over the mess so he can place the kid down on it. He pinches the amniotic sack to tear it and starts working the baby out so he can start some form of modified CPR. I reach for a neonatal BVM and hook it up to the other O2 line. I hand it to Ben and ask, "Want me to call for another unit?"

"How far out are we from the ER?" Ben responds.

"Less than two minutes code-three."

"Just fucking go. I got it for now."

Shorty screams and pulls her oxygen mask off. I yell at her to stay still because the cord is still attached. I don't know if she hears me, but she stays reasonably put.

Ben wipes the kid down and starts the best compressions that he can on the prematurely stillborn child. Shorty continues to scream. I throw my dirty gloves down in the street and jump out the back doors, slamming them behind me. I jog to the driver's seat, and put the rig in gear, burning the roof and let the siren wail like Shorty did a few moments ago.

I pick up the radio and get a channel to St. Rose.

St. Rose answers. A bored sounding nurse says, "Go ahead."

"St. Rose, this is Oakland 527. We have an explosive delivery of what I assume to be a preemie from a heavily intoxicated mother. Baby appears stillborn and was in the amnio-fuck!"

I barely avoid a car that just stopped in the middle of the roadway. Ben bounces off the side of the cabinets and also yells, "Fuck!"

"Sorry, 527 continuing. We had to strip the amniotic sack off the kid. CPR is now in progress. We are less than two minutes out."

The nurse answers, "Can you re-route to Children's?" She already knows the answer to this but tries anyway.

"Negative. We do not have an airway established."

Ben's voice announces, "She's hemorrhaging from the vag, Harlan!"

I key the mic, "And per my partner, mom is now hemorrhaging from the vag. See you in about one minute."

Sometimes radio etiquette goes out the window. But when a street-drunk fires out a stillbirth on your gurney and then continues screaming and bleeding out of her most private orifice, I can assure you that decorum is the last thing on your mind.

After we drop the baby and mom off to the mildly panicked hospital staff, I set about cleaning up the gurney, a big clean, the kind that takes a long while and makes me inform the dispatcher that we are out of service because of a biohazard that needs to be controlled, lest we all be sued for spreading some horrible new pathogen to an unsuspecting populace. First, I wash my hands a few times and put a pinch of chew in my mouth. Then I strip the sheets and throw them in a red biohazard bin. I take off the mattress pad. I grab the foaming kill-anything-spray and douse both sides of the pad, which I lean against the side of the rig. This is followed by dousing the gurney itself, straps and all. I let that sit and use chlorine death-wipes on every surface I can think of that we touched: door handles, the O2 nobs, cabinet doors, etc. I take my time wiping the foaming kill-anything-spray off, making sure I get down in the cracks of the gurney. There's always old blood in there that someone missed from some emergency before. It produces a rust color when mixed with the foam.

When I am satisfied with that, I take a mop from the janitorial closet in the ER and give the ambulance floor a once and twice over with it. I put the mop back and sneak a pillow and a blanket out of the ER from the linen cart (the hospital people hate when you do this). The pad goes back on the gurney. The sheet goes back on the pad. The blanket on top of the sheet. The stolen pillow on top of it all so we might be able to offer the next patient some comfort or use it ourselves if we want to nap.

The gurney goes back in the ambulance. The ambulance doors stay open until the last possible minute to ventilate the various noxious gasses and lingering odors. Ben finishes the first PCR, for mom, and then the second, for baby.

The hospital staff never got a heartbeat on the neonate. They pronounced the kid dead mere minutes after we arrived, before I'd even gotten to the mopping part. There's no surprise there. Mom will probably survive the sudden blood loss, but we bug out before we get the news either way. I spit my dip out the window as we leave the driveway.

"Fuck San Leandro, this bullshit, trash-ass town," I say to nobody in particular for a reason unknown.

Ben concurs, "Fuck it, indeed, my friend. Fuck it indeed."

22.

The sound of the front door closing far too quietly wakes me up out of a shitty dream about work wherein I was trying to give CPR to a person who was pulseless and not breathing but still yelling at me to stop. Obviously, in real life, when they tell you to stop, you don't need to keep going with CPR. But Dreamland has an entirely different set of rules from those in conscious moments. In the real world, there are no talking animals. Your ex-girlfriend doesn't let you have sex with her while your family watches and throws tennis balls at you like it's a kinky version of *American Gladiator*. You can't leap from rooftop to rooftop and then miss one, falling to the pavement below where you are run over by a horse-drawn carriage driven by Bryan Cranston.

The door closes and I stir briefly before realizing that I have to pee. I get up and let my sleepy-time boner point me in the direction of the bathroom. I pass Ben's open bedroom door and notice he's absent. I look around the living room and see his helmet is gone as well. The clock on the microwave displays that it is eight in the goddamn morning. I'm confused by Ben's absence but try not to think about it. I want to go back to bed and don't want to risk taking my mind too far from Dreamland.

I take a leak. I go back to bed. I have brunch plans in a few hours that I am excited about. I drift back to sleep thinking about that *Simpsons* episode where Marge meets the French guy who tells her brunch is not quite breakfast and not quite lunch, but you get a good meal and a slice of cantaloupe. I'm not really a fan of cantaloupe.

Three hours later my alarm goes off. I trudge off to the shower and see that Ben's door is closed. His helmet is back. I briefly contemplate running into his room, putting my balls near his face and interrogating him as to his whereabouts. But I have a place to be.

I race through my routine. I shower. I shave. Brush teeth. Deodorant. Brush hair. Put on my nice jeans. Leather belt. Wife-beater undershirt. Black shirt over it. Leather jacket. Motorcycle helmet. Extra helmet just in case. Sunglasses... did I mention sunglasses? These are really important when the bulk of your waking hours are spent in darkness.

Then it's down the stairs. I straddle the bike, fire it up and rev it 'til it's warm. I roll out of the parking garage and gun it down the street towards destiny. I pop the front tire up for a bit for kicks and to show passersby how cool I am. I don't look back to see if anyone notices.

I get to the brunch spot in less than ten minutes, so I'm early. Ben and I live in the "Uptown" district of Oakland, just north of Downtown but still basically downtown, which is confusing. We are in a development by the newly remodeled Fox Theater; it is completely awesome. I highly recommend you go there at some point. The empty vibe of the area at night is a bit weird, but it has some good stuff and the Fox Theater is one of those things. The only real downside to the neighborhood is the intermittent rioters who vandalize private property in the name of overthrowing The Man, a faceless puller of strings who probably doesn't have any concern as to the windows of a storefront being smashed, as he does not own said store. Good thing we have in-building parking.

The restaurant is called something in Italian that has the word *pizza* in it. I think it's called *Pizzalooloo* or something similar. I've seen the place before, but never been in, just passed it in an ambulance and laughed at all the very, very Caucasian people crowded outside. I figure it's just freaking pizza. Why wait? You can get that delivered to you, and my favorite Italian deli is across the street.

You may be familiar with the area as it is in the same complex as the parking lot where we were smoking the cigars the other night and talking about going to Hawaii. We have yet to revisit that conversation, by the way. Note to self: add Hawaii planning to the agenda.

I park the bike right out front of the eatery, making sure to let my loud engine idle for longer than I need to, so I can relish in the stank-faces the very, very Caucasian people waiting for tables out front shoot me. I'm tired and kinda ornery. I get that way when my sleep schedule is messed up.

My watch says that I'm eleven minutes early. I reflexively reach into my pocket and grab my can of chew. I start to pack the can, another thing I just love to do in front of people because of the look of horror your average urban dweller gives you when you put tobacco under your lip. But then I remember that I am on a date and Dr. Vivian Lopez M.D. is probably one of those urban dwellers that doesn't want to make out with a dude with tobacco breath. I sigh audibly and put the can back in my pocket.

I goof around on my phone for a bit until I hear a familiar voice say, "Hey, Harlan. Glad you could make it."

I look up and see my date. She looks hot, really hot. I want to pump my fist like I just scored a goal in the Stanley Cup playoffs. But I play it cool and say, "Howdy. You look lovely."

She smiles and asks if I had trouble finding the place. I answer in the negative. I tell her I'm a pro at Oakland navigation. She asks if I grew up in Oakland. I tell her that it was regrettably Berkeley, but I moved to Oakland as soon as I could. I don't bother telling her that I technically lived at my mom's house into my twenties. Some people think this is quite sad. They do not realize that we home-dwellers generally use this time to save up tons of money to either purchase a home, an entry-level luxury automobile, or in my case a sweet-ass motorcycle. Imagine my mom's enthusiasm in regard to my choice!

We check in with the hostess. The place is jumping. It has a full bar. I need coffee before I hit the hard stuff, but I won't pretend to argue that a cocktail is far from my mind.

It's at that point that Dr. Vivian Lopez M.D. tells me something that almost makes my heart totally sink: "So, I am *so sorry* to spring this on you, but I have some news."

"Ah, fuck. You're married, aren't you? Look, uh, unless you have some sort of arrangement I don't know if we should make out then."

She laughs for a second and then goes, "Okay, wow. No, Harlan. Um, glad to know you are so, uh, *open-minded* on the issue, but the bad news is that I have a college friend in town so I can't stay out too long today."

"Oh, well. That's cool. Guess we can still make out for a little then." Subtlety is not my strong suit.

We order from a waitress who has a really low-cut shirt on that I'm doing my best to completely ignore so I don't look like a pig but if my date goes to the bathroom, I'm gonna glance at least three times. I knock back some coffees and then join Dr. Vivian Lopez M.D. in a mimosa, which I don't usually drink but she kept telling me how good they were at this place and she slammed her first one so I need to catch up. I don't really know how they could be bad, as they only have two ingredients, but I don't bother asking as that will no doubt betray me as not being a sophisticated and worldly individual.

I learn the following about Dr. Vivian Lopez M.D.:

- Vivian is from Arizona, Scottsdale to be precise.
- She is twenty-eight years old.
- She went to UCLA's medical school.
- Her father is an attorney in a private firm and is a through-and-through republican who was weary of her choice to move to the liberal bastion we currently are inside of.

- Her mother was his secretary (scandal!) but hasn't worked since she had her first child and didn't really need to because dad sounds pretty loaded.
- Vivian is the middle kid and she has a brother and a sister.
- She loves baseball.
- Her team is unfortunately still the Diamondbacks, the name she thankfully uses as opposed to the rather obnoxious *D-Backs*.
- Growing up in Scottsdale, the Spring Training crowd annoyed the crap out of her, especially Giants fans. I tell her that's okay, that I am a green-collar A's man and have been since birth because, "East Bay Pride, Mother-effer!"
- She thinks that the West Bay/East Bay rivalry is kinda weird.
- She is El Salvadoran, on her father's side.
- She gets her lovely tan from spending hours on her roof sunbathing. I immediately picture her naked on her roof.
- She's been in the Bay Area for two months.
- She hasn't been on a date since she arrived. She has been asked by several people, and wasn't interested, but thought that I seemed, "Cool and different than my normal type."
- This makes me want to hire some yahoo with a Cessna to drag a banner around the sky denoting that this clearly sophisticated and beautiful doctor lady just deemed me "cool."
- She mostly listens to whatever is on the radio. She reads things on the NYT Best Seller list. She watches all the Oscar contenders.
- She has a dog, a Corgi named, "Sprinkles," because of course that's its name.
- The dog has outfits, because, of course it does.

Dr. Vivian Lopez M.D. asks what my ancestry is. I tell her I'm Japanese on mom's side and that my dad is North Atlantic-Islander-white and he lives in San Raphael and my mom is in Las Vegas and blah blah blah. You know all this already.

We get our food. I scarf mine down in accordance with the way I normally eat, ambulance-trained to do so. She eats pretty fast too, hospital-trained obviously. The mimosa makes her look at me in that way which leads me to believe if I keep up my current level of charm and personality that I will at some point be solidly inside of her no doubt magical lady-parts. I smile thinking about this.

"What are you smiling about?"

I look her in the eye and say, "Just happy to be here with you." I *am* happy to be there, so this is not technically a lie.

We talk more about normal stuff. She learns that Ben is my housemate. She remembers him being kind of a dick and I tell her that's normal. She lives alone on the island of Alameda. She has a nice little house rented, one with a yard for the dog. She tells me that she also wanted to have a yard for herself. She loves to garden. She says I should come over for a drink sometime, meet her dog and see her backyard. She doesn't flinch at all when she says this, and I don't think she got the innuendo, or she played it like a pro. I try not to snicker. Anyhow, that's my in. She just invited me over.

Houston, we are clear for launch.

We part ways after sharing a dessert and solidifying plans to have a drink as soon as possible, definitely before the rapidly approaching holiday season. We hug and she kisses me quickly on the lips. The visiting friend from out of town might be a lie in case I was terrible, but I think maybe it isn't and doesn't matter either way. I knocked it out of the park.

God, I'm good.

23.
December 25th, 2009

We worked last night, Christmas Eve, and it was completely fucked as usual. Busy as hell. There was thunder, lightning and rain blowing hard like a screaming goddess with a serious sayin' and sprayin' issue.

Christmas Eve is always the same on an ambulance in Oakland. It's cold and dry or cold and wet. There are domestic disputes wherein someone gets hit over the head with a serving tray or fire poker by a member of their immediate family. A guy gets shot or stabbed, because why take a day off shooting and stabbing to celebrate in safety? A homeless person is found dead via alcohol, heroin, exposure, murder or a myriad of other possibilities. Every driver after 2200 hours is hammered, carrying multiple passengers, and mashing their cars into pedestrians, guard rails and other vehicles. There are residential fires. There are commercial fires. There is brimstone. It's the most holy of all alcohol-fueled debacles.

We were held over two hours. We ran fourteen calls total. We both slept until about 1600 on Christmas Day.

Currently, Ben and I are seated on the couch on this day, the day of our Lord and Savior's birth. We are both making obligatory phone calls to our family members. We both have our laptops open on our laps and are sending gift cards via Amazon.com to said family members. We open our Christmas cards. We each get slightly over $100.00 from our parents, in checks of course. We have a tradition with this money. Tonight, it shall be upheld.

After all the pleasantries are completed, Ben and I race to get ready, and then ride our bikes into the twilight across the Bay Bridge into The City. We shall eat, drink and be merry... and by "be merry" I mean that we are going to blow all the money that we were given by our loved ones on lap dances in North Beach. Tonight, we shall view the glory of strippers!

But first, a visit to the ATM.

Ben and I rocket across the Bay Bridge with boobies on the brain. Dr. Vivian Lopez M.D. and Kaylee are at their respective familial domiciles in their respective home states for the holidays. I didn't want to go to Vegas and Mom is even less filled with holiday cheer, which I didn't know was possible, now that Mr. Man is around. My dad is visiting an army buddy in Chicago. Ben's parents are god-knows-where and I don't ask because it's a sore subject. He's an only child, like me. We are the closet things one another have to a sibling.

We start the night off in Chinatown, where we eat Chinese food (surprise!) with various Hindus, Buddhists, Muslims, Jews, agnostics, atheists, tourists and miscellaneous strays not celebrating the day at home. Then we go to Buddha Bar and drink the mystery booze out of the brown jug that tastes like it is made from prunes and demon piss. Until it gets past 2100 or so, we nurse beers and play Midnight, a dice game, with the bartender. He clearly wants to start betting more than a buck a roll with us. We don't bite. We have limited funds. We are saving these funds for the ladies.

Ben and I are well versed in stripper etiquette. We tip two dollars per song, per dancer, minimum. We try not to let girls seeking to give lap dances take too much of our time if we aren't ready for one yet. Better to let them wander off to richer prey. We buy drinks for the girls if they ask. We tip the bartenders well. We always spend more than we planned on.

We do have a few minor strip club issues, though. Namely, Ben hates the bouncers almost universally. I hate the DJs, universally. Between the two of us, male employees at strip clubs have few ways to win our good favor.

After pitched victories and losses at the dice game, Ben eventually asks, "You know how I know that you're gay?"

"No."

"Because you are still here playing dice with a dude and not looking at a stripper."

"Fair enough. But that means you fit the bill too."

He doesn't argue.

We walk a few blocks away and emerge from Chinatown onto Broadway, where the titty-bars line both sides of the street for several blocks, sandwiched among a few nightclubs, the tiki bar that smells bad, a restaurant or two and the North Beach museum.

We decide to go to Condor Club, as it has a full bar in addition to plentiful ladies. Due to California law or something, for the ability to drink, we lose visual access to the naughty bits below the waist, but that's a small price to pay. The girls are wearing thongs. We can imagine the rest and don't have to be taken aback by the occasional realization that having a strange anus shoved in one's face is kinda gross if you think about it too much. Not that such a thing is a deal breaker, but you get to be picky when there are so many options.

The bouncer dude at Condor Club says that the entry fee is twenty bucks per head. He's got overly gelled, black hair slicked back and is wearing a black trench coat and black gloves.

"Hey, we just went to mass and gave the Holy Catholic Church a few bucks. Can we make it twenty for both?" Ben asks. I immediately start laughing.

The doorman does not start laughing. He deadpans, "The cover is twenty dollars a person. If you don't got it, you don't come in."

"You are lucky I just got my inheritance from grandma's death," Ben says and produces forty dollars from his pocket.

The doorman makes a thumbs up and points over his shoulder with it like he's telling Dick Tracy where the crime boss with the ridiculously huge forehead is seated. We both roll our eyes and mosey on in. Every bouncer at a North Beach strip club thinks that they are one dickhead move away from getting "made" as a real mobster.

As I walk by, I ask, "Hey, you like *The Sopranos*?"

Bouncer Dude doesn't answer. He just snarls.

"I'll take that as a yes. Stay warm out here." I can already tell I am on thin ice.

I head to the bar, heeding the unspoken social contract among men that if one takes care of the cover charge, the first round of drinks is bought by the other. At the bar I also get sixty bucks in one-dollar bills. The bartender counts them out slowly for all to see like he's adding chum into the water for the bare-breasted lady-sharks.

I head back to our table with the money and two beers. I give Ben a beer and thirty ones.

Two beers, a few rounds of dancers later, and Ben and I have both made stripper friends for the night who have camped out at our table. One girl has a toned body, dark brown skin, raven hair and a few tattoos. Her name is "Shiva," or so she tells me. I assume she's of Pakistani or Indian descent. Her other friend, the one with her legs draped across Ben, is a white chick who has purple-tinted hair, big boobs and a big butt. She says her name is, "Holly."

Ben scored big points with the girl correctly guessing that her name was derived from *Breakfast at Tiffany's*. He also tells Holly that she looks like Jayne Mansfield, another huge score for the man with the unusually silver tongue this evening. He's not lying, though. She does kinda look like Jayne Mansfield but like a rocker version. Ben is on a roll, but I know he will torpedo it soon by telling her he wants to drink champagne from her dirty shoes and then some other graphic stuff that is far crasser but actually true.

Shiva tells me that she's from Indonesia and moved to

SF a few years back. I do not totally believe her, as she has no trace of an accent, but it doesn't matter. I find this to be confusing, the Indonesia thing, and then remind myself that this is a fantasy identity made to keep at bay sexual predators and weirdoes, bills that I hope we do not fit. In the age of the internet, anyone can be tracked down. It's best not to leave a popcorn trail. She can be from wherever she says she's from. So, I play along. She seems to dig on me quite a bit. I don't bother saying this out loud. Because that's what a strip club patron is supposed to feel like and to mention this to fellow patrons will be met with laughter and accusations of naivety.

Ben and I both get two lap dances each from our respective friends. Each dance lasts for two short songs. Ben pays for both for a grand total of eighty bucks. High roller apparently. They tell us that they hooked us up with the second dances for free. This could be true. It could not be. It doesn't matter.

We share a few more drinks with the girls. We tell work stories. Ben tells them about Darryl crashing his bicycle into the car, right before our eyes. They laugh nervously. As the night progresses, they take their turns on stage and always come back to us to chat for a while. Shiva does crazy, high-flying acrobatic moves on the pole, ones that make me worry she's gonna fall and injure her spinal cord. Holly is more of a slow, swoopy dancer type. Both are fun to watch.

Before we know it, the club is closing early because it is Christmas. I run to the bathroom to pee before we head home.

When I come out of the bathroom, Shiva meets me at the door and puts a piece of paper in my hand. She smiles and says she liked hanging out with me. I look at the paper and see it's a phone number with "Saachi" and "XO" written under it.

Merry Christmas to me. Thank you, Good Lord Jesus, for being born.

Ben and I say our goodbyes and then walk out of the place heading to our bikes, which are parked a few blocks away. As I leave, I resist the temptation to do the "How do you like them apples?!" line from *Good Will Hunting* to the doorman out front with Shiva/Saachi's phone number. But I badly want to.

The doorman guy gives us a hard look and says, "Don't let the door hit you on the way out," for no reason that I can tell. I assume he's still pissed at the crack I made a few hours earlier.

Ben stops. He turns around and walks up to the dude. Bouncer Dude folds his arms across his chest. Ben drops his back leg to the rear a bit like he's about to hit the guy. I've seen this before. Bouncer Dude is oblivious to the body language. I can only assume he's new. I really hope Ben doesn't punch him.

I say to Ben, "Please don't."

"You both best get the fuck out of here before you get hurt!" Bouncer Dude orders in his best Italian gangster voice.

In a flash, Ben tosses me his helmet, lunges forward and grabs the dude in a bear hug repeating, "Just let me love your pain away!"

I aggressively roll my eyes and backpedal away.

Bouncer Dude freezes and screams, "Get of me, faggot!"

Then, Ben moves like he's going to kiss the guy, who contorts his face away from Ben's pursed lips. Ben uses his ridiculous clinch strength honed from years wrestling in high school stay latched onto the poor man.

I can see through the door the other security guards running our way. Behind them, I imagine that Shiva/Saachi and Holly Golightly Mansfield are wondering what the commotion is about. I grow uneasy and announce, "Ben! Uh, he's not that into you, sweetheart!" thinking of nothing better to say, really.

Ben manages to plant a wet one on the guy's cheek and then releases his hold. The doorman shoves him back with both hands. Ben staggers and almost falls, but he regains his footing.

Bouncer Dude advances like he's ready to throw hands but three security guys pile out demanding to know, "What the fuck is going on?!" and that makes him stop and turn to them.

"This fucker kissed me!" he says to his comrades. They all begin laughing hysterically.

Ben asks, "How come you won't let me share my love, you big, Italian sausage?"

Bouncer Dude says, again and rather unoriginally, "Fuck you, faggot!" and advances forward once more. The other bouncers are still cracking up.

An electronic air-horn makes its loud farting noise in the background, startling us all. A SFPD car rolls up and stops. The cop in the passenger's seat asks through the rolled-down window, "There a fuckin' problem here?"

Ben shrugs nonchalantly. I clam up.

This isn't good.

Bouncer Dude exclaims, "That faggot piece of shit tried to kiss me, dude."

In response to this ugly statement, the cop closest to us winces and says, "Uh oh."

"Correction, I did kiss him," Ben adds, unhelpfully.

The driver's side door opens, and another cop gets out of the car. He's huge, well over six foot and on the healthy side of two-fifty. He points at us and says, "Get your asses out of here. Go home. You two are done tonight. Don't let me catch you back." He looks at the doorman and says, "And if you say *faggot* one more time, we're gonna have words." The cop grabs his baton as he slams his door closed.

I see a little rainbow flag pin on the side of the cop's patrol cap. I smile sheepishly at him and say, "Yes, officer. Thank you. Uh, sorry."

Ben smiles and winks as I grab his arm and pull him into the crosswalk. We hightail it to our bikes, laughing maniacally as soon as we are out of earshot. The bullet has

141

been dodged. I thank the Good Lord again for his timing, and suddenly realize it's time to stop saying things like *faggot* because it just makes me sound like that bouncer asshole.

24.
Mid-February 2010

My final points of the game *almost* come after a fast break. I get a rebound off a missed shot and jam down the court with everyone in pursuit. But with only a few seconds left on the clock, I lose control of the dribble off my foot like a total spaz and consequently miss the opportunity to make an easy layup while trying to get control of the ball before it bounces out of play. I manage to avoid this turnover for a moment by tossing the ball towards our center, but it bounces off his ass and then promptly flies out of bounds. The Berkeley Fire Department team gets the ball and just runs the clock out as they have a two-point lead. Game over. AER North's intramural basketball team has lost its third game of the season because Harlan couldn't finish a goddamn layup. I'm pissed at myself. We suck worse than the goddamn Golden State Warriors.

Our team is not the collection of professionals that we would all like it to be. It generally is comprised of those who bother to drag themselves out of bed at 0900 on Tuesdays and Thursdays. Many of our players have just gotten off night shifts. Some have to work right after the game ends.

I am the only die hard who makes practically every game. I am basically the team captain by default. And, though I am not any genius at basketball, I did play in high school, even though it was viewed as terribly uncool by my fellow angsty malcontents. I like to think that I was a decent player, but maybe that's fooling myself.

Unfortunately, my prior basketball experience puts me among a minority. And it seems that our better players are constantly getting hired by local fire departments and becoming difficult opponents. Though it doesn't really matter in the long run as none of us are going to be scouted by the NBA, every victory against the firemen who are able to work out and practice on duty is a little victory for my soul.

We are now 0-3. I take the loss rather hard. If only more players would show. If only we had more than one sub to their five. If only we had some dude who played in the D-League but didn't get called up to the NBA and decided to work for AER like a schmuck rather than play professionally in Kurdistan. Whatever, I'll get over it.

Ben came to the game. It is the first time this season he has done so; he slept through Opening Day – Ben didn't miss much there unless you count Samir from 514 lightly pulling a hammy in the tipoff – and then did another one of his weird, unexplained morning absences on the second game. But he showed up today and logged about three minutes total of playing time before he subbed out and warmed the bench, spitting tobacco juice into his empty water bottle.

Ben is by no means talented at basketball. He wears old Converse and some cut-off camouflage pants with tube socks. This is his normal workout gear. He basically just jogs from three-point line to three-point line and per my instructions stays on the opposite side of the court as the ball. I have not yet begun to explain to him how a "pick and roll" works. He has seen me run many a screen play but probably does not know that's what I was doing.

In today's game, he got possession a few times and passed the ball to the next open man. Nothing fancy, but a contribution none the less. I like it when he shows; people talk less shit. This is probably because Ben leads the league in flagrant fouls and ejections. The guy is all elbows and the occasional head-butt. He takes his shirt off, so people won't touch him because he sweats like crazy. He purposely coughs on people if they get in his face. He is a master at fucking with bros because he is himself, part bro. But I suppose I am too, as is anyone who would partake in intramural basketball.

There was only one notable occurrence along these lines: a bodybuilder-type fireman with obligatory tribal tattoos on his arms and a fauxhawk haircut tried to violently strip the ball away from Ben, so Ben "accidentally" spun away really fast and cracked the dude on the chin with his elbow. This made the fireman reel back, yell out, "Motherfucker!" and summarily shove Ben with both hands (seems to be a pattern developing here). Ben might have charged the guy and was luckily intercepted by Jamal McKinney from 535. McKinney is a rather large dude, so he was able to hold both Ben and the Nu-Metal firefighter at bay.

The other firemen got involved in the fracas by verbally doing the exact opposite of attempting to calm the situation. The refs came over to squash the beef and Ben put his hands up and said, "My bad." He then walked to the bench, chugged his water, put a huge wad of chew in his mouth, and began yelling words of true inspiration such as, "Go team. Woooo. Yay." Ben was clearly defeated by the fact he didn't get to finish a fight for the second time in recent history. At least he didn't kiss anyone against their will.

There was another noticeable occurrence in the fourth quarter: Ben and the fireman he elbowed wound up shaking hands. I saw this as I was attempting to hit my layup on the final fast break. This event was probably why I lost control of the ball. I'd be pissed at Ben if I wasn't so taken aback by his semi-good behavior. Maybe the guy is just getting older and more mature, but the changes in the way he's acting as of late are truly tripping me out.

After the game, we go to Zachary's Pizza for lunch and stuff ourselves on deep-dished, meaty heaven. We share a pitcher of beer. Ben tells me that it feels good to be the "star player" on the team. I tell him that he's extremely terrible at basketball, but I thank him for coming none-the-less. I also tell him with a mouth full of food, "Don't shake fireman hands. They will get their bad medical juju on you."

"Those Berkeley guys aren't that bad. Most of them used to be *real* medics."

"I'm aware. But now they aren't. They sold out, dude, for better pay and benefits and retirement and all that great stuff that we will never get. It's very not punk rock to be so financially secure." I shake some more red pepper flakes on the pie.

"Funny, sure. But how is it a bad thing to be a paramedic firefighter, to still work on an ambulance or, fuck, even on an engine, and make a decent living for once? Are you really gonna work for The Borg for the rest of your life? Please shoot me if I do that. I would rather go quickly then wind up one of those crispy burnouts just waiting for their shitty 401k to kick in." Ben shakes more parmesan on the pie.

"Yeah, dude. I am. If the city or county wants to take over as and pay us more, great, but I'm not going to work for a fire department. I don't want to be in the boy's club. I don't want to spend all day in a recliner trying to watch football and acting pissed off that I have to go on a medical call a few times a day that the ambulance medics are going to handle for us anyways. That's just not me... I don't know. Maybe I'll take a police department test? They hired fucking Dougie and he's, well... Dougie."

"He is eccentric for a cop; I'll give you that."

Ben gets a weird look on his face like he wants to say something but instead finishes his beer in one gulp. He says to a passing waiter, one who isn't ours, "Can we get another pitcher, man?"

25.

Ben is in his room. I am in my room. We have our doors open so we can yell to one another, but this is unnecessary as we both have our online gaming headsets on. We are playing the game *Gears of War 2* cooperatively. His character is Marcus Fenix, the main protagonist. I am Cole Train, the big, black, badass comic relief dude. Wave after wave of enemy fighters assault our fortified positions. Wave after wave fall to the fury of our gunfire and superior strategies.

Our bedrooms are oriented in such a way that Ben and I have figured out how to bank tennis balls off the living room wall into one another's open door. We do this frequently between matches. We started doing this with a lacrosse ball but Ben broke my lamp so we switched to the tennis ball thinking that the decreased weight would help avoid further destruction. We are both aware that this is probably not true, seeing as we now throw it even harder.

I hear the *pong* sound the ball makes as it banks off the living room wall and cover my head reflexively. The ball sails into my room, knocks a pinup girl calendar off my far wall and comes to rest in my bookshelf.

"Dick!"

"Heads up," Ben deadpans.

In the past thirty days, several things have happened:

- Ben has had more of his weird absences that he has not yet explained.
- Ben went on several dates with Kaylee/Hippie.

147

- They have really loud sex several times a week and I also know they go to her place and likely do the same.
- Kaylee/Hippie has on two prior occasions brought other girls home and they have been indulging in the beast with *three* backs.
- Ben feels like the King of the World when this happens and has several times announced that out loud like in *Titanic*, waking me up or otherwise annoying me.
- He is not the King of the World; don't encourage him.
- I have been dating Shiva/Saachi and Dr. Vivian Lopez M.D.
- I have been having very loud (to get back at Ben for the threesomes) sex with them, individually, several times a week, usually at my place.
- Shiva/Saachi has roommates and doesn't like to hang out with me over at her spot so she comes to my place or we meet up somewhere. Also, I've discovered that she likes to hump in her car in semi-public places. I'm down.
- Dr. Vivian Lopez M.D. isn't so much into the public sex but does like to choke me (I really didn't see this one coming either) when she orgasms. I don't mind this because her grip isn't that strong, and it really turns her on. Fine with this too.
- The loud sex thing has kind of become a contest between Ben and me and I'm pretty sure Kaylee is aware of it.
- Because of this unspoken battle, Ben now threatens to bust into my room and take pictures of me mid-coitus, so I now wedge a chair under the door handle as part of the foreplay process.
- Not that you care after all the sex talk, but our basketball team is 2-5 and I'm not feeling too hopeful about our playoff contention.

As I concentrate mortar fire onto a group of bad guys,

Ben asks me, "So who was that in your room last night? Which one is the squeaker, and which one is the squealer? I keep forgetting. That was definitely the squealer, though."

Ben/Marcus chainsaws an enemy's head in half and I double down and offer a challenge, "Which one do you think it was? Choose wisely, and you shall be rewarded."

"Ooh! I like this game! Do I get clues? If so, how many? Will there be visual aids?"

"Eh, I don't know. You have a fifty-fifty shot at the right answer. Why would I give you better odds? And, no, I am not showing you naked photos of the doctor, for the last time. You already saw Saachi naked."

"Who is Saachi?"

"Shiva is Saachi; that's her real name."

"Oh, well, first of all, that didn't count because she is a stripper and that was at her work. Second of all, she was only topless. And you should give me clues because it's more fun that way," he says and charges an enemy, skewering the foul beast with a bayoneted rifle. "Aww shit! Did you see that? I'm on fire with the executions!"

"Yes, that was pretty sweet. Well done. Don't get cocky, kid. Also, check this move out." I affix a grenade to a baddie and then jump-roll out of the blast radius. The monster explodes leaving a bloody mess of guts and limbs in its place. "You may ask one question. You get *one* only, and it can't be about a distinguishing physical feature or the name of the subject in question because that's way too easy."

"Okay," he says, "now cover me while I go blow up that enemy spawn point behind the shipping container."

"Copy, I'm covering." I pop out from behind a concrete wall that's about waist high to pour down harassing fire in the general direction of the advancing enemy force. The enemies run for cover as Ben sprints in behind them.

Ben/Marcus bullseyes the crater with a frag grenade, shutting it down for the duration of the match. "Boo-yah!" he celebrates, only to suddenly cry out in horror as his character's head is split in two by an enemy chainsaw from behind. "Fucking fuck balls! I swear to god the computer cheats! We need more players if we are gonna survive longer."

I snipe the guy who just killed him; the assassin's head explodes in the crosshairs of my sniper rifle. "Well, that's what I keep saying about the basketball team, but so far my efforts have been for naught. Anyhow, I have avenged you. All my other Xbox friends are offline. And I would be shocked if you had any friends but me so what we got is what we got. Now ask your question while you wait to respawn."

"I will, but you should know that, believe it or not, Kaylee also has an Xbox and is down to play. She's working right now, though. I already checked. But here goes my question…" Ben/Marcus appears back on the screen. He takes cover behind a burned-out car and pops up with a machinegun mowing down bazooka wielding bad guys. "Okay, did the girl last night have a medical degree?"

"Damn you."

Check and mate. I should have thought of that one. Just then I am killed by a rogue grenade that I failed to notice nearby, and my screen displays the red skull image of death. I wait to respawn. "She did not. It was Shiva… Saachi, she is the squealer, as you so eloquently put it. And good choice of questions."

"Thank you. Any idea if you are leaning towards one or the other in the girlfriend race?"

"Honestly, I am getting pretty confused as to which one I like more. I mean, it would make more sense that the doctor is the better call from a stability standpoint but Shiva/Saachi has her shit together, even though it might not be as respectable a profession. Anyhow, I'm gonna have to make a decision soon, aren't I?"

The match ends. Our final kill and death tallies are displayed. He leads in kills.

"Eh, probably. If only you could do both at the same time…"

"That's your thing, dude."

"Yeah, I know. I'm King of the World!"

26.

The 911 call is for an altered mental status patient in an industrial park just off Hegenberger Road near Oakland International Airport, *International* because they fly to Cabo and probably one other place in, like, Canada. The dispatcher tells us that the cops are on scene and advising that the patient is very combative. At least one of them has theorized that the altered person in question is having some sort of diabetic emergency. This is good and bad. It's good because it means the cops understand that the crazed man in front of them is in dire medical distress and not just some jackass on PCP in dire need of jail. It is bad, because they can't really use any of their normal instruments for subduing combative people lest they wind up on CNN and forever known as the asshole who used as stun gun on a potentially dying man. Accordingly, OPD dispatch requests that we hurry because the officers are dog-piled on the patient and doing their best to hold him down because he was trying to run away and probably into traffic wherein he would be mowed down by a drunken American frat boy who is late for his flight to contract chlamydia at Sammy Hagar's resort. It's Sunday evening.

Prior to this call coming out, I was looking at my phone and scrolling through my Facebook feed. Mom and Mr. Man were apparently at dim sum this morning and Mom posted a selfie wherein she was smiling somewhat unconvincingly, which is how she always smiles. Mr. Man displayed his usual unreadable expression.

I saw that Dad went to the horse races at Golden Gate

Fields and apparently bet on a beast named, *Pappa's Mustache.* I can only imagine how many dollar beers and hot dogs he consumed while there. Dad loves a bargain. It's one of the few things he had in common with Mom. I'm guessing he spent at least eight dollars on food and libation but no more than ten.

A girl I dated when I was seventeen who went to an affluent private school in Orinda is very, very pregnant for the second time and wrote an entry in what can only be described as the most painfully dull, public journal of the experience one could have the displeasure of reading. Typically, she drips with adoration about her *wonderful* husband. She boasts ad nauseam about their *wonderful* home. She beams with pride about her *wonderful* family and uses words like *blessed* on the reg. She is a super-fan of the exclamation point. She is a full-time, stay-at-home mom who is therefore a Facebook terrorist. Because I am a negative prick, I like to think that her husband is some sort of sexual deviant who pays women in high-heeled leather boots to step on his balls and call him a "limp-dick scum-worm" before teasing him to orgasm with a kangaroo pelt and a bullwhip or the like. But this probably isn't the case. He might simply be a *wonderful* husband. They might indeed be equally happy and content.

Puke.

Dougie's status update from 1044 hours was a picture of a vodka-cran and read: *Breakfast cocktails – because vitamins!* I imagined him seated on an outdoor patio somewhere and felt great jealousy. Brunch has clearly gotten popular in my social circle.

Tay-boobs posted a photo of himself two hours ago at (drumroll) 7-11 holding a (drumroll) gigantic soda. He did not look attractive. I pine for his level of self-esteem.

Kaylee posted a photo of herself in hospital scrubs and a surgical mask. Accompanying text made a playful reference to the coming zombie apocalypse and her readiness for it. She tagged two other women who I could only assume to be coworkers. I made a mental note to revisit this post and see if said coworkers are hot.

Shiva/Saachi, full name of Saachi Saxena (as displayed on her profile) made a reference to her line of work by noting that her feet were sore from dancing all night in heels. She wrote that drunk men said gross things to her, she was burned out, and bruised from a fall a few days back, which I didn't hear about before. I felt a flash of protective anger.

Dr. Vivian Lopez M.D. posted a photo of her brunch at about 1330 and tagged a male friend who seemed, after a bit of digging, to be another physician that she works with. I recognized him as an ER resident at Haven. I felt a flash of jealousy but knew this to be hypocritical. Besides, he's probably just a friend... maybe.

This dude, Terrell, from OPD posted a photo of his infant son in a tiny Niners jersey. The photo was adorable. I hit the *like* button.

Brian, who always demands people call him (I swear I'm not making this up) Redneck Brian, a bartender at the always-gross Merchants Saloon down by Jack London Square, posted a photo of his infant daughter and their dog. I hit the *like* button even though I refuse to call him by his made-up nickname and am somewhat horrified that he is responsible for another human life.

There was an advertisement for the new *Number One Dating App* for Facebook users. I prayed to never hit the level of desperation required to use an online dating service.

HBO posted a shot of Anna Paquin looking sexy as hell in a scene from *True Blood.* I thought about her in *The Piano* and that was weird. I was not totally prepared to sexualize her in my mind. I felt guilty. I kept scrolling.

Kevin, who I haven't seen since sixth grade and whose friend request I accepted not expecting to have everyone else I knew in sixth grade friend request me as well, posted a photo of his infant twins in his wife's arms. Pretty much every "friend" from that era has a photo of a child that is less than two years old.

The last thing I saw was that Becky, who curiously has not unfriended me, posted a quote about being in love from some poet I didn't know. I felt like I got kicked in the chest. I felt my mood instantly sour. I was definitely not prepared to see this.

Thinking about Becky's allusions to romantic love, I exclaim, "What the fuck?!" as we arrive on scene. Ben regards me with a raised eyebrow as we come to a stop.

I open the ambulance door and there's a male voice screaming bloody murder. Voices yell over the screaming. I hear, "Calm down!" and, "We are here to help you!" None of the assurances seem to have any effect on the relentless screaming.

The voices grow louder as Ben and I wheel our gurney and every portable piece of equipment we have through the open roll-up door of what appears to be a machine shop. My eyes adjust to the change in lighting and I view about thirty feet into the shop space a mix of firemen and cops trying to hold down a rather large Latino gentleman, the source of the relentless screaming.

The fire lieutenant holds a clipboard and a radio and has a foot on the guy's right bicep. He addresses us doing his best to be heard above the racket, "Known diabetic. This isn't the first time he's gone AMS, but this is the worst so far per the coworkers. He's been fighting everyone who has touched him for the last ten minutes. Got a blood sugar on the third try and it's not even registering.

"Gotcha," Ben answers.

We set to work. Ben digs the leather restraints, ones that we stole from the psychiatric emergency facility, out of the jump kit. He tosses one near each of the patient's limbs and announces, "You guys keep holding him down and we are gonna try to get these on him ASAP."

More screaming.

Ben gets the first restraint on the patient's right wrist

155

without much difficulty. The left wrist goes a bit slower when the cop kneeling on the guy's left arm suddenly stands up as if to make way for Ben. This act frees the patient's arm which then flails about wildly, causing the cop to kneel back down on it a bit too roughly and to bash his knees on the concrete below in the process. The cop exclaims, "Shit-balls!" He's clearly in pain but doesn't yield the hold again.

I get the restraint on the left arm. The fire guys get the ankle cuffs on without too much difficulty. They use a coordinated four-man attack and have clearly done this before. Two hold the legs down at the knee and two work the restraints on.

After that's done, I say, "Okay, on three we are gonna lift him up and put him on the gurney. You guys ready?"

More screaming.

The fire lieutenant reiterates, "Gonna lift on three!"

I go, "One… two… three," and we lift the screaming, squirming, sweat-covered and clammy man airborne where he continues to scream, squirm and sweat. With a mild thud, we set him on the gurney. He immediately manages to kick one of the firemen away and that leg goes bananas as soon as it's free. A female firefighter who tries to buckle the restraint to the metal rail of the gurney orders her coworker, "Grab that leg, Thompson!" The guy who got kicked away, Thompson apparently, grabs it again and smothers it with his upper body.

While the team secures the leather restraints to the gurney, the patient must realize through the fog in his brain that his chest isn't being pinned down. He immediately sits up and continues to thrash and scream. Spittle flies out of his mouth. One of the cops who was previously holding the guy's upper body down prior to us lifting him on the gurney asks, "What should I do? What should I do?"

Ben says, unhelpfully, while wrestling down an arm, "Feel free to lightly taze him."

The cop looks confused. I throw him a roll of cloth tape

and instruct, "Don't do that. Push the head of the gurney up and tape him to it so he can't wiggle so much.

The cop complies and pulls the red lever at the top of the gurney to elevate the upper half of the gurney's bed. He uses wide circles of tape to secure the patient as best as he can. This doesn't go well at first, but then the FD lieutenant, a fire-plug looking man with a bushy, graying mustache in a white uniform shirt, uses his ape-arms to shove the patient's upper body back to the pad of the gurney and hold him there.

We get the leather restraints secured to the gurney. Soon the man's upper body is taped down. I toss another roll of tape to the same cop and say, "Now tape the right arm but leave some skin showing on the underside of the forearm."

There's more, unrelenting screaming.

"What?!" yells out the cop as he catches the tape.

I repeat myself a bit louder and he nods in agreement.

Ben readies and IV bag. I grab the comically large vial of dextrose out of the drug box and get it set up in a syringe. It's sterile sugar syrup. If the IV line isn't securely in a vein and the solution leaks out, it'll kill the tissue cells around. You have to be careful with the shit, which is hard to do when it counts.

The screaming becomes somewhat muffled. I glance over and realize that this is because the female firefighter has taped an oxygen mask to the man's face by going around the head with in much the same manner as the rest of his upper body. Did I mention the patient has long hair? That's going to be problematic for him later. Oh well. First things first.

Ben gets rest of the IV supplies together and says, "I stick, and you push."

"You and your three-ways."

Ben smirks like Han Solo and says, "Envy doesn't suit you." Ben coordinates as many hands as possible to still the patient's arm, the one that's already taped up. Ben does a messy job with some betadine and then deftly threads in a large bore catheter into one of the patient's forearm veins, which bulges as his muscles strain against the restraint, tape and collective bodyweight of the surrounding emergency personnel. Ben says, "Bingo," like a total dork. There's more muffled screaming. He hooks up the IV line and tapes it down, wrapping an elastic bandage around the site to secure it further.

The patient still thrashes but we are making good headway.

I pierce the IV tubing's injection site with the dextrose syringe. I announce, "Pushing," and the IV-line clouds ever so slightly as the thick solution trickles in. Ben squeezes the bag to speed up the delivery. The patient manages to rip his oxygen mask off of his face by scraping it against his shoulder. He lets out one final climactic scream.

"Jesus, you are fucking loud! It's amazing Harlan isn't, err, *dating* you."

If people get the inside-joke, they don't let on. I chuckle. I keep pushing. The vial is halfway empty now. The patient slows his thrashing and stops screaming. He blinks forth some awareness in his eyes, a higher level of consciousness igniting as he surveys the faces around him.

The vial is three quarters empty. The patient formulates his first words, "Where… am I?"

"You're at work," a cop answers.

"You've had a diabetic emergency and we gave you sugar in an IV," the female firefighter says.

"You put up a hell of a fight, son," the lieutenant goes.

The vial is empty. Color soon returns to the patient's skin. He looks at me holding the empty syringe. He looks at Ben holding up the IV bag.

The newly aware man, still dripping in sweat, still taped down to a gurney and restrained at the wrists and ankles asks all of us, "I don't have to go to the hospital, do I? I don't have insurance."

27.
March 17ᵗʰ, 2010

More Facebook bullshit: I see a photo of Becky on a tropical vacation. There are two pairs of feet in the sand, her feet and some hairy, gross dude's feet. There's also a photo, probably on the same beach, of Becky kissing her apparent new man-friend. He is, quite simply, incredibly handsome and I hate him.

Becky is now listed as "in a relationship" with Esteban Manfredi. Who the holy fuck is Esteban Manfredi? This requires further research into the matter.

I double click on his profile. It's set to public. What a sucker. Any ex-boyfriend plotting the murder of the love of his life's new boyfriend has carte blanche to gather a treasure trove of intelligence.

A goddamn amateur.

Through my detective work, I learn that Esteban Manfredi is a forty-year-old ex-college soccer star who went to Yale and works for some Silicon Valley startup, which I have never heard of. The company seems to be in the business of filling its employees' pockets with loads and loads of venture capital money. How this is possible in the current recession, I have no idea. But the proof is right in front of me. It seems that they are involved in "The Cloud." I have no idea what The Cloud is.

I find a photo of Esteban shaking hands with Larry Ellison at some sort of party wherein they have a backdrop for people to take photos in front of, one emblazoned with a corporate logo so everyone knows where the photo was taken, as if there's any great mystery as to why Pink, Joe Montana, Carrot Top for some reason and Larry Ellison were at the same party with a bunch of Silicon Valley types.

Here's a shot of Becky and Esteban with friends on a sailboat in the bay. Becky and two other women I have never seen before are holding wine glasses no doubt containing a New Zealand pinot grigio. Esteban and two other douchebags are drinking Heineken. Heineken: the official beer of wannabe Euro-trash, the male equivalent of Stella.

What an ass.

I find more boat shots. It's Esteban's goddamn boat, I think. He owns a goddamn boat. I own a motorcycle. He's not cool enough to own a motorcycle, I decide.

I find photos of Esteban's home remodel. That he's remodeled means he owns the house as well. I cannot remodel my apartment lest I lose my lease. Esteban has granite countertops. He has a Wolf range and a Sub-Zero fridge. He has one of those sinks that's recessed into the counter so you can just wipe shit off the tasteful granite countertop directly into the sink. That's good news; I bet his garbage disposal can dispose of his dismembered body. I think how easy the cleanup would be.

Esteban's house looks like it's in Redwood Shores, an exclusive area south of SFO that's right on the water. It's a million-dollar home, easy, probably more. A million fucking dollars. I rent a room in a two bedroom for like a grand a month (my half) and that's tough to swallow. Water and trash are included, but I have to hear my gross roommate having gross sex, blowing up the bathroom after a night of questionable delivery food or listening to porn way too loudly.

Esteban's house is surrounded by trees and shrubs. They are perfect for hiding in, until the cover of darkness, stalking one's prey. I wonder if he leaves his sliding glass door to his redwood patio unlocked when he sleeps. He doesn't seem to own a dog. Good.

Oh, and hey, look, there's Becky and Esteban on a bicycle ride together, and then wine tasting in Napa on the same lovely weekend! Esteban has a convertible BMW! Oh, good for him! Thinks are just A-OK in Estabanville, aren't they?

Could he be any more cliché?

Now they are on a road trip to visit his family in San Diego, probably the nicest part of San Diego where Phil Rivers lives, wherever that is. They stop at Disneyland on the way down. They buy Mickey and Minnie ears with their names embroidered on them. Isn't that cute?!

Here's a photo of Becky and Esteban kissing in front of Cinderella's Castle. I can see Goofy in the background surrounded by happy children. Next to Goofy is a cart selling ice cream and probably those frozen bananas that I loved as a kid. I bet they are like $50.00 a pop now. Anyhow, that's the last Disneyland photo I find. They don't even hit any of the good rides. I'd kill Tay-boobs to be on Space Mountain rather than here.

Then it's Becky and Esteban holding hands at a family BBQ. Esteban's family, a goddamn collection of attractive Argentinian-American success stories. High cheek bones abound. All the men are tall, toned and handsome. All the women, gorgeous, tan and effortlessly elegant in that manner that makes one think they have never farted. Not one person is absent a nice watch.

I click on more profiles of family members tagged in said photos. Everyone is educated and successful. It's a tight family that seems to spend every major holiday together and live in beautiful houses and make glorious feasts and sing songs and dance with their perfect children. Elegance, love and joy are captured everywhere.

I would kill my entire family to eat at one of these parties they have. The food looks incredible. There is a mound of caviar like Scarface's cocaine. Everyone is drinking wine that probably costs more than the frozen bananas.

"Frigging bullshit," I mutter, and I hear Ben close the refrigerator door in the next room.

161

"What is?"

"Um, nothing. This, uh, news story I'm reading."

"Oh, really? What's it about?"

"Argentina."

"Is it about the Nazis who fled there after the war? That's why there are all those German names there, you know?"

"Uh, yeah."

Suddenly Ben appears in the doorway. I look over the top of my computer screen at him. He regards me suspiciously.

"I don't buy it. What are you really looking at?"

"Uh, fine. I lied. I'm looking at porn... Argentinian porn."

"Let me see," he says and takes a step forward.

I quickly start trying to close browser windows but he slams his palm down on my hand and holds it in place so I can't raise my clicking finger and then spins the monitor around. Though I closed several windows before having my hand apprehended, I failed to close the initial one: Becky's Facebook profile.

Ben looks at it. He sees the photo of Becky and Esteban kissing on the tropical beach. He shakes his head at me disapprovingly and says, "If you don't get up and roll out with me to get this St. Patrick's Day going, I am going to tell Becky you are stalking her."

"I wasn't stalking..."

"Yes, you were, Captain Stalky-Stalk," and he gives me a wet willy with his right pointer finger. I jump from my chair and tackle him down to the carpet. We roll around and slap one another unit I wind up in a headlock getting the life squeezed out of me.

"Ahhhhh uncle!" I blurt out.

Thirty minutes later we pull up to The Ruby Room on our bikes and the Jameson starts flowing. We behave irresponsibly until well after sundown.

28.
March 18ᵗʰ, 2010

I'm deathly hung over. Ben is deathly hung over. We have been guzzling water and Gatorade since our shift started. We've downed Ibuprofen by the handful since our alarms woke us up like the heralds of impending doom. That was two hours ago. We are posted at 10ᵗʰ and Clay, downtown.

Why the hell did I drink so much? How could I have done this to myself when I knew I had to work the next day? Why does every March 18ᵗʰ feel this way? The thought of chewing tobacco makes me want to vomit. But, then again, everything else does too.

It couldn't have been my fault, this feeling. It had to be because that damn bartender and his insistence on doing shots – shots of, like, anything: first Jameson... and then tequila... and then something that tasted like one of those orange slushy things you get at the mall because he made too much of it for some already drunk girls that wandered into the bar for a bit. Then more of everything.

I don't remember feeling anything more than buzzed at the end of the night. But, then again, I wasn't entirely sure where I parked my bike when Ben and I begrudgingly walked out the front door to make our ways to our first shift of the week's watch. That was stupid, to ride my motorcycle home. I shouldn't have done that. I should know better. We both should know better. Everyone should, but especially two dudes who pick up the shattered pieces of the aftermath of drunk driving gone bad, predictably bad.

But in the moment, the intoxicated mind tells me that

Oakland is a place where petty crimes go unpoliced. There are so few cops. There are criminals killing and robbing and raping, what have you. On the bell curve of criminality, are we really that bad? It was only a few blocks. Whatever, it is justification, the lot of it. No excuses. Nobody to blame but ourselves. I'm not gonna do that shit next time. I could have easily just walked to where my bike was parked and picked it up this morning.

"Where are we eating? It's time, man. I gotta get something in my stomach. The Advil is eating its way through my organs and is no doubt spilling shit into my gut, which can't be good," Ben says, as we both sit in silent remorse for the previous night's deeds. Saint Patrick's Day, what a goddamn shit-show every year.

"I don't know... you wanna do one of the food trucks?" I reply, knowing that as it is Thursday, there will be a variety of them around town.

"Eh, I don't know, dude. Which one are you thinking?" Ben asks, sounding less than enthused.

"How about that new one that has the Indian burritos?"

"Um, if I have Indian food, I'm gonna shit my pants. Too spicy. I can barely do an actual Mexican burrito right now."

"Okay, how about the Korean-American one, the one with the burgers and fries and shit?"

"First of all, and this is gonna sound racist..." Ben says but then I cut him off.

"*Sound* racist? Gimme a break. You're an ignorant dumb-shit."

"I am *not* racist. I just get annoyed with people sometimes."

"Uh, when you get *annoyed* with people and then say something that sounds racist that kinda makes you a racist. At least right then."

"No, it doesn't; I say mean shit because I know it is the

164

meanest shit I can say. Why pull punches if I'm trying to offend someone?"

"Do you realize that to the average person that makes no sense whatsoever?"

"I don't give a shit what someone I'm trying to offend thinks. I'm out here saving lives of all types. The proof is in actions, not words."

"Would you say the N-word?"

"Hell no, I wouldn't say the N-word."

"Case in point. Why is that word worse than other slurs?"

"Because it's like the worst word that exists, dude. Duh."

"So, you shouldn't say other shit because someone is going to think you are serious and a racist."

"Look, I'm not running for public office anytime soon."

"Whatever. You are an idiot. I don't even know why I bother. Why don't you want to go to the Korean truck?" My head hurts more now.

"Because if I have kimchi right now, I'm gonna shit my pants. The burger and the fries sound good though."

"Why don't you just order the burger and the fries without the kimchi?"

"That's what makes it the Korean truck! They make greasy American food and then do a thing to make it kinda Korean, often with kimchi, and I don't want to insult the chef by having him hold the kimchi and have him go all crazy on me and do whatever it is that crazy Korean truck chefs do – which I imagine involves a meat cleaver."

"See, right there; that was pretty racist, dude!"

"What was racist? Was it because I said *Korean*? I was being descriptive. The Korean truck has a Korean chef. I've literally seen the guy before."

"You know what you said: you said that Korean people put kimchi on everything, which is a stereotype, and stereotypes are intrinsically racist."

"Am I wrong about the Korean truck and the kimchi though?!"

"Well, no… in this specific instance, not really." Shit, I'm getting backed into the ropes here.

"Ha!" he says and holds up two fingers in the victory sign before spinning his hand around and flipping me off like British people do.

"Keep your voice down; my head is still pounding. I'll admit that they put kimchi on *nearly* everything at that truck. And I *have* seen a meat cleaver in there; they use it to hack up the short-ribs for the deep-fried short-rib and mozzarella melt on brioche… with kimchi… burger… thing. I don't remember what all is in it, but I do know that it isn't at all good for you and you should never eat it and oh god I want one now."

"Boom, bitch! Not a racist." Ben celebrates by putting his arms in the air and raising the virtual roof and then noticeably wincing because the sudden movement probably made his head hurt too.

"You get off on a technicality, but barely. You are definitely on my Asian racism radar at the minimum."

"Fair enough. I can work with that. Seriously, though, I don't want to shit my pants."

"You dirt-eating redneck, is there anything you can think of that will not make you shit your pants? I'm really starting to get hungry here despite the repeated mention of excrement."

"Hmmm. How about, like, a grilled cheese? One with ham and maybe pickles. Let's go to that grilled cheese truck."

"You mean the one that has the grilled gruyere on a baguette with truffle oil fries and, like, goose liver pate? If I eat that, I'm gonna shit *my* pants."

"Then get the one that has the pulled pork… and also kimchi… huh, they have that there too, don't they? Is that cook Korean too?" Ben asks but before I can answer the female voice on the other end of the radio asks, "Oakland 527, can you copy a code-three fire standby?"

166

Truth be told, before Dispatch even said anything, I smelled the faint odor of a burning residential building in the air but didn't mention anything of it because, a) I really didn't want to think about having to run any calls due to my general state of malaise, and b) On any given evening in West Oakland there's a good chance that some structure will be fully engulfed in flames due to a myriad of reasons. These reasons can, and frequently do, include:

- Arson
- Electrical issues
- A vehicle pursuit by OPD of a stolen gas tanker truck that terminated when it crashed into an orphanage
- A natural gas explosion due to issues with the line, or someone was heating their residence with the oven and the pilot light went out but then Uncle Jesse came by and decided to light up a cigarette to cover up the fart smell and BOOM!

We roll over to 11th and Wood, in the part of West Oakland that's filled with beautiful, old Victorian houses. There a few types of them: derelict houses falling apart from neglect, those occupied by a large amount of young hipsters trying to convince themselves that the neighborhood isn't *that* dangerous, or ones being restored by prospecting contractors who are betting on the economy continuing to pull itself out of the tailspin of the previous few years.

It's anybody's guess as to which specific type of Victorian is on fire, but the one in front of us that we observe is probably going to remain a mystery to us as it's more or less "fully involved", which is FD-speak for being on lots of fire.

"They better get off that roof soon," Ben says gesturing towards the top of the structure. "That thing looks like it's made of kindling. Not gonna have much time to vent it."

"What do you think the over/under is of injured firemen on this thing?"

"Hopefully, none… but if they don't get off that roof… significantly more, I predict."

"I think they know when they should get off the roof. They live for this shit." I see one of the three firefighters on top of the building hand his power saw to another firefighter who is standing at the top of an aerial ladder. The guy on the roof climbs onto the ladder himself and the other two follow.

"See?" Ben gloats. "Time to get off that thing."

"Yeah, yeah, yeah. Since when are you such an expert?"

"Since I – uh oh!" Ben points ahead.

I follow Ben's excited gesture towards the source of his concern and see a group of firemen in SCBA masks emerging from the front door of the burning house carrying the limp body of a rather large, naked man. I pull the shifter down and throttle the rig forward into the inner perimeter bouncing over a hose line in the process.

"Guess we gotta go to work now?" Ben asks, rhetorically.

"It would seem so."

We drive towards the now hurriedly waving rescuers, one of whom initiates chest compressions on the supinated, nude figure in front of him.

Ben picks up the radio mic and advises, "Oakland 527, we seem to have a full arrest on scene. Send another unit to pick up the standby."

"Copy the full arrest," the dispatcher answers. "Oakland S5, copy 527's status?" the dispatcher relays to our field supervisor, Millard Powell.

"S5 acknowledged and show me responding."

"Copy, S5."

Ben and I see another rescue crew emerge from the burning building. They are inconveniently carrying another body, this one a skinny female who is naked from the waist down and wearing a soot-covered pajama top, the top of the unbuttoned shirt exposing her breasts to the news cameras and onlookers on the outer perimeter. They put her down next to the first patient.

Ben says into the mic, "Oakland 527, can you send *another*-another unit? I think we have one more full arrest on scene now."

"Confirm two full arrests, Oakland 527?" the dispatcher asks with obvious surprise in her voice.

Millard transmits, "S5 acknowledges. I'm expediting my response." There's a crunch of jammed transmissions that follows which I hope is another rig or two starting our way, stepping on the radio traffic of the other.

A fireman pulls his SCBA mask off and casts it aside along with his helmet. He drops to his knees and initiates chest compressions on the female fire victim.

"Yeah, that's confirmed." Ben puts the microphone down, looks at me and says, "I am *way* too hung over for this."

We go to work. I intubate the male patient. Ben tubes the female. We put EKG pads on sloughed-off, burnt skin. We start IV's. We push assorted cardiac drugs through the IV lines. The EKG monitors show pulseless electrical activity on the female. We later learn the PEA persists until the backup crew that we pass her off to drops her off at the closest ER. She doesn't make it.

The male starts off at asystole, a totally flat line, and that never changes despite my best efforts to bring him back. After exhausting all our tricks, I call the time of death out loud and the fire crew use random heavy objects like tools and bricks to weigh down the yellow plastic sheet covering the dead man's naked body. The burning hair smell makes me want to vomit. I do so into a basin in the back of the ambulance, away from the news cameras' impolite gaze.

As we clear the scene to go back into service, safely out of earshot of anyone with decency or taste, Ben tells me, "I kinda want barbeque."

29.

Shiva/Saachi lays next to me, sweaty in the afterglow of sex before dawn, after each of our respective shifts at work. We've had these booty-call sessions a few times now. She doesn't usually leave work until about 0300, so it's not too hard for her to stay up an extra hour or so to come crawl into my bed. She brought a bottle of wine this time, which we have yet to open.

Shiva/Saachi, having been very recently in full Shiva-persona as she was at work projecting the illusion of a relentless sex kitten, smells of vanilla and whatever else it is that strippers put on them to make men desire to empty their pockets and pay outrageous ATM fees so they can once again empty their pockets. She's not more than 5′4″ or so and I'm spooned behind her.

She feels small in my arms. My right arm is under the pillow that's beneath her head. My other arm is around her midsection. Her breasts rest atop on my forearm. Her toned rear end is pressed into my crotch. I have my nose buried in her black hair at the crown of her head. This, truth be told, could be a lot worse.

Here's what I've learned about Saachi "Shiva" Saxena in the time we have been hanging out:

- She is twenty-five years old.
- She grew up in Freemont and has a gigantic family.
- Her family hails from India.
- Her parents moved here in the Eighties. Dad works for Apple. Mom works for Hyatt Hotels.

170

- Most of her siblings, of which there seem to be several, went into medicine or business.
- She went to art school and studied sculpture.
- Her parents think that she is a cocktail waitress, and she prefers to keep it that way. How they haven't figured out the truth via Facebook, I do not know.
- She loves dance music of all kind but is partial towards more Industrial sounding stuff like Nine Inch Nails and Ministry.
- She's been telling me about something called "Dubstep" and says I really need to hear it.
- She's super into horror movies.
- Her favorite comic book is *Johnny the Homicidal Maniac* by Jhonen Vasquez.
- She has a few small tattoos and wants more.

Shiva/Saachi is still wearing her stage makeup and I wonder if that comes out of pillowcases in the wash. I don't really care either way, though. It's not like I have silk sheets.

I can faintly hear sounds of sword fighting coming from Ben's room. Periodically, I hear his voice say a muffled, "I kill you! I kill you!" in a weird accent that he always uses when he plays *Assassin's Creed II*. It's coincidently the same generically foreign accent he uses when he portrays any character from any country of origin not the United States. I've heard him use it when mocking the Irish and/or Canadians. It's very weird, like that of an Algerian who grew up splitting his time between Portugal, Quebec and Russia. There is no place on earth where people talk in that accent. It's ridiculously stupid, but it also makes me laugh.

"I really like the way you smell," I tell her in the soft voice I reserve for when I am trying to sound sexy and romantic.

"You like that I smell like tequila, pussy and money?" she asks in her raspy voice that is pretty damn sexy because she doesn't smoke. I wouldn't really care if she did but over a long enough timeline that tends to turn the sexy raspy thing into Joan Rivers.

"Well, I enjoy all three of those things, so yes," I say, chuckling.

"Works out for me just fine," she laughs back. She adds, "You smell kinda like a barbeque."

"It was the fire."

"What fire?"

I start the fire story by noting that Ben and I were both very hung over. I describe the building being really, really on fire. Then I talk about how not one, but *two* bodies got dragged out by the firemen. She's says, "Oh my god. That's awful."

I tell her how Ben and I bravely ran to the downed victims. I tell her how I intubated the male patient, and Ben intubated the female. She asks, "What's *intubated*?" I inform her that's it's the placement of a tube into the trachea, the thing that leads to the lungs, in order to keep an airway open. I tell her how difficult the process was because of the swelling and soot in the airway. I tell her that the patient obviously had been inhaling superheated, smoky air prior to going unconscious.

She asks if we saved their lives. I tell her that we tried. I tell her how S5, the saltiest ex-Army medic, Detroit native, black and proud supervisor we have, showed up on scene, looked at the EKG monitors affixed to both patients and announced, "I'll get you a transport unit for the female. Brother-man is dead as a doornail, though."

I tell her I pronounced him dead. I don't bother explaining how paramedics technically *determine* death and don't *pronounce* it because it's overly technical and doesn't add to the story at all.

I don't tell her how lifeless eyes look straight up into the air. I don't tell her about the awkward tent that's made by the yellow sheet resting atop the tube sticking out of the dead man's mouth. I don't tell her about the wails of surviving loved ones.

"I think what you do sounds crazy. I mean, two of my brothers and sisters are doctors but they don't do the stuff that you do. My brother is a plastic surgeon and my sister deals with feet, which sounds totally nasty but probably isn't as gross as being on an ambulance."

"I suppose it's all relative. Those are important fields too."

She changes the subject and says, "I really like being with you."

"I like being with you too."

Soon we open the wine. We talk until after sunrise. We have sex again. She straddles me while I'm seated with my back up against the headboard. She bounces up and down on me and then grinds herself against my pubic bone. She orgasms twice, though I can't take much credit for it. On the second one, I hear Ben's voice call out over the cacophony of continuous sword play from his room, as if he's watching a Steelers game, "Squea-leeerrrrs!" I ignore it and we make out while I am still inside her, until I go soft. Then we doze off again.

Eventually, she heads home. I get to bed around 0900 thinking that we might have made love. I'm honestly not sure.

30.
April 2010

Ben has been running almost every day. This is abnormal. This is not to say that it is abnormal for Ben to exercise. He always worked out with relative frequency. But he's been running/jogging/whatever almost five days a week now, usually after he wakes up but sometimes right after we get off work.

Ben insists that this is all quite normal. He told me last week when I asked why he had been running so much, "Because I want to get better at running," as if I was supposed to just act like that was totally in character for him, which it isn't. I pressed the issue further because I didn't buy his answer. He told me, "Kaylee has been running with me a lot too."

Could it be that Ben is attempting to better himself for a woman? Is this symptomatic of the new Ben? Are the few years he has on me age-wise showing in his recent behavior?

No. No fucking way. I still don't buy it. Something is fishy, but I can't put my finger on what it is. I vow to remain vigilant for additional behavior changes. If he finds god or gets sober, I'm kicking him out of the apartment or calling 911.

It's just after 2200. Right out of Deployment, we got sent down to Hayward for coverage and started running calls in South County. We have yet to make it back to Oakland. Ben has already called the Dispatcher on his cell phone and complained. The dispatcher informs Ben in so many words that shit happens and that we should suck it up.

174

We start the shift with back-to-back rush hour fender-benders. On the first one, all parties refuse to be transported. On the second one, we take a whiney commuter who was driving a BMW 3-series with pretty insignificant rear end damage, the result of which somehow triggers *terrible* neck pain, to St. Rose. The nursing staff seems very un-thrilled to see us again.

Instructions in the event of a car accident:

- If you or another party appears injured, and/or one is in an unsafe situation (i.e. upside down in a rollover), immediately call 911.
- Even if not an injury/serious accident, if in doubt, call the dispatch center for guidance.
- If uninjured and able, note the license plate and description of the other involved vehicle in the event the driver takes off.
- If in an active lane of traffic, alert the other driver and pull to the shoulder.
- Safely exit your vehicle.
- Attempt to locate witnesses and obtain their contact information.
- Photograph the scene and/or any damage.
- Exchange contact, insurance and driver's license information.
- If the police respond, inform them what happened to the best of your recollection without exaggeration.
- Obtain the police report number if applicable.
- Notify your insurance provider via their 24-hour claim report number.
- Definitely *do not* be a giant douche and fake having a real injury to try to screw over the other driver in the ensuing insurance settlement battle.

Our third call is in a residential neighborhood in Castro

Valley. A six-year-old kid who was riding a scooter surrounded by other neighborhood cul-de-sac kids in the warm, suburban twilight tried to jump the curb and instead totally ate shit and managed to get a pretty decent Colle's fracture of his right wrist. His parents are understandably freaking out, because those injuries look ugly and hurt like hell.

By the time we arrive, ALCO Fire already has the kid's wrist splinted and he has calmed down considerably, no doubt distracted by the big, fancy fire truck. Ben and I basically give an ice pack and a ride to the (now very curious about ambulance equipment) little dude and his noticeably upset, thirty-something father while mom rides our bumper in her minivan with the baby sister hastily strapped to a car seat therein.

We bring the kid and his entourage to Haven. Triage goes smoothly and they get the kid in a room right away. Even jaded triage nurses have soft spots for injured kids, it seems. It's Ben's tech so while he does paperwork, I wander off in search of Dr. Vivian Lopez M.D. and locate her with the assistance of a nurse and a desk clerk.

She is in the break room on the surgical floor. She's got a cup of coffee and a bag of peanut butter pretzels on the table in front of her. They're the ones from Trader Joes. She holds a chart in her hands. The same male physician I saw her getting brunch with on Facebook a while back is seated at the table with her. He's also looking at a chart. There are like eight chairs at the round table but he's sitting right next to her. Neither of them notice when I walk in.

"What's up, Doc?" I ask and she looks up and seems startled to see me. The physician dude glances up, then his eyes track to her and back to the chart in front of him.

She stands up and walks over to me. I move in with my lips and she offers me a cheek, which I kiss somewhat awkwardly, and then briefly hug her.

"Sorry to interrupt. You look busy," I say.

"Yeah, yeah. Been a crazy few shifts. What brings you to this neck of the woods?"

"Too many people called out sick in South County so they got us covering. Hopefully not for long. It's weird interacting with suburban folks."

"Oh, good luck getting back to the mean streets, then," she says, smiling. "Well, not that Hayward is that great, but you know what I mean."

"Thank you. Thank you. So… are we still on for dinner this week?"

"Yeah, yeah. Absolutely. I can't wait," she says and smiles.

I look over her shoulder. I see male physician's eyes glance up to us. His gaze momentarily meets mine and then he looks away.

"Well," I say, "I won't keep you. Just text me."

"I definitely will." She seems just a tad awkward in her delivery.

We hug once more and I walk out of the room thinking that was kind of an uncomfortable situation but remind myself that I have no right to be jealous. Dating is as dating does and neither of us are beholden to the other. Plus, for all I know, they are just friends. I don't 100% believe that though.

Ben and I pack up the rig. He drops off his report with the desk nurse and no sooner does he pick up his aluminum clipboard off the triage station's counter then we hear, "Hayward 527, copy code-three?"

The dispatcher is saying "Hayward 527" to fuck with us. It's the same dispatcher that Ben called and complained to. In hindsight, that was a bad choice.

I pull my portable radio out of my pocket and speak into it, "*Oakland* 527, go ahead."

"Yeah, Hayward 527, this is code-three for the shortness of breath…" and he sends us lights and sirens ablaze to a spot in the boring, working class suburbia area of Hayward, which comprises everywhere in the city that isn't a place where one can get one's car fixed, which is the rest of Hayward.

It only takes us about five minutes to arrive on scene, but Hayward Fire is already on there. Ben and I roll our gurney to the open front door and leave it just outside. We don't bother bringing any equipment in a passive-aggressive way to make a big production if the fire guys didn't bring theirs, which they are supposed to do, but are known to neglect.

I hear a commotion coming from the rear bedroom area of the single-story house. The aging furniture, random household medical equipment, wall decorations and that smell of old, sick people indicate the patient is an old, sick person of Mexican ancestry. Ben and I make our way to the source of the noise and find our target surrounded by the fire crew. A barrel-chested man in his forties, probably the patient's son, is standing off to the side looking concerned. She's seated in a wheelchair. She's your archetypal grandmother – proud in appearance despite her years, tiny and frail despite her want to be less of a burden. One hand clutches a rosary.

Grandma is drowning in her own body fluid; I can hear it from the doorway. The sound of severe pulmonary edema sounds like trying to get the last drops of a smoothie out of a waxed paper cup with a plastic straw.

I ask out loud, "CHF history?"

The patient's muscles strain in her neck. She leans forward like she's trying to rise up, away from the suffocating feeling in her lungs.

A fire medic with a stethoscope looped around his neck looks at me and says, "Yeah, heart failure history but this is apparently an acute onset. Takes a slew of meds for the CHF and other stuff. No known allergies." The fireman points to one of his comrades who reads off medication names to a coworker with a clipboard. "We will get you a med list." No sooner does he say that then a fourth firefighter who is crouched down at the patient's side loops the elastic band of an oxygen mask around the poor woman's head and affixes it on her face. I recognize him from basketball. Think his last name is Corter.

"You guys got your drug box?" I ask. They don't know that this is a test question.

"It's right here," Corter says.

I give an imperceptible shrug that I know Ben will pick up on if he sees it. Hayward Fire has passed today's test.

The patient is working hard to breathe. It's no easy task for anyone with her symptoms, but especially not for an elderly person. I feel the pulse in her wrist. It's humming along at about 140BPM. The fire medic already has a pulse oximeter on the patient's right pointer finger, and it reads 87 out of 100. Not good. At this rate, she will not be conscious soon.

"You get a BP yet?"

"No, I'll do that now," Corter answers.

Ben taps me on the shoulder. I look back and see him hand over our EKG monitor. He must have immediately walked back to the rig to get it when he saw the patient, in violation of our *No Equipment Shall Be Brought When an ALS Engine is On Scene* policy but a smart decision because changing over EKG monitors is a pain in the ass.

I affix our EKG leads to the patient. The white one goes on the upper right chest. The black one on the upper left. The red below it, and I have to awkwardly lift and move Grandma's sagging breast to put the final lead in its place. "Excuse me, Ma'am," I say in the process, but I don't think she cares. She's too busy concentration on not dying. That tends to throw decorum out the window.

"200 over 110," Corter announces.

"Gotcha," the fireman with the clipboard says.

I grab a nitroglycerine spray container out of the FD's drug box and give it a shake before quickly spraying two puffs into the patient's mouth, hoping that the vasodilation effect will cause some of the fluid to drain into other areas of her vasculature.

The fire medic asks Ben, "You got an IV bag?"

Ben's voice answers behind me, "Ready to rock and roll."

The fire medic puts a latex tourniquet around the patient's somehow simultaneously flabby and frail right arm. She has terrible veins. The fire medic feels around her forearm and then looks for the AC vein in the crook of the elbow. I see him push up and down lightly on a spot. He quickly swabs the same area with an alcohol pad and then says, "Stick," before he pushes in the tip of a small gauge needle. I see him stop and start moving the needle around under the skin slightly. He's hunting for a rascally blood vessel.

Soon he seems to re-find his intended target and advances the needle forwards slightly. A red flash of blood appears in the clear plastic of the needle's housing. He pushes the catheter forward, apparently into the vein. When he withdraws the needle, blood comes out of the catheter slowly. He's in. The fire medic hooks up the IV.

"Nice shot," I tell him.

"Thanks. Tough one."

I draw up forty milligrams of Lasix out of the FD's drug box and hand it to the fire medic. He pushes it into the lowest port on the IV tubing and then flushes it into the patient's body with a small amount of saline. I listen to the woman's congested lungs with my own scope and hear that they are about half full. Must be miserable, but the pulse oximeter says that she's now saturating in the low nineties. Not perfect but coming up.

I say, "Let's get her out of here before the Lasix kicks in." The action of Lasix is that it will kick her kidneys into higher gear and make her body expel more fluid. But that means that she will have to pee, and the likely situation there is that Grandma will pee all over whatever she is sitting on because she's too weak to control it.

The fire medic holds the IV bag and Corter pushes the patient in her wheelchair through the house to the front door. Ben and the fire crew lift her onto the gurney while I hold it still.

The patient's son tells us that she's a Kaiser member. That works out fine because it's pretty much an even split in distance to get there versus Haven. We roll her to the ambulance and Ben loads her in. I jump into the back, and without even a hesitation, the fire medic hops in also. Ben makes eye contact with me, shrugs, and closes the doors. The fire medic tells me, "Figured you could use a hand"

"Yeah, absolutely, thanks," I reply, caught off guard by the man's continuing eagerness to help. "Can you handle the airway?"

"No problem."

Ben takes us on a slow code-three trip to Kaiser Hayward. He uses the siren sparingly, in an effort not to spook the patient too badly. I don't think she really notices it regardless.

I count her respirations. She's slowed a bit but seems just as labored as she was before. Her oxygen saturation hovers at a score of 93.

I glance down at the EKG and notice the large, dagger-like pinnacles of a supraventricular tachycardia tracking across the display. Crap.

"Ben, she's in SVT now," I announce calmly.

"Crap," the fire medic says, and I shoot him a look.

Keep calm.

I ignore the SVT. The med that I would need to give Grandma to correct the arrhythmia needs a much bigger IV for a very rapid infusion. And that isn't an option. I spray two more puffs of nitro into the patient's mouth. As I do, I say, "You are doing great, Ma'am. Hang in there. I know this is hard, but the oxygen level in your blood is at a good spot."

Grandma's eyes make contact with mine. She's tired and looks at me as if pleading for solace that I cannot give her.

I wish there was more that I could do, and there is, technically, but I still think she's too alert to assist her breathing with a BVM. Or maybe it's time to be a little more aggressive in my treatment. I can't decide.

I go over this internally for a few moments. Ben's voice snaps me back into the moment by saying, "She needs to be bagged, dude."

And then the fire medic says, "Yeah, I agree."

"How far out are we?"

"Two or three," Ben answers.

"Well, we have a quorum." I tell the fire medic, "It's all you. I hate doing that."

The reason I hate doing this is because forcing air into a frail old lady's lungs with a BVM is in practice as horrible as it sounds. It requires a firm but gentle hand and lots of timing to make sure one isn't trying to inflate the lungs while the patient is trying to deflate them. If done incorrectly, it can cause the lungs to tear. It tends to make people who are already short of breath panic, which makes the problem worse.

So that's why I'm relieved when the fire medic grabs a BVM from the cabinet above his head, hooks it up to the oxygen output and then says to the patient, "Ma'am, I am going to help you breathe with this mask. It is going to feel a little strange at first. Just try to breathe at the same tempo as you are now, and I promise it's going to help."

Grandma looks me in the eyes, and I ask, "Understand?"

She doesn't nod but I think she gets it. The fire medic puts the mask on her face and starts off gently squeezing the bag in time with the patient's inhalation. As the two of them synch up, he squeezes a little more. Her oxygen sat immediately goes up to 97%.

I draw up another forty of Lasix push it in. I listen to her lungs. It sounds less wet in there. Her systolic blood pressure has come down to 170. She's still in SVT. We pull into the driveway of the ER a few seconds later. The HFD engine company is right behind us. After we drop the patient off in the ER, the fire medic helps me clean up. Before he leaves, I tell him, "Hey, you kicked ass. Thanks."

He smiles and says, "We heard from the truck company that ran on the MVA with you earlier that you two were down here and knew we had to be on our shit."

I laugh and think for a moment that maybe firemen aren't so bad... sometimes.

31.

Instructions in the event of an impending deer attack:

- Don't run. You may not correctly surmise the source of the deer's aggression and, say, put yourself closer to the angry parent's little Bambi offspring, thereby making the situation worse.
- Attempt to figure out why the deer seems so pissed off and slowly back away, making sure you aren't backing towards the giant bear.
- Yell, scream and flail your arms as much as possible. Try to be large and scary.
- Try deer-jitsu, I guess. Honestly, I'm not much of an expert on this subject.

"You are fucking high, dude," Ben tells me.

"Nu-uh," I answer back.

"Yeah-huh, jackass."

"No, you are just an idiot. And I am entitled to my opinion on the matter."

"I am not an idiot, and your opinion is wrong."

"Yes, you are times a million-infinity an idiot."

"Real mature."

"Fuck you. You are in zero position to say anything about maturity. You are practically a giant baby, a giant, racist, dumb-shit baby."

"You are a homophobic, anti-American pile of ass-garbage."

"What is ass-garbage?"

There's a brief pause in the argument as we both think about what to say next. We are posted in a parking lot in the pitch black of the night sky, surrounded by the cool stillness of a small park a few blocks off of Highway 13, a park that feels about a hundred miles away from the urban sprawl we can't see below. I think I spot movement in the trees across the lawn in front of us. I illuminate the area with the ambulance's spotlight and three startled deer look straight at us before running off into the bush.

"Bingo! Three down! Mark 'em," I tell Ben. He begrudgingly removes a small notebook out of his pocket, takes out his pen and makes three hash marks on the side of a page divided by a single line with our names on either side, respectively.

"Dude! You are *killing* me this month," Ben says and puts the notebook back in his pocket. "Now gimme that thing. It's my turn."

Ben and I have for the last several months played this game. The goal of the game is to "shoot" as many deer with the spotlight as possible. At the end of the month, a winner is declared, and the game begins anew. Last month, we only made it to this post once and Ben won the game with a pathetic 1-0 score. But a win is a win. It's a deer-eat-deer world out there.

I toss the spotlight to Ben without looking. He catches it and holds it at the ready. Again, we sit in darkness.

"I am not wrong," I continue arguing. "Cloth seats are superior to leather seats because they are more comfortable. They don't get as hot in the sun and your ass sweats less if you have to sit in them a long time. Plus, they feel better against your bare skin. And leather seats get to be like waterslides if you put that slippery cleaner stuff on them."

"You, again, are clearly confusing genuine leather seats with that vinyl faux-leather crap. Genuine leather is amazing and luxurious. It's also easier to clean than cloth seats, which I would think would be preferred in an ambulance as opposed to these MRSA coated shit-seats we are sitting on now. I'm probably gonna get some new ass infection that nobody has ever heard of because of these gnarly cesspools. That's ass-garbage."

"Oh, you're gonna get ass-garbage alright, but it isn't because of these sheets. It's because of some handsome fella."

"Ah, a gay joke from a known homophobe. Real creative. Can we not have a civil debate, free of your prejudices?"

"We make those jokes all the time."

Then he gets serious, takes a deep breath and says, "Sure, but, I don't know, dude. It's just that lately I've been a little gun-shy about them, like using *gay* in a negative context just seems wrong when we have friends who are gay and I think both you and I would get pissed if someone called one of them a *fag* or whatever."

"You are making good points; however, I cannot help but ask if you are talking, or Kaylee?"

"If you must know, she did point out that I use certain words in a way that could be offensive. Specifically, the gay stuff. Got me to thinking."

"Hold up! You of all people 'got to thinking' about offending people?"

"Yeah. I just am trying to avoid using certain words because I don't want people to think that I'm a bigoted asshole. I'm fine with being a regular asshole, but not a bigoted one."

"I need to find some balloons to blow up. This is a noteworthy occasion, a radical change in worldview. This is like the Berlin Wall coming down. So what words aren't we using then?"

"You really want to know?"

"Yes."

"*Gay*. Stuff in a similar vein, such as *fag*. And *retarded*. That's also super rude."

"*Gay*, and *retarded*, eh?"

"Yep."

"Even if we meet a retarded gay guy and need to describe him to other people?"

"We can cross that bridge when we come to it."

I sit there for a while thinking that he's absolutely correct and that I have no viable argument for any disagreement. As a matter of fact, I am shocked to realize that he has made nothing but extremely valid points and now, as a result, I am going to adjust my behavior. Kaylee must be some kind of a witch. And as I sit in silence knowing full well that Ben is aware that he has called me out, and that I have no possible counter argument, which might just be his only motivation for this and the Kaylee thing is just a cover story, it suddenly hits me: the one and only thing I can possibly say that will be appropriate for the subject matter.

"If I can't say *those* words, then how am I supposed to describe lacrosse?"

"Ooooh shit! Boom, son!" and we fist bump, laughing.

"Sorry. Last joke like that from here on out."

After a few beats he asks, "Have you even sat in an actual leather seat?"

"Back to this, eh? Yes. Yes, I have sat in an 'actual' leather seat."

"When?"

"My mom had a Lexus growing up."

"If you have been in Lexus, you should know what I'm talking about. Clearly, you are willfully ignorant in addition to being wrong."

"Whatever."

And then Ben goes, "Ah ha!" and raises the beam of the spotlight forward, illuminating the same spot where I scored three deer moments ago. There's nothing there. "Fucking... shit! Stupid deer, show yourselves..."

After about an hour, we get sent to post downtown. I'm still up three deer by the time the shift ends, just down a few archaic vocabulary words.

32.
Early June 2010

The needle scratches across the proverbial record when Dr. Vivian Lopez M.D. asks, "Are you seeing anyone else?"

For a moment, I think about lying. You know that feeling when you first start to sweat, and your skin gets all tingly? That happens to me. I don't know why I am panicking in the face of this inquiry. We have no obligation. There's been no mention of monogamy. None the less... I don't know what to say.

Perhaps it's because I suspect there's a right and a wrong answer. But is there? Is there, really? The Good Doctor could be the town harlot for all I know, like me. It's not like we really ever talk about these things. We hang out once or twice a week. We go on dates. We laugh. We eat. We see movies. We have sex. We text a few times a day.

I'll concede that it's been months since we first went out. And, yeah, we are both busy people with our own hectic schedules. But now that I think about it, there is kind of an unwritten equation I can't ignore: time + familiarity + regular sex = relationship.

Truthfully, and you already know this, Shiva/Saachi is the only other woman I'm seeing. I started dating her not long after Vivian. And it's the same story there. We hang out once or twice a week. There are dates, sexing, laughing, texting, etc.

Though suspiciously long in coming, I choose the moral high road and blurt out, "Yes, there's someone else I'm seeing." I then involuntarily clench my ass cheeks.

"Can I get you another beer?" the waiter asks from my

right. Thank god.

"Yes, please. And a little Jameson." I make the small sign with my thumb and middle finger. I'm pretty sure he rolls his eyes.

"Madam, another glass of pinot? Or a *Jameson* perhaps?" he asks the (suddenly unamused) woman at the other end of the table who I can now tell was not expecting my answer.

"No, I think I'm okay." Her delivery is terse.

We are at Bay Wolf on Piedmont. It's a fancy place. I'm wearing a shirt with buttons and leather shoes. Dr. Vivian Lopez M.D. is wearing a little black dress and looks fantastic. When I first saw her in that dress, I wanted to tear it off her. That statement stands.

The night started off well. We met out front. We embraced and kissed. I made a reservation so we got a table right away. I had the duck cassoulet. She had the Petrale sole. Everything was delicious.

We are currently splitting the final bites of a chocolate caramel tart that the waiter insisted was way better than the fruity pot de crème thing that I don't remember the full specifics of. I take another bite and decide to hold it in my mouth as long as possible, so I don't have to say anything just yet.

Things took a bad turn when I told a story about going to a concert at the Fox Theater last week and eating at a restaurant across the street from the theater called Flora. I mentioned that Flora and the Fox both have great Art Deco architecture and styling. I like Deco because it's both iconic and uniquely American and I can recognize it when I see it. I talked about how good the restaurant was. I mentioned it had a full bar and fancy cocktails, the kind that have egg whites in them for what the bartender said provided better mouth feel, which was a silly thing to say and it made me laugh.

Dr. Vivian Lopez M.D.'s demeanor changed while I

conveyed this story, her deductive reasoning skills no doubt figuring that I didn't do this activity solo or with my best buddy whose idea of fine dining is Korean BBQ – which is delicious but you see what I'm getting at here. She knows that neither of us drink fancy cocktails nor give a shit about "mouth feel" unless it's in reference to something involving boobs.

Now, well, it's awkward. Thanks for tuning in for this part. I didn't want to be going this alone.

"What are you looking for out of our relationship, Harlan, or whatever it is that we have?" she asks. "Do you want anything more than this 'friends who fuck' thing we have been doing?" She says "friends who fuck" at a volume that is sufficient to make one or more fellow customers glance in our direction. I doubt this is by accident and deliberately an attempt to make my ass clench even further, which it does!

Out of the corner of my eye I see a dude in his fifties, who is clearly on a date with his wife, smirk. He's thinking, *That dude is fucked.*

I'm fucked.

"Uhhhh, I don't have anything specific in mind. I'm just enjoying the time we spend together and hoping to keep it going. I like you a lot and think we have a good thing here."

She just looks at me clearly expecting that I'm going to continue.

Accordingly, I ad lib: "I'm still trying to make sense of my last failed relationship, I guess. I suppose I'm a bit skittish at times. I don't mean to be. I'm sorry."

What I have just said is the truth and surprisingly introspective, coming from me. However, this was not a good answer. I already figured this out while saying it, but I was totally put on the spot and tried to power through it. How I could be caught off guard this completely is just as confusing to me as it is to you. God knows I carry a mountain of programming to get married, have babies and do all that shit that a person approaching thirty is supposed to do. What the hell is wrong with me? It's not like I haven't had time to think of all this.

"That's not an, uh, *ideal* answer for me," she says, kind of chuckling. "But I appreciate your honesty. If you haven't figured out your own situation, then I can't expect you to figure *ours* out, I suppose."

I do catch the thinly veiled insult there, by the way.

The waiter arrives with our drinks and I take a long pull off my new pint of Anchor Steam, buying time again. I think of Becky. I conjure a mental image of her shaking her head in a condescending manner as she watches me flail. Then I push her out of my mind. I down the shot.

"Look, I don't know what I'm doing when it comes to stuff like this, which is probably obvious to you. Half the time I freak out that I'm not on my way to getting married and having kids and the other half of the time I talk to people at work who are married, have kids and are miserable and then I'm so stoked on the freedom I have."

She doesn't say anything.

I continue. "Do I think I could see you and me getting serious? Yeah, absolutely. Does that idea kind of freak me out? Yeah, it kind of does. Does that make any sense at all?"

Do I normally talk like this?

No, I don't.

"Harlan, I like you. You are sweet and fun and… and I'm sure you could make a hell of a husband if that's what you wanted. But I don't really think you want that yet. I don't think you, and I don't mean this to sound condescending, are quite mature enough yet to get serious with, at least not at this stage in your life. I'm not upset you are seeing other people; I figured you were. And, honestly, there's someone else in my life too. That's one of the reasons I brought this up."

"Oh," I say. I want to tell her that she *was* being condescending, but I do not. I'm a bit offended maybe… or jealous?

191

"I'm in the process of making some decisions about my future. Now that I'm established in my career and in the Bay Area I want to start a family sooner than later, you know? I want to have children while I'm less at risk of the developmental health risks that tend to materialize as we get older. I've got to start planning now. And that takes a willing partner and adherence to a somewhat strict timeline. At least, it does for me."

Now I start stutter. "I guess I just... you just... I mean you are a freaking *doctor* and so smart and normal and... well, look at me: I don't make much money and I look like a hooligan and I ride a motorcycle and I hunt friggin' deer with the spotlight—"

"Huh?"

"I'm not, like, respectable compared to you. I live with my best friend. We play video games and throw tennis balls at each other and shit. You and me, we are kind of an odd couple, you know?"

"Oh. Okay. That kind of makes it sound like you think I'm a square."

I continue my downward trajectory. "No, wait... I guess one of the reasons things have gone so slowly between us is that I'm kind of insecure about your station in life versus mine. You've accomplished so much already. It's kind of intimidating."

"Well, you shouldn't be intimidated. I didn't agree to go out with you to fulfill some sort of fetish while I looked for someone else. I liked you for you, not because of the clear image that you try to present to the world."

"I don't know if I *try* that hard, I just..."

"There's nothing wrong with you, Harlan. Take away the motorcycle and the leather jacket... the hair... and you are still the same good person. You could make someone very happy someday, if that's something you choose to commit to."

"Thanks. Glad to know I'm still a catch if I'm hairless."

"Don't be snarky."

"Sorry."

"Harlan, I've really enjoyed our time together; I really have..." she continues for a while, but I don't really listen because I know what's coming. She breaks up with me, in case you didn't call that one already. I keep my cool, I guess. We split the tab. She says we will still be friends and doesn't want it to be awkward at work. I assure her it won't be. I give her a quick hug and a peck on the lips and am first to leave the restaurant. The married guy gives me a nod. The waiter shoots me a look.

Fuck that guy.

I ride down to the Ruby Room. The motorcycle helmet keeps anyone on the road from being able to tell that I have a few tears in my eyes. When I take the helmet off, any ocular wetness is easy to explain away as a side effect from the cold air coming off the bay on a chilly Oakland evening.

I get to the bar. I walk in the front door and let my eyes adjust. I look down at the end of the bar and smile. Ben is sitting there with a beer and a shot in front of him.

He looks in my direction and smirks. He flips me off. I flip him off and make my way to the barstool next to him. He looks in my eyes and asks, "You alright, dude? Date not go well? Only been like an hour, right?"

"Three hours."

"Close enough."

"She dumped me. I don't blame her, but it sucks."

"Sorry, man. But I'd be even sorrier if you didn't have a hot stripper on your jock. I would also be shocked if you didn't trip, dick first, into some new girl when you get up to take a leak."

"Well, thank you for that remarkable self-esteem builder, truly. It's just that I'm still not over *You Know Who* and I think it's made me skittish to commit to a relationship."

"Stop talking about her. She should and could make anyone skittish. She was a pain in the ass, and you know it."

"I don't really want to have this reta… err, dumb conversation again. How about we change the subject?"

"Fine, I don't either. So sorry one of your *two* attractive lady friends dumped you. There's plenty of fish in the sea and all that jazz, man." He raises his shot glass and then downs it. Then a beat later he adds, "Though not everyone can be as awesome as Kaylee." Something weird happens as he says her name this time. His eyes light up.

My eyes narrow as I look at his face. "Umm… dude?"

"What?"

"Are you in love?"

Ben appears to take mental inventory and then all nonchalantly, like it's a thing that I have *ever* known to happen before in the history of our friendship, he says, "Yeah. Seems that way." Then he takes a sip of his beer and does an exaggerated, "Aaaah," as he puts the bottle down.

I'm speechless. I am also no longer thinking of Dr. Vivian Lopez M.D. or Becky. I think my brain might be short-circuiting.

The female bartender walks up, my new favorite one, effective immediately. She just started a few weeks ago. She's a short blonde with a Bettie Page haircut, tattoos and giant boobs. She's from Oklahoma or Arkansas or Iowa maybe, if I recall correctly from the few conversations we have had. She's wearing a black tank top with the logo of the punk band The Dwarves on the front. The logo consists of a skull with giant, crossed penises behind it instead of crossbones. She has on really tight jeans accentuating her rather generous rear end. She asks, "What can I get you?

I nod towards Ben and say, "I'll have what he's having."

Before she can answer, Ben goes, "And I'll have another round… on his tab."

"Dick."

"It's okay. You love dick."

"No more homophobic put-downs, dude!"

194

"Slipped out."

The bartender groans, laughs, and turns to get our order. I check out her butt. I look at Ben. He's also looking at her butt. I give him a little nod and he returns it. The bartender turns back around. We both look up immediately. It's unlikely that she doesn't know that we were looking at her butt, but we uphold the social contract of not being overtly creepy when clearly the truth is to the contrary. She puts down two bottles of High Life and then two shots of Jameson. I pay and tip six dollars. I do this because we are regulars and want to stay in good standing. Also, because she is attractive. If she was one of the male bartenders, I would only be tipping four dollars. Them is: the breaks.

She says, "I'll get your next shots. Cheers."

I tell her she should join us in our next shots by saying, "You should join us in our next shots." I drop my voice an octave or so when I say it, so I'm more mysterious and sexier, and wave my hand across my face like I'm Obi-Wan. I doubt this works but it's basically uncontrollable.

She says she will and then asks, "I've seen you here before, right? What was your name again?"

I tell her.

She tells me I have a unique name. She says her name is Les.

In my head, so I don't forget it, I go, *Les, Les, Les, Les, Les, Les...*

33.

The power is out in the apartment when we get home from Ruby Room. I have the bartender's number programmed in my phone. This has raised my self-esteem a bit. I needed that.

Neither Ben, nor I, are ready to crash out yet but it's 1:43 in the morning. We cannot watch a movie we have seen a million times already or play video games. We just have to hang out at home and make small talk by candlelight, I guess. Out of habit, I check the fridge for another beer out of and unsurprisingly there is none.

There is never any beer. Between Ben, Kaylee, whoever they bring to bed with them (Did I mention that I sleep with earplugs in at least once a week?), and me, beer is a rare commodity in this domicile. There are, however, pickles and chips, so after a long, resigned sigh into the dark refrigerator, I bring both out to the living room with me. The power outage has brought us to hang out in the living room, a scarce occurrence.

A brief summary of items in our living room:

- Sectional couch, with an attached recliner which we fight about who gets to sit in during the infrequent times we both are planning on using the couch simultaneously.
- Table strewn with comic books, the second *Song of Ice and Fire* novel, the cordless phone, Kaylee's spare bong, a random bra that looks to be too big to be Kaylee's, but I assume has to be, and a few coasters.

- A fan-bike that Ben bought recently and we both have used a few times. It's surprisingly hard. Also, it makes my taint hurt if I sit on it for more than twenty minutes.
- Truth be told, looking around, that's really all that is worth mention. We don't spend much time here, like I said.

Ben emerges from his room and hands me a cold, red and white tallboy of Budweiser. He presents it to me with a smug expression on his face as if to convey, *You are welcome, Peon.*

My eyes widen and I demand to know, "Where the fuck did you get tallboys from?"

"The store. Duh."

I am not satisfied with this answer and say, "Asshole, that's not what I meant."

"I know that's not what you meant."

"You are dodging my inquiry, but I'll just assume it a miracle."

We drink the first pair of tall boys and he doesn't let me talk about Becky.

He doesn't let me talk about her new man, his perfect house, or his perfect face, or his perfect boat or his perfect anything else related to the general subject that I would like to slander. It's because I am now sufficiently drunk, hurt and pissed that I was just dumped by Vivian, who I mention had such potential, who I rightfully note was gorgeous and had her shit together and would make a perfect wife and mother for my children. I tell him all this and he just nods and listens. He doesn't say much at all.

"Since when are you a good listener?"

"I've always been a good listener. I'm just pretending that I want to fuck you and that means I'll listen to your bullshit for days."

"You are so romantic."

"Damn right I am."

Our eyes meet. He puts his hand on my knee. I put my hand on his thigh. I tell him, "You have never won Gay Chicken before, and today is not your day. Come at me, bro."

"Oh, I'm gonna come right up that pert ass of yours," he taunts.

"I thought we weren't doing gay-joke stuff like this anymore?"

"Like what, taking care of your carnal needs, the ones that you dare not speak of in front of your parents?"

Gay Chicken is a game we sometimes play when drunk. If Dr. Sigmund Freud was in the room, the field day he would have with this situation would be one of historical proportions.

Ben slides his hand down to my inner thigh with his pinky just brushing my crotch.

I slap my hand on his balls and give a little confident squeeze. I can tell it hurts. Because he inhales sharply.

He grabs the back of my head and tries to shove his tongue in my mouth succeeding only in licking my cheek.

"Oh god, Dude!" I yell and jump up from the couch. I run to the sink and throw water on my soiled face.

I look back and Ben sits contently – nay, proudly – on the couch. He takes a long pull off his beer and says, "Don't act like you didn't love that, you sexy beast."

I have decisively lost Gay Chicken.

"Alright. You win. I really didn't think you would go that far."

He laughs and says, "You mean farther than you straight up grabbin' my cock and balls through my pants? Because, uh, you went pretty far."

"It was just your balls. And there are no body fluids involved in that move. Trying to French kiss me is, like, another level."

"Whatever helps you sleep at night."

He's got a point, I suppose. I tell him, "You've got a

point, I suppose."

"Yep. I'm going to celebrate my victory with a shot of whiskey. Would you like one to numb the searing pain of your loss?"

"Where the hell did you get whiskey?!"

He produces a bottle of whiskey from his room. We drink plenty of it and bullshit about nothing I remember later. And, I don't know how it happens, but we toss down what is probably the millionth shot of whiskey of the night and then suddenly we are seated side by side on the couch in a pause to our normal, juvenile banter exchanging an awkward, open-mouth kiss by candlelight.

It's a real kiss.

My stubble rubs against his stubble, and it is very strange. Though it's only for a few moments he starts to push against me like he's trying to bed me, and I push against him in the same way, a de facto power struggle between two men who have never done anything like this before. And then suddenly we break apart when my hand finds his flank, and instead of pushing against him, it pulls him closer. Then I realize what the fuck I'm doing, and he does too.

He jumps up to his feet and goes, "What the fuck are we doing?!"

I jump up from the couch, at a true loss for words, except for a panicked, "You started it!"

Instructions in the event of a power outage:

- Try to keep the fridge and freezer closed as much as possible (I screwed the pooch on this one already).
- Unplug any appliances previously in use to minimize any damage from power spikes.
- Leave one light on to let you know when the power has returned.

- Avoid driving/traveling. There is a good chance that traffic controls will be out as well making driving conditions hazardous.
- Probably don't make out with your roommate.

In the wake of our collective horror, Ben and I stay up until sunrise. We finish all of his tall boys, at least all he's willing to share… I think. The Jameson is gone from the bottle. We pass out on the couch. He gets the part that converts into a recliner. I get the longer part. I opt to keep my feet closest to him rather than my head. After a few hours, his snoring wakes me up and I trudge off to bed with a giant glass of water taking three Advil on the way and still wondering what exactly happened, unsure if it really did, and hoping to forget about it entirely regardless of the veracity of the experience.

The loud ring of the landline wakes me up in the early afternoon. My head is full of hot fog, but the ringing stops on the fifth or so one and I hear Ben's voice speaking in an overly deliberate and professional manner. I clearly hear him repeat, "Thank you. Thank you. I'll be there," excitedly, with far too much enthusiasm considering how his head no doubt feels because he drank just as much as I did. He puts the cordless receiver back in the cradle.

My door opens. Light pours into my room. Groggy, I say, "Go away unless someone is dead and never speak to me again about anything in the last twenty-four hours."

Ben says something to me, he shares important news, but he shares it like this isn't news that soon sends my heart down into the pit of my stomach and causes a dark wave of betrayal to grow behind my eyes, like this is something I was totally expecting, like I would be completely okay with hearing it, and which I am absolutely fucking not.

"Dude, I just got hired by the Berkeley Fire Department!"

"It's too early for this shit. Go away."

"I'm serious."

I don't totally believe him until the letter announcing his academy start date arrives in the mail the following day. Then I feel like I don't know which way is up and utterly confused about not only my sexuality but also what I'm going to do with the rest of my life.

34.
A Few Uncomfortable Weeks Later

We change guard every morning, the two of us. I'm usually playing video games or watching TV and having after work beers when I hear his alarm go off and the shower start a few moments later. The hum of his electric razor harkens the sunrise and lets me know I need to get to bed. Then the front door closes. His bike scares away the birds that just started to chirp in their unique manner that lets the world know they don't give two shits about shift workers.

Ben leaves by 0645 and presumably somehow makes it to his 0700 muster at the Berkeley Fire Academy.

Ben is already a few weeks into his sixteen-week training course. He and his fellow recruits do jumping jacks, pushups, sit-ups, burpees, mountain climbers, and march around like they are in the army. They learn how to raise ladders up and spray water or foam on burning stuff. They carry hoses up flights of stairs. They fold those hoses in a precise and unwavering manner. They learn rudimentary first aid despite the expertise in that area of pretty much everyone present, as all of them are culled from private ambulance services or smaller fire departments that pay less. They talk about things like *joists*. They learn what all the nobs, dials and little spinning wheels on the outside of the fire apparatus are for. They learn the difference between fire trucks and fire engines. They learn what the guy is called who steers the back part of the hook and ladder. That guy is the *tillerman* in case you were wondering.

Those that know how to cook are already more popular

among the instructors than those who do not. Those students that were paramedics share a bonding gratitude to no longer be working for AER or whatever other bullshit company they came from. But to the training staff, they are all *boots* or *FNG's*. It doesn't matter to the training staff where the recruits herald from or what they did before the academy started. The recruits are just fresh meat for the grinder.

Ben's hair is buzzed and kind of flat top like the crazy PE teacher from *Beavis and Butthead*. He informs me early on in our alternating sunset/sunrise cycle that Kaylee kind of likes the new hairdo and is getting off on how "square" he looks. She also likes that he has evenings free, even though he has to study.

Ben says the classroom material is way easier than the curriculum in paramedic school, but still new to him regardless. He makes flash cards like he did in paramedic school. Often, he studies at Kaylee's house and then they have sex in her new hot tub, which he helped pay for, which is the single most commitment-oriented thing I've ever known him to do. His paycheck has already nearly doubled his one from AER and he is still a trainee. It's only gonna go up from there.

By the way, it isn't a redwood hot tub but it's nice enough, I hear. I've yet to be invited. I don't know if I would accept the invite regardless. So much jizz probably afloat in there. Presumably that's a thing I'm still disinterested in.

Kaylee is excited that Ben is going to spend his first few years on a BFD ambulance, and he will see her more at work. None of the academy trainees really care that they will be back on the ambulance after graduation. They will be perfectly happy because they've made the Big League. They won. It's all downhill to a great retirement now.

Did I mention that I know most of this only from the occasional text message exchange? I rarely see the dude.

I am beginning to feel not unlike Martin Sheen in *Apocalypse Now*. I long to get drunker and higher than I have ever been before and do naked karate facing a mirror while weirdo 1970's Francis Ford Coppola watches from his director's chair in his Dolphin shorts with his gross beard and offers helpful notes like, "Make your balls swing more on the front kicks, Marty! Yes, that's it! I want to see the sweat droplets impacting on the mirror! Now punch it with your bare hand, you beautiful bastard! More blood!"

To make matters worse, for some ungodly reason and in defiance of all that is holy and pure, approximately ten days ago, Tay-boobs decided that he wanted to work a later schedule. In Ben's absence, he has been made my partner. I had no say in the matter. I was the odd man out, as was he.

It is only a matter of time until I detonate a bomb while we are on the way to a call. I don't know how much longer I can take it. I am already having suicidal thoughts every time that fat asshole speaks. If I have to go meet my maker, be he God, Satan or Travolta's Guy, Tay-boobs is coming with me.

By the way, if you have it handy, please put on "The End" by The Doors before this next part, because Tay-boobs is my Colonel Kurtz. His sloth and avarice insult my very soul. I long to venture up a hazy jungle river to smite him with my rage and then disavow all knowledge of the operation when called before the inevitable military tribunal. I will have no knowledge of such clandestine operations, nor if I did would I be able to speak about them.

Intellectually, I know that Ben has not done anything intentionally to harm me. I repeatedly try to remind myself of this every single minute I stare at the third hand of my watch while Tay-boobs blathers on about his views and gripes and offers his "helpful" suggestions regarding all efforts at ambulance navigation or patient treatments that I dare endeavor in without.

I further know that Tay-boobs has not chosen to work nights in an effort to ruin my calm, or further aggravate my tenuous mental state. I know that Tay-boobs doesn't want me to drown out my memories from the previous shift by drinking whiskey far past sunrise. I know he isn't technically responsible for my bouts of yelling, "Fuck you, you little motherfucker!" numerous times per day over the Xbox Live headset at children half my age who dared to have smote my character by camping out at a spawn point in a multiplayer round of *Call of Duty: Modern Warfare 2*, stabbing my hapless avatar and then doing the crouch move over and over again on top of my lifeless corpse.

Ben cannot be a modern-day Andy Kaufman, can he? This isn't all some elaborate practical joke, right?

Yet the evidence speaks for itself: I knew that Ben wanted off the ambulance at some point. He said as much to me more than once when we looked around at the medics nearing retirement and knew how insane, bitter, angry and unhealthy they were.

I concede that I told him I didn't want to end up like those guys. I just never thought that actualizing that idea meant that I wouldn't be a medic, by trade. I never considered leaving the job entirely. I thought I could do it better than the aging lunatics, burnouts and malcontents. I thought I could minimize the damage to my mental and physical health and make it to retirement as a shining example of success.

Ben figured out the end game I had pushed out of my mind for years, choosing instead to concentrate on the moment. Ben made the right call. He found the greener pastures. His very act of becoming a fireman means that my hatred of firemen was probably misguided.

Intellectually and as much as I hate to admit it, I know Ben made a good career move. I know it's a good decision for him in the long run. I know he'll have a guaranteed pension now and better benefits and shit like that.

In moments of clarity, I exhale deeply and think, *Nobody is out to get you, Harlan.*

I also know that Tay-boobs wanted the night shift bonus pay and to not deal with daytime traffic, because he really hates traffic. He never shuts up about it, and attributes its primary causes to "the damn illegals and foreigners without licenses." Then I call him a Nazi, and he gets all pissy like *I'm the one* in the wrong.

Tay-boobs probably isn't trying to ruin my life, even though he's a dipshit and I hope he chokes on his own micro-dick. In moments of clarity, I inhale deeply and think, *Tay-boobs isn't out to get you and Ben isn't either.*

I know I shouldn't secretly fantasize about taking both of them out in a suicidal hatchet attack, but I do. Or maybe I could use a sword. Or maybe I could do that thing where you hide in the rafters and drip poison down a thin thread onto the lips of a slumbering enemy? That could work.

But fucking Tay-boobs' ghost would no doubt find a way to make a bigoted crack about that too, something Japanese-ninja-blah blah blah related. I'm sure he'd do that thing where he uses his hands to make his eyes slanted while he said it. Then he would go to whatever 7-11 is called in Hell and get another sugary death-snack but it wouldn't matter because he was already passed into The Darkness and calories don't count there.

Saigon.
Shit.
I'm still only in Saigon.

35.

Despite all of these troubling things upsetting the stability of my day to day existence, there's still Shiva/Saachi, a beacon of golden light shining down from Nirvana. This morning, we lay in my bed in the lazy, comfortable time between sex and sleep. It's my day off after a date night that consisted of eating good ramen from a place downtown and then watching anime in my room. Both of these things were her ideas, might I note, but I was more than happy to partake.

Earlier she asked me what my favorite ramen place was, and I didn't have any input on the matter.

"Your Japanese half needs a little work." Because she is not Tay-boobs, and not a racist dickhead, I laughed. After dinner she said she would pick the anime because I "clearly" was "not qualified" to choose.

Before she could follow that statement up, I said authoritatively, "Not so fast. We are gonna watch Cowboy Bebop."

Her eyes lit up. She said, "Perhaps I should retract my previous statement?"

We held hands silently through the movie, feeling no need to occupy the dead air with chatter. It felt good. It was nice to know she was there next to me in the darkness illuminated only by the light of the television screen as Spike Spiegel Jeet-Kune-Do'd his way to victory over the forces of evil.

Now, I'm spooned up behind her small frame, my nose

buried in her hair. Her brown skin casts a contrast to my inked-up pallor. I can feel her heart beating. Her chest rises and falls. Somewhere in the space behind my sternum there's a pleasant flutter.

She whispers, "Can I tell you something?"

"Yes, of course."

And she tells me something that makes the feeling in my chest wash over my entire body, she says, "I know this might be a little sudden. I just think I might be in love with you."

A smile bigger than I've let creep across my mug in a long while plasters itself there and it makes me want to weep because I had no idea what a relief it would be to hear such a thing.

I'm overwhelmed. I'm overjoyed. I'm ready to throw caution to the wind. I had no idea how heartbroken I was over Ben being, for all practical purposes, gone from my everyday life. I had no idea how much damage losing Becky did to my idea of emotional normalcy, at least, not until I heard this beautiful person in my arms say such a wonderful thing to me.

I'm in awe. I breathe in the positive feeling and breathe out the negative energy. I decide it's time for me to answer even if I'm not 100% positive of the situation. But I my left brain says that I should tell her, unequivocally, that I love her. Because I probably do at least a little, and nothing ventured, nothing gained.

Before I can say anything, in the same whispered tone of voice, the same one that just sent my heart aflutter, she says, "But I don't want a boyfriend. And it isn't fair to you or me. I don't think I can see you any longer, and it really hurts." Then she starts to cry and gets out of bed so now she's crying naked, hastily gathering her clothing from the floor.

I blurt out, "What the fuck?!"

36.
Sunday, July 4th, 2010

This is the second day in a row that I've called in sick. Calling in sick to an overtime shift though, one on a busy holiday, that's a big no-no. I did it anyways.

I know that everyone will assume it's because I got loaded at the bar after watching Germany trounce Argentina in the World Cup. Or maybe I watched that game and went to another bar to view Spain edge out a one goal victory against Paraguay to the surprise of absolutely nobody. But the reality is that I couldn't take another night on the rig with Colonel Kurtz, who was to be my partner because the overtime gods hate me as much as the other gods. At least, not this night, not the night where assholes shoot roman candles and throw M80's at the ambulance when we go to one of the seven thousand 911 calls that inevitably happen.

I couldn't deal with having to duck stray gunfire that always seems right around the corner, muzzle flash from automatic weapons strobe-lighting the streets with cracking staccatos. I couldn't deal with getting held over until after sunrise and then have to go home to Ben and Kaylee having a nice, home cooked brunch on the couch in the living room, one that now has an arrangement of goddamn flowers on the coffee table, while I go jerk off in the shower and then shoot computerized enemy soldiers while yelling at obnoxious children that I can't see. Because inevitably that's what would happen as the Berkeley Fire Academy is not in session on holidays and Ben thinks that I'm gonna work late anyhow, and now he's *really* into brunch, which drives me crazy for no goddamn good reason.

I wasn't technically even scheduled to work. It was a volunteer thing. Someone else will fill the vacancy.

I tell myself this to feel less guilty about calling out and burdening a peer with having to suffer through a shitty night with His Royal Fatness. It was an overtime shift I for some reason agreed to on a random night last week when Tay-boobs was slightly less annoying than usual, and I figured I could use the money.

I should have known that there was no way he would be less annoying than usual on a night like July 4th when he would show up with some weird, bitter attitude like he was being forced into the experience at gunpoint and didn't let greed surmount his desire to be at a backyard barbeque with family. I mentioned that he's married, right?

That man's wife must be a saint… or she's in a coma. Anyhow, someone else can make the blood money.

I needed a mental health day. I needed to do something healthy for my body and my soul. I needed to not see suffering and pain on a day that's supposed to be a celebration of our rumored freedom.

So, what, you ask, did I decide to do with my time? What constructive endeavor did I partake in rather than suck it up and go to work on a night when both North and South Counties need all the help they can get, nights when people like Dr. Vivian Lopez M.D. are hard at work saving lives and people like Shiva/Saachi are hard at work saving marriages?

I decided to call Becky.

And I was stone sober when I did it.

37.
A year ago, Mid-July 2009

Ben and I have all the ambulance doors open. We just dropped off Darryl at Kaiser before our lunch break and he clearly shit his pants while we were transporting him as indicated by sound, smell, and the creepy smile that crept upon his face. I don't even remember what malady he claimed he had when we picked him up but I do remember that we took him to the hospital and then drove to the top of the parking garage immediately after dropping him off to take our lunch break and air out the ambulance.

We're once again listening to Loveline and throwing the Frisbee around having hastily eaten gigantic burritos earlier in the shift because we missed our bagel orgy due to catching a run right out of the gate.

Ben goes, "You heard about these adventure mud race things?" He hucks the disc.

"Huh?" I catch it overhead and on the move with one hand.

"It's like a steeple chase but with more stuff you gotta do and you get dirty, not just wet."

I throw the disc back. "What the fuck is a steeple chase? Sounds pretty dumb."

"Steeple chase is an Olympic running event involving a few obstacles, like a puddle and a hurdle and shit." He throws the disc. It does a long, lazy arc right to where I'm standing. Good shot.

"So, it's a running course with a few things that make it hard to run? It sounds like an obstacle course." I throw the disc.

Another good shot... if he was standing like thirty feet away. Ben displays an unexpected acceleration and manages to snag the thing out of the air with his left hand, upstaging my earlier grab. He says with some difficulty as he's rapidly decelerating, "It's that plus mud."

"Good grab!"

"Damn right."

"Let's remember our humility. Tell me more about the mud. You keep mentioning that."

He stands there for a second catching his breath and goes, "I don't really know about the mud. I just hear that people do an obstacle course except there's shit like mud and tunnels and pools and electricity that you gotta run through." He throws the disc.

"That sounds weird." I catch it after taking a few steps to my left. "So, basically you are describing to me a thing that you can get paid to do in the military and should not venture to do unless you are in the military... unless you want to sound like a complete dickhead?"

"Yeah, totally. That's why I brought it up. You can literally get paid to do that shit and get a cool gun but instead weekend warriors spend their money to get sweaty and have to pull wet dirt out of their labias and balls... I assume they do it to get laid or whatever."

I throw the disc. "Am I correct in assuming that you are wondering why people would pay presumably hard-earned money   to   suffer?"

"Yes. I mean, dude, what the actual fuck? Is it *that* hard to get ass?" He makes another running catch with one hand like he's born to do it.

Fucker.

Meanwhile, in the background, a female Loveline caller with a baby girl voice is talking about how her boyfriend will only ejaculate on the outside of her body, like every time, apparently, and it's really messy. The physician/counselor host, Dr. Drew, takes vehement umbrage with this practice while the comedian host, who isn't nearly as good as Adam Corolla or David Alan Greir, takes a counterpoint noting that things could be far worse, in that she could not be getting any action at all so maybe it's to be appreciated as some sort of offering to the Sex Deity.

Ben tosses an offline throw that I briefly jog towards but then it goes skipping across the pavement and winds up under a parked Honda Civic, the worst case Frisbee scenario that doesn't involve getting mortally struck by said Honda Civic or other sensible car, one probably driven by a certain ex of mine who is texting her wonderful new man.

The mental image of all these weekend warriors jogging in a giant mud puddle makes me unreasonably annoyed. I kneel down on the pavement and use my flashlight to find the disc. Then I reach my arm under the car trying to not get it all covered in road grime. I retrieve the disc with only a bit of cross contamination to my uniform sleeve.

"I'm telling you, that shit is popular because you fucking people never had to suffer. You never had to deal with being poor or underfed; you were never put bondage; you never had to deal with the concept of mortal terror at the hands of white masters. You exist sheltered in your blissful ignorance, free to spend your money to do dumb shit like jogging in mud puddles."

"Easy there, Hirohito," Ben says in a historically astute attempt at a burn.

"There were never redneck internment camps, buddy. You put on a suit and get a haircut and you can blend with the ruling class." That comes out harsher and less in jest than I meant it to. I huck the disc at him. I slice it heavily to the left because I am a failure at sports, apparently.

Dr. Drew and the comedian I don't know the name of are belly laughing at a joke I missed, and it adds to the embarrassment of my shitty throw.

Ben doesn't move. The disk skids across the pavement

and Ben doesn't pay it any attention. He stands there with his hands on his hips and an odd expression on his face like he might have to poop or something.

Ben says, "Look, dude, I didn't have a lot growing up. Mom did the best she could and, God rest her soul, I love her for that. Shit wasn't exactly normal, though. Every couple of years, Mom used to bring my brother and me by my dad's house where his wife lived with his *real family* to steal his other kids' bikes and stuff. She would smack the shit out of us if we were too scared to do it."

I realize that I honestly have little information about Ben's upbringing. I ask, "That true?"

He laughs and says, "Yeah. We usually had to give the bikes or whatever it was back a few days later and pretend like we were just bad, random neighborhood kids from the trailer park. Thing was, we lived in the projects. We would have loved to live in a trailer park because then at least you own something."

"No shit?"

"No shit."

"Anyhow, Mom was always doing shit like that to fuck with my dad."

I hear the Loveline caller laughing on the radio after some mention of a tarp being used during sex.

"How come I never knew any of this?"

Ben's drawl comes out a bit. "Because it doesn't define me. I could have been a victim plenty in life and I *chose* not to be. You don't get to act like you know about my life because of the way I look. And fuck Ayn Rand for being the only writer who has good quotes about this shit. And fuck that good-for-nothing asshole."

"Which good-for-nothing asshole? Ayn Rand?"

"My father."

I go get the Frisbee. Then I change the subject because I kinda feel like an asshole too, but I'm still not doing one of those adventure races, even if he tries to guilt me into it.

38.
July 4th, 2010 Again

I go for a motorcycle ride. It isn't what you would call a *safe* one. It isn't one you would want your mom to be witnessing. I ride as an escape from reality, my own little roller coaster of 100+ horsepower.

I'm going no place in particular. The sun has set, and illegal, amateur firework displays light up my peripheral vision as I streak by. I only hear the loudest whistles and bangs over the growl of the bike as I jam down the 580 freeway in the uncommonly brisk summer night.

The conversation with Becky was predictably unhelpful to my sanity. I cringe recalling her statements. She was blunt. She pulled no punches. And she seemed like she had the diatribe rehearsed for my inevitable, ill-advised phone call. I simultaneously asked for it and was unprepared for what I heard. It all rang true. It all cut deep.

The replay:

- I ask her to reserve comment for a moment and hear me out.
- I make a poorly thought out plea for one more chance for the reasons to follow.
- I tell her that things between Ben and me aren't great. I tell her he's moving on from our partnership and in love with a girl who he seems pretty serious with, the evidence being that they recently bought a hot tub together to keep at her house. I tell her that I think he's

grown out of our friendship, at least in the iteration that it was before.

- I tell her how much I miss her. I tell her how stupid I was for failing to commit in the way that she needed, for putting her second to my dumb friendship with my dumb friend.
- I tell her I can be different this time.
- I tell her that I know I don't own a boat, and I know that I don't make a ton of money, but I can be the husband she wants. I can be the father to her children.
- I tell her I'm ready to settle down. I tell her the old me is on the way out. Meet the 2.0 Harlan, the new, improved and mature version. Gone are the reckless days of yore.
- I tell her that I know there's probably no chance of her letting me close again, but I ask her to consider the idea, nonetheless.
- I make mention of having to go for broke in life sometimes to get what is most important, which is always love, real, honest love.
- I tell her how much I love her and how much I have never loved anyone like her. I tell her how all I've learned in her absence is how much we were supposed to be together, how much better a person I am with her.
- I tell her, "This is for real, this time," which I fail to understand means that I'm implying that everything before wasn't.

She goes silent for a beat and I hear her breathing. And her reply basically goes like this: a one-two gut punch that I run with wild abandon directly into.

"Harlan, please understand that I believe you have a good heart. You've got plenty going for you. You are a good paramedic and you are attractive and interesting. Many women see all that, and frankly that's part of your problem: you notice them noticing you and apparently can't control yourself. You aren't currently any kind of material to be a husband or a father. I'm not saying that you cannot be either of those things in the future. There would need to be some significant changes though. The bottom line is that I don't love you anymore, not in the way that you *think* you want. Now, hear me say this, let me be crystal-fucking-clear: there is no more *you* and me. There is no more *us*. And while I understand that you are clearly having a tough time right now, and I can only speculate as to why, I'm not right for you and you aren't right for me. I have moved on."

I manage a, "But..."

She continues and her tone sharpens, "There's no *but*. Men like you and your beloved best friend aren't compatible with the bulk of polite society when you behave the way you do. At your worst, you are a man-child. You are selfish. Your superhuman ability to compartmentalize and adapt to imperfect situations makes you great at your job but a bad romantic partner because you aren't even honest with yourself about your needs, which is literally the only thing you need to do to fix yourself. But we both know you won't. And until you can be fully present in a relationship, this pain you feel is going to keep happening again and again. You will always be breaking hearts or having your heart broken."

I manage to say, "Babe..."

And she closes with, "Don't you fucking call me that! I'm getting fucking married, Harlan. And I am happy with my life *without* you in it. I don't want you contacting me anymore, so this is the final time I will say goodbye and I *urge* you to respect that boundary."

"Okay."

"I mean it, Harlan. Please just leave me alone."

I hear a strained, exasperated sigh in her voice before she hangs up on me, right as I confess, "It's just... I can't lose him too."

I replay the conversation in my head about ten times until I'm crying beneath the face shield of my motorcycle helmet. It starts to fog up, but I don't slow down. Damn it all.

I can't lose him too.

Anyhow, they tell me that I was doing at least seventy miles an hour on Highway 13 when I hit the deer that I didn't see jump out in front of me. I don't remember my body tumbling and skidding across the pavement. I was just riding my motorcycle, replaying my failure in my head, and then there was nothing but my presumed final journey into The Great Beyond.

How fitting that the first thing I see upon my resurrection, through eyes I'm not totally sure how to keep open, is the sweaty face of Tay-boobs as he yells out, "Harlan! Harlan! Jesus, it's Harlan! McKinney get over here!"

All I manage to say is a groaned, "Fuck."

Of course, this is when the fireworks really start rolling. God forbid the event that might kill me be free of comedy.

39

The situation isn't pretty. I piece this together despite the fact that I'm strapped to a backboard with an oxygen mask on my face, cervical collar around my neck and I don't dare open my eyes because of the garish, overhead florescent lights of Trauma Room #1 at Highland. Multiple voices seem to be yelling my name and telling me to stay awake and keep my eyes open, which is really hard for me to do even if you were to take away the bright lights.

Trauma team protocol is to give each patient a designation that sounds like a codename due to its usage of the military phonetic alphabet. I could be *Kilo, Foxtrot, Bravo,* etc. For some reason I earnestly wonder what my codename is. I hope that it's Foxtrot, but I don't know why. It just sounds cooler. Then I recognize that this display of higher cognition is a good sign. The helmet did its job. My brain isn't totally scrambled. Maybe nothing is bleeding inside of my head. That would be nice.

But I can't say things aren't confusing. The voices of the doctors, nurses and X-ray technicians are seemingly farther away than they should be, like I'm looking up to daylight through an open manhole cover and listening to conversations between people who don't know I can hear them. I think I hear some of Tay-boobs' report to the trauma team, which I don't really need because, though I don't feel much pain, I can tell something is wrong with my right, lower leg. The entire middle part of my body feels like there's ice water running through it, and the ice blood has made me go somewhat numb, I think. It must be cold out.

Cold, a symptom of shock. I hope I am not in shock. Shock is bad. I try very hard to keep my eyes open.

A problem is that I'm tired. I'm more tired than I should be, because I'm sober and I work nights. I shouldn't be this tired right now.

I know I don't want to go to sleep, but the specter of slumber embraces me despite my opposition. I start to fade in and out of the scenario despite the repeated instructions to the contrary. My head hurts.

During one of the moments when I'm present for a sliver of time that I presume is known as an *iota* among those more mentally capable than I am, I hear someone say "traumatic amputation" very clearly despite the distant voices, sounding alarms of the EKG and pulse oximeter machine, and farting noise of the blood pressure cuff inflating, all of it farther away than it should be except those words.

"Traumatic amputation," they say, like it's totally normal. It is not normal.

I think I maybe scream or cry or something because the same voices that I hear down in the manhole tell me that I'm going to be okay. I'm glad they know I'm present in the room.

Another problem is that I know too much about what the voices are saying, and I don't think that I am going to be "okay" because then I hear someone yell out very low numbers that I think are supposed to be my blood pressure, and a very high number that I glean as my heart rate, and that could mean that the leakiness that I don't want to have inside of my skull might be further south, which would explain why I feel so cold: because I'm going into shock and that will kill me way quicker if it isn't surgically repaired. The fact that I recognize this is a good sign for my brain continuing to work, provided it remains profuse with the blood that is probably filling up my abdominal cavity, if I had to take a stab in the dark.

A pair of hands starts at my head and gropes down the front of my body. Whom I presume to be the owner of the hands yells out observations an unseen nurse writing it all down. I don't want to hear any of it. I've heard enough. I want to put my hands over my ears and yell out *blah-blah-blah-blah* but trying to pick my arms up seems like a herculean task.

They keep saying my name over and over up there on the street level and I stop myself from saying that I don't want to die. I know that if I say that, I'm probably a goner. That's what people always say when they are dying. That, or they say that they want their mom. I kind of want to see my mom. I push that thought out of my mind with all my might.

And then what I assume to be the same set of hands presses on the iliac crests of my pelvis and everything goes to white light and maybe I scream again. I don't know. Maybe I cry out, "I don't want to die!" despite my efforts to the contrary. Maybe I just make a terrible sound.

More people say my name and tell me, "It's gonna be okay."

I feel a needle push into my left forearm, though the arm feels like it isn't totally mine, like maybe I share use of it with someone else. Maybe I have it Monday, Wednesday, Friday and every other weekend. I don't know. The arm feels like it's up on street level with the voices.

Someone says, "Unstable fracture," and I assume it's my hip because fireworks explode behind my eyes when the doctor presses down on it again.

Someone puts their finger in my ass, which I totally feel, rather incuriously. And for some reason that feels like it's down in the sewer with me, below my little circular portal to the light and voices. As quickly the finger enters my hopefully uninjured sphincter, it's gone, and I proceed to once again fade.

Out I go.

I time travel to an odd moment of relative silence around me, awoken by a jostling of my midsection that makes me groan and I hear the hum and bark of the CT scanner. For some reason, the awful noise puts me back to sleep despite my best efforts to stay awake.

I time travel to more people back in the room and I hear the words *splenic, laceration, ortho, intubate,* and *surgery.* A doctor I can't recognize due to the mask on his face tells me to count backwards from ten. I don't think I ever manage to say anything. I feel the sensation of motion like I'm falling deeper into my sewer, farther and farther away from the increasingly shrinking circle of light and voices. It all goes dark again and there is no more *me* for I have no consciousness.

I time travel to a much quieter room except for the voice of Eric Cartman giving Kyle Broflovski shit for being a Jew. I manage to open my eyes into little, crusty slits with great difficulty and I can tell that I'm probably alive. I'm definitely still in a hospital, which means none of this was a dream and I am very much fucked up.

The overhead lights aren't nearly as bright as the trauma room. I don't think I'm in a sewer anymore. Whatever underground work I had to accomplish, unconscious me clearly took care of.

I know I don't smell good. I try to speak but my voice doesn't work. The best I can muster is a sound not dissimilar from a dog that wants you to stop stepping on its paw.

I feel a hand touch my head, tenderly, like the times I hurt myself real bad screwing around on a skateboard or trampoline and mom magically made it all better. I look to my right and see Ben sitting there, his outstretched arm clearly the source of the touch on my head, and he says, "It's okay, buddy. You're gonna be okay."

Despite his unoriginality, I think I start to cry when I hear his voice; I don't know for how long though. This is embarrassing. I plea to him, "Don't kill me. I'm not quadriplegic."

"Don't worry about that."

I eventually fall back asleep.

The TV remains on when I wake up again. I don't know what day it is, but *South Park* is still on and the light of day still shines through the window so maybe it's the same evening but maybe not.

I wonder if *South Park* is always on this much. Then I

feel relief that it isn't *Family Guy.*

I'm still not 100% positive that I'm really alive until I try to move and immediately transition from a mere feeling of misery to a total sobbing fit because of the pain. It's fucking Groundhog Day over here, I tell you.

Ben's voice again says, "It's okay, Harlan. I'm here and you are gonna be okay. I promise."

I wonder if he knows that I, like, *totally* hear that all the time, from lots of people.

I can't find my voice. Where the fuck did it go? It seems lost in the fire that is my throat. Then I realize that I'm probably status-post extubation, which really makes me want to know what day it is, and *South Park* isn't helping me figure it out so I continue to sob and Ben continues to whisper calming assurances.

Punxsutawney Phil, you suck.

I'm able to lift my head a little, it turns out, and start to do so but Ben tells me, "Don't. Just rest, man," and gently pushes my head back down on the pillow.

In the background, Cartman complains to his mom about not getting a video game console that he wants. I think that maybe I should see if they can bring my Xbox here, so I don't have to watch the same TV shows all day, but then again moving my hands seems like a lot of work.

As the ending credit song of the episode twangs, I am able to form the words, "How bad?" My voice sounds like Batman's growl. I think for a brief moment that it's kind of cool.

Ben's comforting smile turns to a frown and then he tells me that I don't have a right leg below the knee anymore and I cry for another unknown period of time until I fall asleep again.

Looks like it's seven more months of winter or whatever.

40.

Over the next few days in the moments that I'm awake, I learn the extent of the damage from either Ben or various doctors and nurses, some of whom I recognize and some who I do not:

- Spleen? Lacerated but surgically repaired in surgery #1.
- Pelvis? Fractured iliac wing that was surgically repaired in surgery #2.
- Right radius and ulna? Fractured and surgically repaired in surgery #3.
- Right lower leg? Amputated by the motorcycle and pavement, presumably burned with various other medical waste, reasonably expensive tattoos and all. To be honest, I have no idea where they took it and I don't want to know. I just know I really miss it already despite zero odds of me standing on either leg anytime soon. My spleen and the other stuff are probably going to be okay. I got that going for me, which is nice.

So, it's three surgeries so far in the bag. Hopefully no more on the horizon. Fun fact: there's no bleeding in my skull. I was right. How's that for self-diagnosis? All told, I'm several pounds lighter despite the new metal inside of my body, which sounds cool on paper but to be honest I'm not really that happy about it and I doubt you would be either. You would probably rather have your leg back. We are clearly on the same page in that regard.

I sleep most of the days and nights for the better part of a week. During that time, I leave the relative calm and comfort of the ICU to the much less exclusive med-surgical wing with the rest of the plebeians. Usually it's the hospital staff that wakes me up to be poked and prodded every few hours or so. Every day I stay awake a little bit longer. I think it's a good sign that I haven't been back in my sewer except for having weird dreams about it.

And, boy oh boy, there are so many weird dreams.

In one of them, I'm sexting with Becky when another version of Becky walks into my room. She sees me sending Original Becky a picture of my boner. Other Becky gets super mad at me, screams and throws items like my Xbox controller and the glass of water I keep on my nightstand at me. I tell her that it "isn't what you think!" I'm suddenly mad at Ben because I figure Ben probably let her in the apartment with the express purpose of seeing her catch me being a dirtbag because he's a snake. While I ponder this, Other Becky says that we are "finished forever!" She screams and wails about what a bastard I am and how I broke her heart. I feel utter shame and humiliation. I never make any attempt to ask her why there are two of her and why it would be a problem for me to be sexting the one I thought was the only Becky in existence.

In another dream, I'm immobile in my hospital bed in, what I've now reluctantly accepted to be, reality. Shiva/Saachi is in the room and she dances on the bed with her legs straddling my immobilized pelvis. She wears a short, plaid skirt and black bra under a button-down, white shirt like every stupid schoolgirl porn clip that I love despite the cliché. Some drum-heavy song that I cannot put my finger on but is similar to "Smack My Bitch Up" by Prodigy plays as she sways and bucks in cadence with the rhythm. Then she slowly lowers herself onto me. She isn't wearing panties, which is awesome for obvious reasons that need no further explanation. She proceeds to deftly bounce her body up and down on me without further injuring my broken hip, like a total pro, and whips her hair around like every hot lady in an eighties rock video.

Shiva/Saachi's incredible performance causes me to go completely mad with lust, grab her ass cheeks in my hands and then attempt to drive up into her only to be immediately catapulted out of the fantastic dream because I've moved my hips in the waking, non-pretend world, produced stress on the metal screws holding part of my pelvis together and driven the stub of my amputated leg into the bed sheets. The result of all this is that I scream the exact opposite kind of scream that I want to be screaming. It is the inverse manifestation of an orgasm.

I have this one dream that I hate more than the one with the two iterations of Becky. In the most hated one, I'm at that infamous dinner with Dr. Vivian Lopez M.D. and she's reciting a deconstruction of my persona that's a blend between the speech she gave me and the one Becky gave me over the phone before I decided to use a motorcycle and pavement to remove my leg. Except this time, we aren't in the restaurant on Piedmont Avenue like we were when it really happened. We are in the Ruby Room, Ben is the bartender and he has a huge pair of boobies. Dr. Vivian Lopez M.D. turns into my mother, which adds a special layer of awkwardness. Luckily, I wake up from this one without any new onset of pain.

In between dreams, I hear statements like, "This is healing nicely," and discussions regarding the looming process known as *physical therapy*. The latter topic is qualified with notations about needing to be "better" prior to that being a possibility, like I don't know that already. I am well aware that I cannot go to physical therapy with a broken pelvis and the like, thanks.

At least, that's what I thought. It turns out, they aren't above torturing you while you are still broken. Take that under consideration for your next bone fractures.

Groundhog Day again.

More dreams: motorcycle crashes, losing to foul-mouthed children in video games that don't exist, bloody 911 calls on the ambulance with screaming and wailing children, and sneaky sex with Becky in her car on Mount Diablo, that one time when we got locked in after dark and had to wake the ranger to let us out, much to his displeasure. Did that really happen, or did I dream it?

There are dreams of death, mangled motorcyclists, kissing Ben, the ensuing panic, Tay-boobs farting, fireworks in the sky, dispatchers belting out never-ending calls, and Dr. Vivian Lopez M.D. and I having our first child.

That one comes out of left field. In that dream, she takes the baby and runs away with it, and I feel guilty for feeling relieved that I don't have to imprint the kid with all the shit she said was wrong with me in the last dream wherein she made an appearance.

When I wake up one day, Mom is holding my hand. Mr. Man is seated in the chair that Ben uses more than anyone else so far. He is eating something that smells weird but familiar. There are balloons hovering above my head that no doubt instruct me to "GET WELL!!" Mom looks at me with eyes that are simultaneously, loving, judgmental and sad. As I wake, she immediately scolds me about riding a motorcycle and I start to tune her out by volunteering to succumb to my overwhelming urge to fall back asleep, even though Mom starts to cry and it makes me feel like an asshole. This is probably not the first time my Mom and Mr. Man have visited me since the accident. It is the first one that I am sufficiently conscious to remember, though. It's right then that I wonder where my father is.

I fade in and out as she touches my head like Ben did for what is probably a few hours. In one of the moments wherein I'm awake she kisses my head and tells me she will be back the next day. She says that she loves me.

South Park is not on. Instead, Mr. Man watches Fox News. The severe white lady news anchor seems very angry about something. This discrepancy in TV channel choice immediately becomes a valuable clue as to who is visiting in future, confused moments after first waking.

In response to my mother, I manage to rasp out my best version of, "I love you too." Mr. Man touches my shoulder. I nod back, smile a bit, and just like that we have officially met one another.

I squeeze Mom's hand and make a kissing motion with my lips that misses her cheek because I don't feel like I have the strength to raise my head. I do manage to turn it slightly and watch them leave. On the bedside table, I see a tiny potted tree. There's a note hanging from its branches and it reads, *From Your Stepfather with Love, Mamoru.* And then I'm like, *Ooh, Mr. Mamoru.* Duh. At least we can close the book on that mystery.

41.

Fun fact: it's been over a week since the deer tried to kill me. Or maybe it's more like *I* tried to kill me? I mean, there's evidence for that theory. I *was* upset and reckless on a motorcycle on a dark stretch of mountain highway. I was having one of those moments wherein I couldn't help but desire an escape from life. I don't think I'm the kind of person to seek such a permanent solution, though. Honestly, I can't really remember either way. Don't suppose it matters in the long run. The damage is done regardless of the motive.

Ben comes and goes daily. He usually shows up in the late afternoon when he's done at the academy and wears his uniform if it's a weekday. On the weekend he's in his civvies. Yesterday, which was a day he wasn't wearing his uniform, Kaylee joined him in visiting me and I was surprisingly happy to see her. I was even happy to see the two of them *together*. I didn't tell them this. I don't know why. Maybe I should have? I suppose it doesn't matter in the long run either.

During the first Kaylee/Ben joint visit, Ben asked me if I remembered the conversation we had about going to Hawaii on the night we smoked cigars in front of the Temescal Walgreens and puffed smoke rings into the sky. I told him I remembered. He said that we should go when I get better. I snapped at him by saying in a rather dickish tone, "You should go without me! Thanks for mentioning it!" after feeling sudden and overwhelming despair that I wasn't leaving the hospital bed for anywhere but the physical therapy wing, shitting without assistance and embarrassment, or even having the catheter removed from my penis, anytime soon.

In response, Kaylee calmly said like the medical professional she is, "You aren't spending the rest of your life in this bed, Harlan. I know there's a tough road ahead and I assure you that no matter what it doesn't end in this room. It's time to start thinking about that."

Then she held my one of my hands while Ben held the other and I was so damn embarrassed, again, because I had to shit and needed the bedpan while they were standing there on their own two feet speaking words of encouragement, words that did not make my leg grow back or provide me with a time machine to take up some other hobby than riding a two-wheeled death machine across the hard pavement.

I almost made a mess of myself before I said something. Kaylee, clearly a veteran of such situations, got my nurse to help me after I insisted Kaylee not do so personally despite her assuring me that it was all in a day's work for her. After I was done, Ben walked back into the room with his shirt up over his nose and said, "Jesus Christ, you're foul. Did they feed you your rotting lower leg?"

I snorted and said, "Too soon, asshole. Too soon."

That was the first time I laughed since the crash, at least the first time I knew about.

Mom and Mr. Mamoru show up every day in a yin and yang schedule with Ben and (sometimes) Kaylee. It's like a changing of the guard. Mom and Mr. Mamoru leave when Ben shows. Ben hangs until visiting hours are over. Then I sleep or watch *South Park* and sometimes *Family Guy* (even though I shudder to admit it) until Mom and my stepfather reappear when visiting hours resume.

I don't know why there's such an insistence on keeping the nonstop vigil by my bedside. I'm clearly out of the proverbial woods and fully above the weird manhole thing that I haven't bothered explaining to them about. I would say something about the support crew not always needing being around in light of the presence of paid medical professionals, but the truth is I like it and don't want it to change. Maybe that makes me a needy egomaniac? Eh, screw it.

In keeping with previous trajectory, thankfully, every day I am awake more and sleep less. The only problem is that as I clearly get less sick, the physical therapist gets more sadistic. It's even worse because her name is Tasha and she's an attractive woman in her mid-thirties with a fantastic afro hairstyle circa 1974. It totally does something for me.

Accordingly, when she does things to me that hurt like a motherfucker and asks, "Does that hurt?" I always pretend like it does not in order to impress her as if she has any interest in a one-legged invalid who pees into a bag involuntarily. I'm pretty sure Tasha is a lesbian too, but that weird thing in my brain seems to hold out hope she'll forgo the torture for, say, a hand job or something, if I can remain stoic enough.

This horniness is probably a good sign. And apparently, I am getting better. At least that's what the doctors, nurses and Tasha say.

Today, which is a day wherein the television screen shows Barbara Streisand in the form of a monster bring about a near-apocalypse unto the small mountain town, one with ample parking, day or night, the little tree sits on the table adjacent to me. I'm staring at it and zoning out thinking about nothing in particular. It's kind of pleasant to tune out all distractions and attempt to be totally in the moment, free of thought, concentrating on the sound and feeling of my own breath. The genesis of this newfound hobby is that after watching *The Matrix* one day, I figured I might as well learn to meditate like Keanu because it might help me be less bored and definitely couldn't make me any worse at kung fu. So, I googled a simple how-to guide on my phone and viola: here we are in a moment of Zen.

Accordingly, because of course this happens right

when I'm about to really master this stuff, Becky comes walking through the door wearing her uniform pants and a black hoodie approximately two seconds *after* Dr. Vivian Lopez M.D. enters the room while clad in her scrubs.

As I'm a smooth operator, I simply blurt out, "Rad."

42.

Yes, you're goddamn right it was an awkward situation. Thank goodness for my dad showing up and making a sufficiently large ass of himself so I wasn't fielding questions about dating timelines from two women who are equally aware of my potential to be a scoundrel. It went like this:

- They walk in, one right after the other.
- They start to say hello at exactly the same time, clumsily cease doing so and stammer telling the other one to go first.
- Then they introduce themselves to one another. Becky says, "Hi, I'm Becky, Harlan's ex. You must be his girlfriend." And then Dr. Vivian Lopez M.D. laughs out loud with a little chuckle and says, "I'm Vivian... no we aren't together and were never that formal. I was going to ask you the same question." I see a look creep across Becky's face (mind you I still haven't said anything besides "rad" and they never finished saying hello to me) like she's using her cop brain and trying to figure out if she needs to punch the woman in front of her in the face for my past transgressions... up until the good doctor goes, "My oh my, what a gorgeous engagement ring! Lucky lady!" And they proceed to have a weird interrogation of one another, like potential rivals to the status of Queen of the Immediate Area. I might as well not even be present. I am but a hapless pawn. I'm part of the furniture. The little tree,

which I now remember is called a bonsai thanks to Daniel LaRusso, is as important as I am.

- Next, Dad walks in and goes, "You son of a bitch, first you nearly kill yourself, you make me sleep two days in this fucking hospital room eating nothing but cafeteria food, and now there are two gorgeous women here fawning over you?" He smiles when he says it like he's expecting the two of them to laugh, but they don't. I cringe and it hurts various parts of my broken body. So, yeah, it's awkward.

- After about ten minutes of small talk, Dr. Vivian Lopez M.D. leans in and gives me a hug. She says she will come back and visit again. She explains that she would have sooner, but she found out through the grapevine (Facebook) "just yesterday" that I was hurt in the first place. After introducing herself to my father, she tells me to check my phone when I have a free moment, says her goodbye and exits.

- Becky and my dad hug. Dad hooks his thumb at me and tells her, "Never thought I'd see you again near this guy after the mess he made." Becky gives kind of a nervous laugh and I want to pull the covers up over my head or strangle my dad with them. Becky says, "I'm getting married in a week. Nothing more needs to be said about what happened between the two of us." Then she grabs my right hand and squeezes it. I squeeze her hand back. We all make idle chat for a while. Prior to her exit, she touches me on the forehead like she's blessing my soon-to-be corpse and says, "I'm feel bad for my tone over the phone. I got angry all over again and you caught me at a bad moment. Get better, okay?"

I tell Becky, "This wasn't your fault. You didn't say anything that was unfair. I am genuinely glad you are happy and hope that your husband treats you the way you deserve to be treated."

"Thank you, Harlan."

Dad says, "Well said, son." I shoot him a look.

"Have fun on the sailboat."

She raises an eyebrow at me.

I say, nervously, "Facebook, man."

She gives a little chuckle and shakes her head saying, "I'll see you later."

I think that last statement probably isn't true but for some reason I'm good with it. Maybe I'm officially tired of the heartache that I manufacture for myself. Maybe it's the pain meds though. They really take the edge off.

I fill dad in on who Dr. Vivian Lopez M.D. is, Dad calls me an "asshole... but apparently an attractive asshole." Seems like a decent compliment in the moment. Then we watch the entirety of the World Cup final. I root for the Netherlands and eventually have my hopes dashed by Andres Iniesta four damn minutes from the end of extra time. Dad roots for Spain the whole time because he has a grand on them with his bookie/bartender friend. Let it not be said the man is a frivolous gambler on underdogs.

During the game, I learn that Dad stood vigil for about forty-eight hours after my injury and when he was officially convinced of my survival, he immediately grew pissed off and decided to go stew by himself for like a week. At halftime, Dad says, "I just remembered, there was another girl here the day after you crashed. Young. Dark skin. She seemed very upset. She gave me a note to give to you."

Presuming he is referring to Shiva/Saachi, I have no idea how she found out so quickly but whatever. I ask, "When were you planning on telling me this?"

"Now. I just did. I'm old; be grateful I remembered in the first place." He reaches into the top drawer of my bedside table, says, "Ta-da!" and hands me a Hallmark envelope that's clearly been opened already.

"You opened this and read the... who does that? That's

not cool, Dad."

"Yeah, I opened it. I was bored. It's *boring* being in the hospital even if it's your only son who is the sick person. One distant day from now when I'm dying slowly from cancer or something, you'll experience it. You should be glad I didn't write *asshole* on your forehead with a marker."

Ben's voice echoes from outside, "Why the shit didn't I think of that idea?!" and he walks in the room with what I believe to be a tall boy in a brown paper bag. He says, "Oh, badass, you got the game on." Ben and Dad give one another the back-patting bro-hug. Ben whips another beer out of his pocket and hands it to my father who cracks it open and goes, "*Now* we can watch the game like civilized people."

"What the fuck? I don't get one?"

Both of them chime simultaneously, "No."

Dad adds, "You can't mix dope and alcohol. You'll wind up losing the other leg or something."

"The hits just keep coming."

I open the envelope and remove the card. It's got a drawing of a bear in hospital bed on the cover and a pun about the bear being injured inscribed inside that's too dumb to mention further. What's important is what is adjacent. There, Shiva/Saachi has written the following:

Harlan,

I hope you will forgive me for not visiting more but I am afraid of hospitals and honestly I didn't know if I was welcome or not. I would understand if that's the case. I have been thinking about you a lot. Feel free to call/text if you want to. I understand if not. Get well soon. I'm glad you are still among the living!

Love,
S.

The fact of the matter apparently is that I am absolutely

slaying the sympathy vote. If you are trying to get in the good graces of exes, I recommend sacrificing one of your limbs. It works like a charm, albeit probably temporarily, and then you get addicted to pain pills.

43.

While Tasha has me hooked up to the electric muscle stimulator so my leg muscles don't atrophy, because apparently hobbling around cautiously like I have a four cell flashlight up where the sun don't shine isn't what she considers to be sufficient exercise, I research on my phone all the things that can go wrong with a traumatic amputation. Surprisingly, this is the first time I have done this. Perhaps I didn't really want to dissipate the bliss of ignorance… or I'm just an idiot? Anyhow, it goes like this:

- Infection at the amputation site resulting (in worst case scenario) in sepsis and then death.
- Thrombosis, AKA blood clots, potentially resulting in pulmonary embolism, myocardial infarction, cerebral infarction and (drumroll!) death.
- Pneumonia due to a combination of a compromised immune system and the shallow respirations common with inactivity/spending so much time in bed in a place full of sick people. This is *probably* not fatal for a person of my age and health. But if I was a child, old, or chronically immunocompromised, I could die.
- Mental health disorders most commonly manifesting as depression, the extreme cases of which lead to suicide… again, death.
- Substance abuse and chemical dependency related to long term use of pain medication. I guess this is why they are weening me off of the opiates, much to my chagrin. Man, that stuff is good. I'm going to miss it.

Much like my legs, God giveth and then taketh away. But there's always the chance I could wake up one day and, on a whim, grab a handful of leftover Oxycontin, wash them down with a tall glass of whiskey and (drumroll, again) there would be death.

- Phantom limb pain. And I mean it when I say it: fuck phantom limb pain. It won't kill you unless you do the pills and whiskey thing to make it go away.

As long as we are discussing it, let me tell you a bit about phantom limb pain: it sucks. See, it isn't simply pain, per se, not necessarily in the classical definition. It's also a tickle, numbness and itching. Can you imagine having an itch you can't scratch or a leg that feels asleep even though it isn't attached to your body? Trust me, it's shitty. You don't want it.

Tasha has taught me the trick to dealing with phantom limb pain: meditative visualization of using the limb like I used to, doing things like flexing my non-existent calf muscle or scrunching my ghost toes. For me, this requires a ridiculous amount of concentration because I am not by any means a Zen master yet, despite my recent foray into the world of meditation. Some other things that I do in Tasha's company are walking on crutches, weird abdominal exercises you've never seen before to activate muscles you didn't know you had, and "massage" that is easy to confuse with an effort by enemy captors to extract information as to troop movements and battle plans.

I could go on about the minutiae of learning to walk again minus half a leg while healing a broken pelvis, but to do so would mostly likely delve into self-pity which Ben, Tasha, and most everyone else I speak to on a regular basis constantly remind me is bad. Ben went so far as to read me a poem by D.H. Lawrence about a bird freezing to death and not feeling sorry for himself. This is who Ben is now, apparently: a person who knows about poetry. No doubt, it's Kaylee's influence again. Kaylee must have an enchanted dream-cave of a vagina. It's the only possible explanation.

Anyhow, rather than speak more about physical therapy, I'm going to tell you about the lovely goddamn wedding that Becky and that douche had because you aren't Facebook friends with her like I am. Let's start with the setting: Hawaii. It was bad enough she got married but she also *had* to go and do it in the one place on earth that I want to go but cannot because I have no income.

Unfortunately, I am out of my own, paid sick time. I'm subsisting on donations of sick leave and vacation hours from coworkers. My medical insurance is paying for *most* of my small bed and bland food, both of which are greatly appreciated, don't get me wrong.

The beautiful Pacific Ocean framed their ceremony and made for ideal, romantic photographs. I'm sure there were dolphins frolicking just offshore, breaching the surface, doing backflips with their cute little dolphin children, and bumping errant beach balls with their noses to the delight of mildly sunburned and rum-drunk attendees.

Her dress, you ask? Oh, it was gorgeous, but you already knew that. Accordingly, she looked gorgeous in it. And the groom? Also gorgeous in his impeccable suit that was probably made by some designer that I do not know and could never afford anyway because I don't have *sailboat money*.

The bridesmaids? Gorgeous. Groomsmen? Gorgeous. Everyone in attendance was as well. Puke.

It looked like a hell of a party too! I could tell people ate delicious foods, definitely not hospital food, and drank champagne and cocktails and stuff, not the brown water they call coffee here. It appeared that everyone had a great time. I'm sure they nursed their hangovers with expensive mimosas in the morning and eggs benedict prepared by Chef Roy Yamaguchi himself.

And did the smiling bride and proud groom love to kiss? Oh, you bet your ass they did. People must have been nonstop clanking their forks on their stemware because it seemed like every photo after The Kiss at the end of the ceremony was of them passionately locking lips, looking ever so in love and perfect for one another. Barf.

And last but not least, guess where they went on their honeymoon? You didn't think that they just stayed in Maui for a week or whatever, did you? No, they went to a whole other Hawaiian island, one I didn't even know existed, a super exclusive and expensive one! Isn't that fun, you guys?! And there they ate, drank, saw *gorgeous* things and, you guessed it, kissed a whole lot. They probably had sex seven hundred times. Becky is probably pregnant with the tan, business school graduate version of Tom Brady. Hurl.

Not that I care about any of this. Like I said before, I'm "good with it." Clearly.

What is wrong with me?

The problem is Facebook. Fuck Facebook almost as much as phantom limb pain. Facebook will only serve to further erode the tenuous mental health of the human populace, mark my word.

In a mental tailspin one night at three o'clock in the morning when I couldn't sleep due to the demons of opiate withdrawal sending imaginary spiders crawling across my skin, I deactivated my Facebook account. I couldn't stand the well wishes anymore, the *get well soons* and the *hang in theres*. And, yeah, I didn't want to see Becky with her two-legged husband.

The bitch of the whole thing is that I tried to delete it entirely but couldn't close the deal via my phone because Facebook is like an adult roommate that you tolerate for no other reason than you have known him since you were a kid, meaning he is entertaining at times, and your family loves him to death. But the reality is that the fucker steals all your food despite repeated instructions to the contrary, is always late with the rent and never pays for any of the shared utilities, instead thinking that leaving a few grams of weed lying around is sufficient compensation.

This is not to say Ben was/is like that. I'm more picturing Tay-boobs as a stoner in his late twenties to be this metaphorical roommate. A stoner who goes to Klan meetings, probably.

God, he sucks.

The bottom line is that I'm going stir crazy in this place and must get out of here. I want to go home. I want to go back to work on the ambulance with Ben. I want to talk shit about Tay-boobs and ride my motorcycle around Oakland without a care in the world. I want my leg back. I want my life back.

Like phantom limb pain, depression is a side effect with authenticity that I can officially vouch for. It's pushed me down into a new sewer. It is just as deep as the one from before except it feels like the cover is on the manhole.

Please give me more opiates.

44.
Mid-August 2010

Ben pushes me around Lake Merritt in a wheelchair that my health insurance bought (most of) for me. He has adorned it with stickers from local bars and local bands I have not heard of. These are stickers that he has probably just grabbed from free piles in coffee shops and such, but I like to pretend they make me look like I'm plugged into the local scene despite my convalescence. It's a sunny and warm Oakland afternoon, and the lake is scenic, smelling only slightly of goose shit and whatever it is that lives inside the water that apparently has a farting problem. I hear sirens in the background. I try to ignore them. I look across the water and see the spot in the lake that we pulled Darryl out of that one time. It happened a few years ago. It occurs to me that if Darryl hadn't T-boned the car on that bicycle, he would have kept going straight to the spot where we previously found him sans pants splashing about in the mud and sludge. Perhaps repeating that experience was what Darryl had in mind when he took off down the hill in the first place.

I make a mental note to ask him the next time I see him and then immediately feel my eyes start to dampen and a knot form in my throat because I do not have any idea if this will ever happen. My stump is still too tender to wear a prosthetic and the pain in my hip when I hobble around on crutches is enough to let me know that I have a long way to go before I can think about working any kind of job other than panhandling.

Ben says, "I think one of the reasons you are depressed

and haven't gotten better faster is because you aren't using the magic spray, dude."

I contemplate not answering him because I'm for some reason wrought with grief at the thought of being unable to work. I have no idea what to do with myself now that I've been discharged, well, other than go to my outpatient physical therapy appointments five days a week and apply for government assistance. Then there's the crushing medical debt! Not sure how that's gonna get paid for!

Ben puts his hand on my shoulder and commands, "Magic spray. I've given us a topic. Discuss, dude. Do your breathing exercise too."

I look up at him and a tear rolls down my face involuntarily. I know he sees it and he just smiles. I swallow the knot down a bit and say, "Sorry. I was just thinking about that time Darryl was in the water with his pants off and I got all choked up I guess."

"That is ridiculous, and I am buying you a beer."

I give a half-hearted smile back and ask, "Aren't you not supposed to put depressants in very depressed people?"

"Sure, and I'm sure those same pussies say you aren't supposed to ride motorcycles or you might lose a leg or whatever."

I laugh a bit for real and it feels good.

Ben wheels me in the direction of the Grand Lake Theater. As we pass the pull-up bars, I say, "Stop."

"Why? We are getting beer now. Remember?"

"Just wheel me up to the pull-up bar, okay?"

Incredulously, he asks, "What are you planning? Are you sure this is a good idea?"

"No, I'm not but I want to see if I can do it and it can't be any worse for me than going into a bar after kicking opiates, so wheel my ass to that bad boy and let me grind out some reps." I flex my left bicep and say, "Boom."

"Alright, but if you fall and break your ass, I'm gonna say I told you so."

"Fair enough."

Ben wheels me to one of the wooden posts holding up the shortest bar. With the assistance of the post, and Ben, I pick myself up onto one leg – not that I had a choice otherwise – and grab the bar with both of my hands, which I realize have become soft and lame during the last month of being an invalid.

Regardless, I use a double-overhand grip and center myself under the bar. I take a deep breath and I pull. The motion causes my surgical scars to stretch a bit and I wince, but I know they are past the point of being in danger of ripping, and my atrophied arm isn't broken anymore, so I keep pulling until my chin is over the bar. Then I lower myself and do it two more times before I decide that is plenty for now and move myself back into the wheelchair. As I do that, I hear the electronic air horn of an emergency vehicle and look in its direction. I spy a police cruiser with its passenger side window rolled down. I look inside and see a cop whose assailant Ben and I did a medical evaluation of. The cop leans in my direction as he slowly drives by and says, "Glad you are alive, bro! See you when you are back out there!"

I smile and wave back to him. To my horror, I call out, "You too!" and then I want to die of embarrassment. I look to my left and see Ben drop from the highest bar.

"I did ten just so you know who the top dog is still." He then flexes both biceps, triumphantly.

About fifteen minutes later, Ben and I sit in the back-patio area of the Heart and Dagger saloon right at Lake Park and Lakeshore, about 200 yards or so from the pull-up bars. I'm having a Budweiser and Ben has a pint of some hoppy nightmare from Dirty Hippie Brewing Co. in Arcadia or the like – Kaylee's influence again, I assume. The Bud feels lonely without a shot next to it, but I haven't had any alcohol in a month and have lost twenty pounds in addition to the weight of my leg, so I figure I should ease into boozin' even though Ben could just load my drunk ass into the chair and push me home if it came down to it.

"What's up with the magic spray you were talking about? What is it?" I ask.

"It's that shit from the World Cup!"

"Refresh my recollection. I don't remember it, per se. You may recall that I was in a serious traumatic event and hospitalized for a month while all hopped-up on goofballs, so things tend to be a little fuzzy about the World Cup other than Spain winning."

"I don't know if they used in that game we watched in your room with your pop, but it's amazing. It's my new favorite thing in sports. Basically, one of those soccer sissies... sorry, *dudes*, soccer *dudes* I mean, acts like he got shot by a sniper and rolls around on the ground holding his knee for a ridiculous amount of time. Then some medical staff guy runs over with this silver can of spray and just hoses the soccer dude's injured knee with it, and then the guy is able to get back up and do wind sprints for the next forty-five minutes like he wasn't *just* acting like he was mortally wounded."

"Hmm," I say and take a sip of my beer. It tastes like carbonated water with a touch of cereal grains and corn syrup... in other words, it is glorious. "What do you think is in it? Think it's like something that feels cold? That's what would make the most sense."

"It's fucking water, dude. I swear. Maybe it's like Evian or something fancy like that, but that shit is definitely nonsense. There is no therapeutic value to magic spray. It is part of the grand charade that is men's soccer, a bunch of fit Europeans trying to outrun one another for an hour and a half."

"I thought you liked soccer?"

"I like it fine. I prefer women's soccer. Those ladies are tough and don't act like the little bitches that the men do."

"So, I now gather that you watch women's sports, drink hippie beer, dress like less of a slob, attempt to use more politically correct terminology, are in decent physical shape *and* you know about at least one poem? Who are you even? What has Kaylee done with my beloved redneck idiot? Are you even capable of making me uncomfortable around polite society anymore?"

"What can I say, man? I like the broad and I want to keep her around." He takes a big gulp of beer and winks at me. Then he stands up and says way too loudly, "Let's do some shots and make out again, faggot." At least three people in the immediate area hear it and look at him disdainfully.

Much like a turtle trying to hide, I attempt to pull my head into my Iron Maiden shirt that's now too big for me and say, "Jesus, dude! Take it easy."

He pounds the rest of his beer and says, "I was only serious about the shots but, see, I still got it!"

45.

Because I am apparently a glutton for punishment, I am playing *Modern Warfare 2* online and getting destroyed by foul mouthed, racist, homophobic children, children whose absence I didn't bemoan one iota, children whom I relish in occasionally being able to kill with grenades, guns, knives and – my favorite – rocket launchers. I have the house to myself, so I have cranked up the volume and I'm sure to the neighbors it sounds like Armageddon. But it's only 2000ish hours and I don't feel like attempting to take my crippled ass down the stairs again to seek entertainment outside of the domicile. I descended the stairs twice today for PT, and to pay the pizza dude, and that's it.

The pizza served as lunch and dinner. Ben left fancy gin, fancy tonic and organic limes on the kitchen counter. Why he feels the need to spend the extra money for an organic garnish is beyond me, but I'm not one to complain about his benevolence.

Ben is at work on the BFD ambulance with his new partner, who he insists that I met at a basketball game, but I can't quite picture his face. Oh well. I'm sure I'll meet him eventually.

When Ben graduated the academy, I attended the ceremony and watched the recruits march around in their blue uniforms and get their badges, which I don't know why they need. It's not like people are confused about who you are when you wear that funny hat.

The event was kinda cool. The mayor of Berkeley

spoke. Kaylee wheeled me around the place and then we all went to Jupiter on Telegraph for beer and, of course, pizza. All in all, a nice night only mildly tempered by my occasional bouts of glowering, ones which I was pretty sure I was able to successfully manage without bringing anybody else down with me. If I was a total Debbie Downer, nobody broke the social contract by acknowledging so. All in all, success.

As I run through an open area between a warehouse and a series of shipping containers attempting to find cover from harassing sniper fire, my phone lights up with a text message. Right about then, I get brutally assassinated via Rambo knife by an unseen enemy. I pick the phone up as I wait for my character to respawn. It's Shiva/Saachi. It reads: *I want to see you.*

I type back, because I've had a few gin and tonics, a thing I really didn't know I liked until I had the fancy tonic water: *That so? Naked?*

Fortune favors the bold, or so I've heard.

My character respawns and is immediately sniped by some asshole with a scoped rifle who is camped out somewhere in view of a spawn point, one of the most hated and disreputable things one can do in multiplayer gaming… but also one that I would totally do if I could bother to remember where the spawn points were.

Another message arrives: *You don't beat around the bush. LOL. You sure you are up for it?*

I figure that now isn't the time to suddenly be embarrassed by my own words, despite a creeping desire to do just that, and I type back: *I haven't been laid in two months. My right hand is twenty times more moisturized than my left. I don't need your love, but I really want to touch your body and then I would like to catch up with you if such an arrangement is amendable. I understand if it is not.*

Immediately after sending this message I regret coming on so strong. I begin to feel a vague sense of panic.

Her next text is a picture of her topless body, which was clearly taken in the locker room at work because she's all made up and wearing her stripper underwear. There's a caption written under it: *Tomorrow afternoon before work?*

This is a very interesting development. I write back: *I'll be here waiting with bells on.* I then immediately send a text to Ben that says: *Please, please, please bring home a box of non-latex condoms. This cripple has a laaaaaady coming over tomorrow!*

The response arrives a few lives later: *Roger. On a call. Some street kid fucker slashed a whiney college type with a broken bottle in front of the Walgreens on Shattuck. I'll get them now because I can't stand this guy and it's not my tech.* Then another message arrives: *You need the small ones, right?*

Friendship is just the best.

Another hour and many more horrible deaths pass by. I see a notification on my TV that Dougie, who has the Xbox username *Admiral Assrock*, is online. How he was able to circumvent the Microsoft Fun Police and obtain such a username, I will both never understand and be eternally jealous of. Moments after the notification pops up, another appears stating, *Admiral Assrock wants to chat.* I plug in my headset to the controller and accept the invite.

Dougie starts in with, "How's it going, Stumpy?"

"A little soon for that one, don't you think?"

"I'm sure you've heard way worse from your feral roommate. At least, he's made way worse jokes with me via text."

I suppose I should have figured that Ben was keeping the people in my life in the loop. I have not really been the most communicative with anyone not in my immediate presence.

"Yeah, he has continued to bust my balls per standard operating procedure. The guy isn't exactly one to add fuel to the fire of self-pity."

"I never saw a wild thing sorry for itself – "

I cut him off, "Yeah, yeah, yeah... birds freeze to death and don't give a shit. I know the poem."

"I wasn't aware that you were a D.H. Lawrence fan. Ben must be lying about you not getting outside enough. Seems you live near a library."

"I'm not. I don't know any of his other stuff. Ben just said that poem over and over again while I was at the hospital. Frankly, it got a little annoying because I knew I had heard it before and couldn't figure out where from until I was up at like three in the morning one day watching AMC and the movie *GI Jane* came on. The drill instructor guy recites it to all the wannabe Navy SEALS. Then I got sucked into the flick and wound up watching the whole thing before realizing that it still sucked regardless of how sexy Demi Moore is with a shaved head."

"I've never seen it. I'll take your word for it."

"That's for the best. Though, Demi Moore *is* fantastic."

"That could sway my vote. I am definitely a fan of her. Did you ever see the stripper movie she was in?"

"You bet your ass I did. They also showed that on AMC when I was in the hospital one night but had all these weird edits so you couldn't see her boobs. It was really frustrating. I mean, I know that I could look at a naked picture of her on my phone but it's the principal. It's disrespectful to edit out such a rack."

"I can only imagine the struggle you must have had. It seems that *American Movie Classics* are rather loosely defined these days." Dougie changes his tone to one a tad more serious and asks, "How are you doing otherwise?"

"I'm okay, I guess."

"I imagine you have good days and bad?"

"I think that's a fair summary. But, I'm going to get laid tomorrow by a girl who I fell for kinda hard a while ago and then she broke my heart a bit, but that's all good now. She's really hot and I am officially hard up and ready to have the first sex of my life as a cripple."

251

"You sure you are, well, emotionally ready for that?"

No sooner does he ask that then suddenly I have a tremendous feeling of dread about Shiva/Saachi coming over. It crashes down on my chest and I do not understand why. I reflexively answer Dougie by saying, "Yes." But then I say, "Or no. Or maybe. It just seems like something I should get back into doing if I am going to have any semblance of normalcy in my life again."

"I get you... sex is good. Let me just say this about normalcy: don't be afraid to find a new normal. Remember what led you to where you are now and don't repeat the choices that were damaging. If there's a cycle you need to break, then break it. You shouldn't have to lose another leg to learn your lesson."

"You think maybe I should start something new and not revisit old flames?"

"Get laid if you want, Harlan. Fall in love with the girl all over again if you want. Just make sure you are doing something because you want to do it and not out of some hormonal compulsion of being near thirty and single, because you are basically becoming the poster boy for that. And I'm a reformed version of Jimmy-fucking-McNulty from *The Wire* so don't think I'm talking out of my ass here when it comes to recognizing one's own bullshit."

"Okay, wow. You aren't invited to my birthday party anymore."

"I call them like I see them, sorry."

"It's fine... I never watched *The Wire* but thanks for reminding me about it. I'm running out of shows and this game is starting to suck out what little will to live I still have."

"Definitely watch it. It's fantastic. And stop feeling sorry for yourself."

"Noted."

"And I'm just saying don't set yourself up for heartbreak. And also listen to the voices in your head and not assholes like me who think they know what they are talking about."

"Okay, fair enough. I'm going to see her. We will probably have sex, but I'll wear a suit of emotional armor when I do it."

"Seems like a fine enough plan to me. Oh, and get a job. That's actually the reason I wanted to talk, believe it or not. You just gave me a nice segue for the other shit."

I am a bit taken aback by this statement. I ask a tad more spitefully than I mean to, "Get a job? How do you suppose I accomplish that? Know anywhere hiring one-legged paramedics with zero other skills than motorcycling, poorly at that, and being marginally competent at video games? I can't even wear a prosthesis yet."

"Harlan, call up AER and ask if there's something you can do. I bet they'll find a place for you. Answer phones or the like. Restock the bandages and urinals until you are better on your foot."

"Nice, asshole."

"Sorry."

"It's... okay."

"If you don't get a job, all you are going to do is sit around, drink, eat pizza and get fat. Ben is probably going to move in with Kaylee one day and you are going to need a way to pay for that place when he isn't living there anymore, which is gonna to be sooner than later, I suspect. The time to mourn is over. You gotta get out there, man."

"Fine. I'll call," I concede. The guy has a point.

"But not before we get a few games in, so hit the invite button and let's use some of that broadband that Ben pays for."

"Sending the invite now."

It is this exact moment that I realize I am officially freeloading off of, and being charitably supported by, my best friend. He hasn't asked me for a dollar either. This means I am forever in his debt.

God damnit.

46.
September 11th, 2010

I'm a dispatcher now. Go ahead, laugh it up. Mock my white uniform shirt with the unsanctioned, blue Dickies work pants that I wear, because I'm not paying for the ridiculously marked up ones at the uniform shop, while I sit down in an ergonomic chair and try not to eat the endless variety of sugary and salty snacks that are constantly available and singing their siren song.

Yeah, because I know you are curious about it, I cut the right leg off the pants at the knee. But I didn't sew the bottom shut to spare everyone the sight of my stub-leg. They have to live with it if I do. Try and stop me, catty, loud and very flamboyant Dispatch Supervisor David (not Dave!), I dare you, you perfectly groomed and coifed man.

He has great eyebrows, seriously. Never even noticed such a trait before in a person. They are that noteworthy.

Another thing that happens with dispatchers, besides constantly bringing snacks and then attempting to avoid the snacks that others bring, is watching TV with the sound off and the closed captioning on. I'm working swing shift so at least I can avoid the endless daytime television that the day shift always has on. I experienced this while I was training, and I still can't tell if Dr. Phil is better or worse when read instead of heard.

Typically, the swing shift tunes into the news. There's an unending war going on between two dispatchers over the correct news channel to watch. I don't know who the participants are as they are both sneaky, but they constantly change the TV from Fox News to MSNBC and vice-versa.

Today, they have apparently called a 9/11 armistice and settled on CNN. On the screen, passenger planes barrel into the WTC towers on an endless loop that I'm trying my best to ignore. Stampedes of people flee the ensuing collapses and fearsome dust cloud that chases after them like something Stephen King was too kind to bother terrifying us with.

Next, we cut to the Flight 93 debris field and it seems too sparse to have been a fully loaded aircraft filled with luggage and bodies. I try not to think of what I would have done on that plane. Would I have had the balls to resign myself to death and participate in the hostage rebellion in order to save an unknown number of strangers in an unknown target in Washington DC? Or did they even know it was to be a suicide mission to stop an apparent suicide mission? Were they convinced of their ability to take the plane back? Did they think about who would fly it, or who would land it? Or did they just take it one crisis at a time?

I see the Pentagon in flames. Stunned soldiers gather outside looking at the gaping hole in the building as cop cars, engine companies, truck companies, and ambulances swarm. Predictably, the Pentagon personnel are the most orderly group of terrified victims of the attack. You can see the look on some of the faces of the Pentagon staff that it's time to go to work and deal with the situation at hand. Leaders being leaders. Fighters being fighters.

It's still so very horrible and surreal all these years later. But enough about that indescribably awful tragedy. I have an important task to do. In moments, a call for service pops up on my screen in West Oakland. Bingo. The mission is a *go*.

I key the mic and at the speed of light from the AER dispatch hub in San Mateo, I facilitate chest pain and dizziness treatment for an elderly woman parked in her maroon Oldsmobile at the corner of 14th and Alice by saying, "Oakland 526, copy code-three?"

In response, I get silence. And I am well aware why that is.

I say it again, "Oakland 526, copy code-three?"

A few beats more of silence. I smile and get ready to transmit to a supervisor that 526 isn't answering the radio. It could be an emergency. We should *definitely* take them out of service until they can be located, hopefully uninjured and just having some sort of technical difficulty that precluded them from being able to answer the call.

Before I am able to proceed, Tay-boobs answers, "Yeah, go ahead," and he sounds pissed. Mission accomplished, just not as perfectly as I would have liked.

"Oakland 526, code-three for the elderly female with chest pain and dizziness at 14th, that's one-four street, and Alice, that's adam-lincoln-ida-charlie-edward. She is in a blue Oldsmobile parked at the corner. Fire is responding with a delay." Though I know I do not need to use the phonetic alphabet, I elect to just savor the moment a bit longer, add a little *je ne sais quoi*.

Tay-boobs responds, unhappily but with faux politeness, "We are en route. Can we have a time check as well, please?"

I am the hunter and he is my prey.

"Yes, 526, you absolutely may. It is currently 2317 hours so this I should be your last call of the evening. Congrats."

Oakland 526 is a twelve-hour car that works noon to midnight. I have just sent him on a call that will undoubtedly hold him over late, because I am evil, and he is a dick. *Muahaha. He* knows that *I* know exactly what I am doing, and you best believe that I know he knows I know it. I bet you anything he complains to a supervisor. This is glorious.

A terse, "Copy," is his retort. Then he keys the mic again, sirens blaring in the background, and says, "Oakland 526 to Oakland S-2."

Bingo. The supervisor, S-2, Julie Fernandez who loves

me, answers, "Go for Oakland S-2."

"Can I speak to you on a tactical channel?"

I say out loud to a busy room, "Aww shit. This is gonna be good."

Bernitha "Berry" Chaplin, the dispatcher with the sexiest voice of all of them who is also the most sexually inappropriate person in the whole cast of dispatchers overhears my excited utterance. (Ask me how many times she uses the line, *The blacker the berry the sweeter the juice*," I dare you.) She's seated directly behind me working South County. She asks, "Did you send that grumpy man on a late call again? Mmm, mmm, mmm, he's gonna hate you, baby-cakes!"

"He already does, my dear. I assure you."

Julie transmits, "Go to tac-1."

Naturally, everyone who overhears this traffic, me included, switches their radios over to tac-1. Eavesdropping on unofficial radio traffic is a widely enjoyed pastime among AER employees.

Tay-boobs breaks the silence first and says, "Oakland 526 on tac-1 to S-2."

"Go for S-2."

He spits out, "A certain dispatcher just sent us on a late run again. That's happened twice this week already and this is my Friday."

"Are you the closest unit to the call?"

Of course, they are the closest unit. You think I haven't made sure of this beforehand? I am already a master of shenanigans as a dispatcher as there is little else to do but eat and watch network news, so I keep track of these things under the guise of being thorough.

Tay-boobs admits, "I don't know. It's possible. But there are a few units that have been out of service on meal break for a while near the 10th and Clay post."

Crap. I forgot about those units. So much for my proclamation of mastery. I saw them on the board in front of me on meal breaks but forgot to see how long they had been on said meal breaks. I cringe at my careless oversight.

The worry is all for naught, because Julie says, "Well, feel free to make sure your rig is nice and clean before you clock out so you can get some solid overtime. Thanks for helping us out on a busy day. S-2 out."

Tay-boobs answers with a forced, "No problem."

Yep, I am a golden god of mischief. It's confirmed.

Now, before you come at me with some weak shit like: *Harlan, didn't Tay-boobs possibly save your life in the recent past? And, if so, shouldn't you be nicer to him now?* Well, I do not blame you for wondering this very thing. Truth be told, I was for a very short time willing to start anew with our chubby pal on 526. This was up until Ben told me when I was in the hospital that Tay-boobs was blasting out text message jokes to coworkers about Asian drivers referencing my motorcycle crash, which was the fault of goddamn Bambi and shitty luck. So, the armistice ended as soon as I heard that. In the immortal words of Buggs Bunny, "Of course, you realize this means war?" And it is a war that I intend to win.

A text message pops up on my phone screen. It's Supervisor Julie. It reads: *I think you are going to drive him to drink.*

I type back: *Probably better for him than all the Mountain Dew. Thanks for having my back. I guess I'm just new at this dispatching stuff. I promise to get better. Honest.*

She replies: *Oh, stop. You know damn well what you are doing. As much as we like having you up there being a terrorist, we would rather have you out here with us.*

I reply: *When I get my bionic leg, I'll make every effort to return.*

I don't know if this is true or not. I can't even begin to imagine how I would manage to squat down with a prosthetic leg and treat Darryl after he got flattened by a newspaper truck or the like.

And what if I've lost my nerve?

47.

"Yes you can work with the prosthetic," Tasha says. "I'm going to teach you to crouch, lift, climb stairs, all the stuff people do on a day to day basis. Now turn around and come back."

I have had my new lower leg on for a grand total of one session and I have already walked the length of the parallel bars. I was not expecting this skill to be quick in coming, but it turns out when you've walked pretty much your entire life on two legs you can pick it up again even after a setback such as losing one of said legs. Who knew?

Granted, I could have done some basic internet research to learn more about the process, which you are no doubt figuring you would do were you in my position, but I did not because I am a medical professional and therefore one of the worst patients one can have due to my predisposition for believing I already know everything about medicine.

The new leg went on pretty easily. Basically, I put this long condom-thingy on that fits super tightly, then a real sock over that and then jam my incomplete leg into the fiberglass and titanium prosthesis. The rest is all self-explanatory: pretend it is a real leg and figure it out. It's wonky and it hurts but it's doable.

I turn around and walk back the length of the parallel bars. Tasha instructs, "Now go again. Hold onto the rails so you don't fall." I comply. It's a little harder because of the pain, but I do it without calamity. Tasha utilizes positive reinforcement not unlike teaching a puppy to not piss in the house, "Good!"

"So, when am I getting my running blade leg? I want to look badass and I think that would help you choose to finally go out with me, if I looked all badass and could run fast, I mean."

She says, "Stop," and rolls her eyes.

I don't stop. "I'm just saying that people love that Pistorious guy. I bet he slays with the ladies."

She laughs a little and instructs, "Keep walking, Harlan. Put enough miles on that one you got there, and you never know what the future will hold. Though from what I hear from your good friend, Ben, you have your hands full already when it comes to dating."

"Don't listen to him. He stretches the truth constantly and is generally a garbage person, unlike myself."

Okay, fine, yes, I did sleep with Shiva/Saachi that day she said she was going to come over. And, yes, I have continued to do so since that fateful day. But I'm not gonna fall for her again, I assure you. Scout's honor. I have accepted the wisdom of Dougie the Xbox Oracle into my life. I don't have time to fall in love between work and learning to walk again. Also, and this stays between you and me, I'm pretty sure she has a boyfriend. She comes over at odd hours and never spends the night. And she seems even sexier now than she was the first time we were doing… whatever it was we were doing. Things could be described as *torrid* now. Maybe I'm wrong. But then again, I might need that running blade thing sooner than later to make a quick escape from a jealous lover.

"Now we are going to work on standing up from sitting," Tasha instructs and demonstrates how to stand in that way physical therapists do that breaks down something you've done probably a million times and somehow makes it complicated.

I practice sitting and standing. Tasha praises my efforts and tells me to keep doing it. I'm a good boy.

I deadpan, "Gee, it is almost like I have stood up

before. Who knew? The other bipeds at the dispatch center are going to be so impressed by me."

"Well, if you are such a pro at it why don't you go ahead and use your handy pocket computer and research the myriad of jobs people with your same prosthesis are able to do? I bet if you google the words *amputee* and *paramedic* you will find a number of examples."

"You seem pretty sure about that. All the walking around on this thing doesn't explain how I pick up a gurney or do CPR on my knees on a city sidewalk."

"I am quite confident. Because I researched it before you got here. And I'm going to send you a link to a local news report of a paramedic who has your same amputation and still works."

I exhale for a long time, put my hands on my hips and say, "It gets kind of annoying when you're right all the time."

"You should be used to it by now. It's part of my charm. Just like being cranky and borderline inappropriate is part of yours."

"Cranky? Moi? Well try this on for size then, lady." I stand up and start shuffling around without the assistance of the parallel bars or a walker.

"Looks like we've found the key to motivating you."

I look at her sideways, dramatically, and say, "Now I'm going to show you my runway strut. Keep your eyes on the booty for the full effect."

48.

"There was this one night in the hospital when I watched *Forrest Gump* on network television, which meant it was an hour longer with all the commercials and they overdubbed stupid words like *crud* and *fudge* over half of Lieutenant Dan's lines because of all the cussing. Dad was there with me and we both got sucked into it even though network television sucks," I explain as I sit in the back of a Berkeley Fire Department ambulance in the jump seat wearing a black baseball cap pulled down low above my eyes and one of my AER uniforms with the patches removed like I'm undercover.

Ben and his partner are letting me do an unauthorized ride-a-long to help me figure out how to be a one-legged paramedic while sparing me the embarrassment of having to flail in front of my AER coworkers, who I do not want to see me as anything less than superhuman. So far, we have only seen a few of them and only one has noticed me and given me that awkward, *"Wow! You are doing so good!"* pep talk.

We are currently at Alta Bates in the ambulance bay waiting for Ben's partner who is finishing his PCR in the emergency department's break room, and no doubt rapping at a cute nurse or stealing food, because it's taking forever.

Want to know who Ben's partner is? Of course, you do. Get this: it's the *swole* dude with the tribal tattoos and almost-Mohawk haircut from the basketball league. Yes, the same one Ben got into the brief shoving match with. Life is a fickle thing and men continue to be simple and dumb creatures.

The guy's name is Brantly, because of course his name has to be just as white bread as he is. Thankfully, he goes by

Brant. Yes, spelled like that, b-r-a-n-t. Sounds like a cereal brand. Whitey leads the race in ridiculous names these days, I swear.

I'm doing my best to give the guy the benefit of the doubt. He's kind of an uber-bro but he's a nice enough guy. And he doesn't have the same haircut anymore. He's doing the shaved head thing now, which vastly lowers the douche-quotient.

Ben asks, "Is there a Nineties movie that you *didn't* watch while you were in the hospital?"

"Eh, a few. I was very shocked that I didn't see *Happy Gilmore* or *Billy Madison* once. It was like a glitch in the Matrix or something. I hope that isn't a bad omen." And then I add, "Come to think of it, *The Matrix* was on too and so were the shitty sequels."

"That is surprising about the Sandler flicks. I would take that as a blessing, though."

I say, mildly offended, "I don't want to have the Adam Sandler argument again. I know where you stand on the issue of his comedic prowess and I vehemently disagree when it comes to those two movies. They are classics. End of story."

Ben shakes his head. "Alright. He still sucks though. *Little Nicky* is all the evidence I need to present on that point. What were you saying about *Forrest Gump*?"

"Oh yeah. So, I'm watching the movie with my dad and then the gnarly Vietnam part happens and in the back of my head I'm always concerned it's going to bring back bad memories for him when stuff like that comes on. I mean, the guy refuses to watch *The Deer Hunter* and *Apocalypse Now* to this day."

"That's a shame. Both are fine films and I think we can agree on that without any conflict."

"Yes, we can. Cinematic achievements, both. So, anyways, Lieutenant Dan loses his legs and for a moment I didn't think about how I was in a hospital bed missing a leg watching a movie where there's a dude in a hospital bed missing *his* legs. Instead I was just worried about my dad. I remember it being comforting for some reason, because I knew the missing leg parallel was something that someone in my situation would probably be thinking about, but I had a reason not to. It was a little emotional escape I guess."

"I don't really know the psychology of why, but it sounds reasonable enough to me, bro," Ben says. I ignore his use of the word *bro* and hope it's not a new thing that he's doing now that he has a partner who *says bro* all the time. I do a quick mental inventory and realize *bro* is something he has always said now and again. I figure I'm just being a jealous ex-partner because that's a thing I do now: look within myself to find the source of my problems as I am totally Zen.

"So, all of a sudden dad starts talking about Vietnam, which he just doesn't do... pretty much ever. I can only think of a few stories from the war that he tells, and they are always about funny things that happened when he was on leave, never the violent shit."

"What did he say?"

"Dad says that the characters in the movie remind him of some of his Army buddies when he was over there and how he knew a bunch of dudes who lost legs and arms, like Lieutenant Dan, including a guy actually named Dan. And suddenly I felt really guilty."

"Why guilty, because you didn't fight in Vietnam too? You weren't even alive yet."

"It's just that I lost a perfectly good leg doing something stupid like riding a motorcycle, which everyone knows is dangerous and is completely avoidable. It's not like I got drafted to ride one against my will. But here's my veteran dad telling stories of braver men than me suffering the same fate or worse."

"Again, that's dumb. I see where you are coming from, I think, but I still deem it dumb."

"I know. Intellectually, I know. And I told that to my dad, about how I felt guilty and he said something to the effect of how people are always going to romanticize war, just like Lieutenant Dan did when he was talking about the generations of men in his family dying in battle before him. Dad said that he went to Vietnam full of patriotic vigor and shit. And he survived when many good men didn't. He said that he got lucky and the dead ones weren't as lucky, and there's nothing romantic about it."

"He would be an authority on the matter."

"And then he tells me that he thinks it was all pointless anyway because everyone my age or younger who talks about Vietnam does so in reference to it being a great place to travel to because the food is amazing. Also, that it's cheap, and the people are nice. But he didn't say it angrily; he was kinda glad about it. He didn't want to think of Vietnam as the same hellhole that he had to be in. He didn't want to think about it at all, which is why he didn't watch movies about it. Then he talked about how he moved to San Francisco to be a hippie after he got discharged. He said he was gonna try to fry the war out of his brain with drugs and women, but he met a beautiful girl, my mom, before he was able to do any real, lasting damage. I realized then that I never really knew that part about why he wound up in The City as opposed to going back to his hometown."

"Can't say I blame him one bit about not wanting to talk about it, even though *they* say that's not good for you."

"How do you mean?"

"It just seems like lots of people did the right thing by going to therapy to work through the shit they went through, but then they never stopped reliving the traumatic shit when it came time to move on. I always wonder if dudes like Darryl Figgus still show up at the support groups."

"Unconventional take on mental health treatment, I'll give you that."

"What I'm trying to say is, you know, get busy living or get busy dying and all that. I'm probably full of crap though."

"You are definitely full of crap, but you still might be

onto something. The last thing Dad mentioned about all of it was that he considered me to be a hero because of the lives that I saved and that he wished he had been a medic in the Army. So that made me feel pretty good, and also panic that I wouldn't be able to be a paramedic anymore and let him down."

"You won't let him down and he's got every right to be proud of you. Because I'm certainly a fucking hero and that makes you one too… even if you are like three-quarters the man I am and aren't a handsome fireman."

"That better not be an amputee joke. You better be talking about muscle mass only."

"I would never mock your condition."

"Liar."

Then an unfamiliar voice says over the radio, "Medic-5, copy code-three?"

49.
October 5th, 2010

Fish, man. Who knew there were so many kinds of fish? Vibrant colors, all of them, the primaries and pastels. Big ones, little ones, ones that are long and thin like reeds and ones that are oddly round. They dart through the water or lazily glide next to corals and volcanic rock. They seem mostly undisturbed by the locals and tourists hooting and hollering as they jump off the lava formation known as *Blackrock* above.

There are so many creatures under the surface of the warm, aquamarine Pacific, ones so beautiful that I cannot imagine how the native people of this island chain ever managed to eat them. Maybe it's because they didn't have snorkel masks and weren't able to fully appreciate the sights? That has to be it. Or they ate different ones. I guess that would make more sense. I'm not much of a fisherman, if that isn't obvious by now.

I always knew this place would be beautiful, but I didn't know how stunning, how relaxing and how far away from my day-to-day world it would be. When I look out across the water, I see the islands of Molokai and Lanai, where Becky went on her honeymoon, turns out. If I turn 180 degrees, I see the volcanic mountain that makes up the second tallest part of the island. The top of the larger mountain, Haleakala, disappears into the clouds to the southeast. I've been here for three nights and every day has been the same slice of perfection so far:

- I wake up to the sound of chirping birds and waves breaking.

- I get a coffee and hit the breakfast buffet.
- I have Ben or Kaylee spray copious amounts of sunblock on my back.
- The three of us stake out some chairs by the pool.
- I rent a kickboard, a single fin (this took explaining to the kiosk stewards, in the form of show-and-tell, initially) and a snorkel mask.
- I snorkel until it's time for more sunblock.
- I have a cocktail while Ben or Kaylee reapplies said sunblock.
- I hit the pool.
- I go back to the beach.
- Cocktail-sunblock-pool-beach-lunch-etc.
- I don't forget to hydrate.
- We head back to our rooms in the late afternoon and we get ready for dinner.
- Ben and Kaylee screw and I know this because our rooms are adjoining.
- We go to dinner and order half the menu, plus wine.
- Hot tub time!
- We have a nightcap on our one of our lanais.
- I fall asleep to the sounds of the waves and wind gently shifting the palms.

I never want to leave here. I imagine that's why there are so many mainland expats. The phenomenon is not exclusive to me.

It hit me somewhere on the plane ride over that this was my first real vacation as an adult. Sure, Ben and I had gone motorcycle camping a few times. There were plenty of long weekends snowboarding in Tahoe. Ben and I went to Punk Rock Bowling in Vegas twice and plan on returning again. This, though, this is different.

I figure if I just work on the tan, I can convince fellow tourists that I'm local and lost my leg to a tiger shark while heroically saving a child. Gotta be worth a free drink. I have all week plus one day to try it. That's five more nights of sleeping in a bed that I never have to make myself. I am unaccustomed to this level of luxury outside of a hospital room.

I find the big turtle after about twenty minutes of puttering around. I build up the courage for the second time since I discovered my newfound love of snorkeling to ditch the kickboard and swim down next to the big guy for a better look at my green, shelled friend. I accomplish the dive without great difficulty. This pleases me. I decide to celebrate with a margarita.

After retrieving my other leg from the beach, where thankfully no joker filled it with sand, buried it, and/or used it as a paddle for their kayak or the like, I meet Ben at the poolside bar, the one that has the grill station behind it. I will spare you the awkward details of how I crawl/scamper across the hot beach to get to my other leg. Basically, it looks like a bear crawl and works the shoulders nicely.

There are two poolside bars at our hotel: one has a grill station which produces good burgers and fish sandwiches, and the other bar has good poke. I already fancy myself an expert at the amenities of this hotel even though I don't know the names of the two bars, just the menu items that I enjoy.

Yesterday, we watched Monday Night Football at 1430 (that's 2:30 in the afternoon) at this bar. Well, we watched a portion of the game between dips in the pool and a halftime snorkel. Ben now has a plate of nachos and a local pilsner in front of him. I hop my butt up into the stool next to him. He's looking at the TV. Ben says, "I cannot fucking believe this."

"Believe it, dude. We are still in paradise and have many more days ahead."

"No. Not that. *This* shit." He points at the TV. SportsCenter is on, because it never isn't. "The fucking San Francisco Giants are in the playoffs. I hope the Braves sweep them."

The bartender, Kalani, chimes in, "Hey, take it easy! I'm a Giants fan."

I ask, "How does that even happen?"

Ben answers, "I'm sorry. A's fan. I can't abide this atrocity. It's not okay."

Kalani says, "It's all good. At least you aren't a Raiders fan. Then I would have to eighty-six you."

I tell him, "That would be perfectly fair. Though if I was a big Raiders fan, it would be a lay-up for me to wear a silver and black pirate outfit because of my peg leg."

Ben nods approvingly. Kalani laughs and asks, "You want the usual, Captain?"

I say, "Yes, please. No salt this time though. I got a few mouthfuls of seawater out there."

Kalani tells me, "That happens to everyone. Don't worry. It's good for you," and he sets about making my drink.

"Where's Kaylee?"

"She went to do yoga and then was going to get a massage, I believe."

"Tough schedule. I'll remember to send a sympathy card."

"You're telling me. Before you scurried up here, I was going to have to eat these nachos all myself."

"You still are," I tell him. "I'm hoping to be a vacationing MILF's skeleton in the closet and need my abs to be on point. I will be drinking my carbs only."

"You are on vacation, which means you get to eat what you want. If you were that worried, you would have gone on a diet beforehand. Now is not the time."

Kalani pipes in over the noise of the blender, "I'm going to have to side with the A's fan on this one."

I say, "I'm an A's fan too. Sorry to complicate things for you."

About a minute later I have a margarita in front of me and my vacation continues to be awesome. I grab a nacho and down it. Ben says, "I knew you'd come around. Eat like you're still in your twenties. This is your last year of being young and relevant, birthday boy."

Kalani looks up from the pitcher he's rinsing the remnants of a pina colada out of and says, "Happy birthday! That one is one me, brah. What year is this for you?"

"Twenty-nine."

Kalani flashes me the hang loose sign. I grab another nacho and many more after that.

After a while I have another drink – also on the house – and then in my perfect, lightly buzzed and happy condition tell Ben, "I'm glad Kaylee is here with us. She's really cool. I can't believe she puts up with you. I vote for you to keep her around."

Ben grins and says, "Funny you mention that. I have a surprise for her."

"I bet you do."

"No, not that. She's seen that already."

"Dude, is it a ring?"

Ben exhales and says, "Yes. Good guess."

"No shit, dude? That was a wild guess. When are you going to ask? Wait, can I the Best Man?! I promise to be the best man that ever manned."

"That spot is reserved for Tay-boobs. Sorry."

"Not funny."

"Of course, you can, dummy. I was thinking of asking her on the sunset cruise tomorrow night. This is where you come in: you gotta take the pictures so I don't have to pay anyone. I didn't tell you earlier because I figured you would blurt it out and spoil the surprise."

Kalani, clearly no stranger to this same conversation tells us, "Should be a good night for it. Water is still calm enough you won't be puking off the side of the boat."

Ben says, "Good intel."

Kalani says, "More free drinks if she says yes. Even more if she says no." Everyone laughs, including the other vacationers at the bar.

I add, "Hell, even if we are vomiting everywhere, it could be worse. The boat could sink and we could be attacked by sharks. This is a situation in which I have an advantage. I can use my prosthetic as a weapon."

"I would steal that shit from you immediately."

"I expect no less." After a few seconds of silence, and gazing at the TV, I vocalize a recent thought, "I've come to the conclusion that life is a string of crises and the lulls between them. The best-case scenario is that the lulls are long. The worst case is that the next crisis takes you out permanently. The rest is just the survival period. I find there's comfort in that."

"That's a damn somber thought to follow my most recent announcement, dude. Get a little introspective during your last snorkel?"

Kalani pipes in while spearing a cherry and a pineapple to top a drink he's making, "Marriage is not a crisis. Divorce, however, is, so only do it once." He's slaying it with good bartender lines today.

I continue, "The point I am making is that it is nice to have partners in the adventure, so you don't have to go it alone. And, I don't mind sharing my best friend. Accordingly, I will allow this blessed union to proceed."

Ben says, "I was wondering where you were going with that. Thanks." He looks at Kalani and says, "Two Fireball shots, please."

I moan, "Ugh," in protest.

Kalani pours the two shots out of a frosted bottle and shakes his head in disgust. "Your funeral, brah. I don't know how people drink this stuff."

A soft arm wraps around my shoulder before I can grab the glass. It's Kaylee. She's got her other arm draped across Ben's shoulders. She nods at the shot glasses and says, "Hey, boys. I see you can't be left alone without bad ideas coming to fruition?" She kisses Ben on the lips and me on the top of the head.

Kalani, who has already established himself to be a huge Kaylee fan because she is fun and looks quite fantastic in a bikini, says, "I tried to talk them out of it."

She says, "Nonsense. Give me one too. I feel way too sober and healthy after that yoga class and my massage isn't for a few hours."

Kalani pours a third shot and sets it down in front of her. We pick up the glasses and Ben says, "To your birthday and this paradise."

I say, "Thank you. Here's to not hearing sirens until we get back to work... and to that other thing that I'm *super* excited about that may or may not happen soon."

Ben glares at me and says, "Shut it. I swear to god..."

Kaylee interrupts, smiling, "I'll drink to whatever it is that you are talking about."

We clink our glasses and toss down the spicy cinnamon sweetness. I try to kill the taste with a swig of my margarita and suddenly wish I had a water or something else handy, as it's a terrible combo, but I survive. Ben chases the shot with his beer, a much better option. Kaylee looks at our faces, smiles and says, "Pussies."

Within the next two minutes, as if a sign from God, a gaggle of three, thirty-something to forty-something women in swimsuits walks up to the other side of the bar and they settle in. Kalani greets them. One of them looks in my direction and smiles. She's got loose, sun-bleached curls, coffee-with-cream skin, a half-sleeve depicting Nefertiti and a turquoise, one-piece bathing suit... which is quite complementary to her shape. I smile back and then avert my gaze so as not to be a total creep.

Kaylee leans in with her arms across our shoulders and whispers the perfect movie quote to her fellow dirty, rotten scoundrels:

"Are you ready? Then let's go get 'em."

50.
Like, twenty frigging seconds later, tops…

Panicked screams of, "Help! Nine-one-one! Help! Mom! Help! Call nine-one-one!" come searing through the air from the direction of the beach. The three of us are awkwardly close to the gaggle of sexy bar patrons, beginning our strafing run of flirtation.

They are immediately startled by the commotion. Smiles vanish. *Oh great.*

Our heads whip in unison to the source of the noise. Collectively, we observe a teenager in a snorkel mask dragging his portly, pale and lifeless father by a limp arm onto the sandy shore. Even from the pool bar we can see dude is *fuuucked* up and probably had a major heart attack in the water.

I look at Ben. Kaylee looks at me. Ben looks at Kaylee and back to me. He gives a shrug, a nonverbal, *Should we?*

Shit-god-damnit-of-course-yes.

I sigh, drop my gaze to the floor for a beat, and take a deep breath as I hear the hot lady who I was gonna flirt with mutter, "Oh my god."

Kalani, now staring at the commotion, gives a drawn out, "Braaah, not good."

Gotta hand it to the dude, he stays in character.

Ben and Kaylee break into a run towards the beach. Ben apparently runs to emergencies now. Hell, maybe he's in the police academy, for all I know. Dress blues, patrol caps and polished sidearms at the wedding, to follow. Nothing surprises me anymore with him.

I turn to Kalani, point to the neon green box affixed to the wall below SportsCenter, knock the dust off my business voice and say, "Kalani, I'm a paramedic. Gimme the AED, now."

Kalani startles into action and responds to my barked-out order. He hands the AED to me over the top of the bar. I start to *walk* my old and new legs to the beach, to yet another disaster, because there's no safe harbor from them, no matter the paradise and regardless of plans or desires.

I announce, "Someone, call it in please."

There's no need to panic. We are professionals. We are trained for this.

In my head, the dispatcher tells us, over the crackling static of wind blowing through palm fronds and the white noise of pounding surf, "Oakland 527, copy code-three."

The End

Made in the USA
Coppell, TX
14 July 2020

30912205R00154